Keith Beal was born in Chalfont St Peter in 1933. He grew up in Potters Bar during the Second World War, went to school in North London, attained a BSc and MA at the London School of Economics and Sussex University, and now lives in Hastings.

Keith Beal

THE DANGER OF LIVING

For Alison

a very good starting partner

from

Keith

AUSTIN MACAULEY PUBLISHERS®
LONDON * CAMBRIDGE * NEW YORK * SHARJAH

Copyright © Keith Beal 2025

The right of Keith Beal to be identified as author of this work has been asserted by the author in accordance with sections 77 and 78 of the Copyright, Designs and Patents Act 1988.

All rights reserved. No part of this publication may be reproduced, stored in a retrieval system, or transmitted in any form or by any means, electronic, mechanical, photocopying, recording, or otherwise, without the prior permission of the publishers.

Any person who commits any unauthorised act in relation to this publication may be liable to criminal prosecution and civil claims for damages.

This is a work of fiction. Names, characters, businesses, places, events, locales, and incidents are either the products of the author's imagination or used in a fictitious manner. Any resemblance to actual persons, living or dead, or actual events is purely coincidental.

Note: The author does not necessarily hold all the views expressed in this novel.

A CIP catalogue record for this title is available from the British Library.

ISBN 9781035870226 (Paperback)
ISBN 9781035870233 (Hardback)
ISBN 9781035870240 (ePub e-book)

www.austinmacauley.com

First Published 2025
Austin Macauley Publishers Ltd®
1 Canada Square
Canary Wharf
London
E14 5AA

Chapter One

"Well, you seem to have done quite well this last year." The middle-aged man from the BBC personnel department leant back in his chair. He glanced lovingly at the briar pipe on the corner of his desk. He found it a bore to have to give annual interviews to young employees. The brown stain on his moustache confirmed to Michael, sitting on the other side of the desk, that he was a heavy smoker. Michael thought his interviewer probably felt that a pipe made him look more grave and gave him an air of authority. He almost certainly was not as old as he looked.

A rather boring series of standard questions were gone through and answered. Then, eventually, the administrator came out with his final question. "How do you see your future in the Corporation?" he asked with a half-smile, leaning forward in his chair.

"Well, I'd rather like to become a director," Michael suggested, seeking encouragement but reluctant to reveal just how ambitious he really was.

"Ooh! Don't you think you're aiming a bit too high?" The bureaucrat's expression became more serious. "Our directors are rather special. We like to get them from Oxford or Cambridge. Perhaps you should content yourself with working up some grades in the engineering department."

Michael did not answer. He knew what idiots came out of the universities who thought it would be "rather fun" to do something in television. He had frequently helped some of them to get out of a fix—those that could not get their studios sorted out and the programme on the air on time. He shook hands and left the interview with a feeling of disdain.

Broadcasting House was in an area of London that had recovered quickly after the war, but Michael caught the Underground to a poorer part of London where he was lodging. There, bomb sites still blotted the district. The rubble had been cleared, but there was plenty of waste ground where scruffy children played. Just a few areas had been developed with prefabs. These temporary houses were greatly appreciated by their lucky recipients, and a lot of their thankful tenants had made a big effort to improve them with lamps over the front door and flowerful front gardens.

Streets were empty except for the odd milkman or baker's horse and cart, so they were given over to children playing cricket or football against a chalked-up target on a brick wall. The only relieving factor was the smell: that of oats spilt from the sacks as they were unloaded from the barges at the end of the street, the sawmill on the corner of Farncombe Street, or, from a bit further off, the Peake Freans biscuit factory.

The next morning, Michael wrote out his resignation and handed it to George Collins, his crew manager.
"What's this?"
"My resignation."
"What! You've got one of the best jobs in the country. Most people would give their right arm for your job."
"Well, I'm not most people."
"It's a good, clean job and very well paid. What brought this on?"
"I can't stand Auntie BBC any longer with its class prejudice. It's riddled from top to bottom with class distinctions. Look how we have to use the middle canteen because, by their criteria, as engineers or technicians, they think we're middle class. What other organisation would have set up three canteens? One at the top for the managers and stars, one in the middle that we can go to, along with lesser actors, and one in the basement for the workers, the doormen, and the extras?"
"More organisations than you think. The war has only superficially changed things."
"It's disgusting now, in the mid-1950s."
"But the engineering department is not like Administration. We have our feet on the ground. Take no notice of those dinosaurs in the offices that are left over from the '30s. Things are changing."
"Not quickly enough."
"Always the radical! I thought our little discussions would have tamed your Marxist tendencies by now."
"I'm not a Marxist. I just believe this whole country is held back by the class system. There must be a better way. I think we chose the wrong side in 1789."
"You forget I've seen communism at work," came back George. "When I was a radio officer on cargo ships, going to Russia in the '20s, just after the revolution, I saw how the people suffered."

"That was not real socialism the Russians suffered then. They had had to fight a civil war, and it might have been different if the Mensheviks had won when the Duma broke up." Michael paused. "Or Trotsky."

Oh! The impetuosity of youth, George thinks, *I was like that once. It's nice to see idealism still exists.*

"But this is not Russia. Things are getting better here. We will build a more equal society."

"Stalin was the problem in Russia," Michael said with just a hint of anger. "He was just like any other dictator. Russia had had no real experience of freedom and democracy. What could you expect? It took us nearly five hundred years to get anything like democracy here."

"Perhaps." George nodded. "Well, I'm not going to pass your resignation on just yet. I think you should go away and think about it. I'll talk to you in a couple of days' time."

A week later, Michael was sitting, drinking his coffee in the canteen. George joined him.

"Have you considered your decision?"

"Yes."

"And?"

"I'm going through with it. It's nothing personal. I like my workmates, and I have no complaints about how the crew is run." He smiled at George. "But I want to do more in life. Other people can have my well-paid, comfortable job. I have always believed in living dangerously."

"Well, what are you going to do?"

"I'm going to Paris to paint. That's where it's all happening these days."

"Peter told me you were a painter. He says you're rather good."

"That's nice of him."

"There's not much money in painting unless you are very lucky. Engineering and the sciences are much safer." He paused. "And better paid."

"I know, but I have to try. Here I work on programmes promoting other people's work. I want to be one of those people. They are doing their own thing—creating art, or directing films—while I am just showing other people's creations. I want to be the person who "does," the creator, not the enabler. I want to express myself and evolve my own creations."

George thought for a moment and then said, "Listen, I have some friends in Paris that may be able to help you find a job, or get some money if the painting isn't keeping you."

He's crazy, but he has to have his head. Youth is so ephemeral. We should all try and keep our ideals of youth and encourage others. Youth should never be discouraged.

George carefully drew out his diary and copied an address on to a piece of paper.

"Thank you. I appreciate that," said Michael as he put the paper in his pocket. "We have argued a lot about politics, I know, but I have always enjoyed your company, even if you are a bit right-wing," he grinned.

George took the remark as it was meant and grinned inside.

Before he could say anything Michael continued, "One doesn't expect to enjoy talking politics with one's boss, but I have found it very enlightening."

"You see. Authority is not always forbidding. You should try co-operation more often. Learn patience. The frontal approach is not always the best way to achieve what you seek."

A week later, Michael emerged from the Gare du Nord into a sunny afternoon in Paris. Once before, he had visited it, and he immediately recognised its distinctive smell. It was difficult to place. Perhaps it was the conglomerated aromas of cooking; the whiff of perfume from the sophisticated women passing by; Gauloises and stale wine; the sweat of the odd horse that still plied the streets; or the leaking petrol from decrepit Citroën cars that were slipping into old age.

Puffs of black smoke coughed out of ancient single-decker buses that were moving off in all directions from the front of the station's façade, their engines roaring and rattling like the bones of a grumpy old man.

He caught a bus to the bottom of the Boulevard St-Michel, standing on the balcony at the back, his arms overhanging the battered tin advert for San Raphaël. The particular one on his bus had bullet holes in it left over from the war.

As Paris sped past, he breathed in the air with excitement, rejoicing in his new freedom. Paris had a visual harmony with the soft pastel grey and ochre of most of the buildings, clothed in peeling paint, and the predominant blue of the workmen's clothes. The women's clothes were more colourful, but only just. The austerity of the war years had hardly receded, and anyway, the smarter upper set always understated colour in preference for line and good taste. The colour, when it came, was at the neck or the cuffs, where a splash of red or gold from under a navy-coloured suit might suggest a wilder character than the cool outer appearance.

The traffic was sparse compared to London. Apart from the buses and Citroën taxis, it mostly consisted of 2CVs bouncing along the boulevards—a lot of which were still cobbled or scooters, often driven by a young man with an attractive girl on the back, pop-popping their way round the corners. The sound was similar to any big city, but with a higher level of motor horns than London and the odd shouting of men selling wares or telling the punch line of a joke rather loudly.

The speed of the traffic was noticeably faster than London, and more of it, but the driving was very skilful. They managed not to hit each other.

He went to a hotel that he knew; that he had stayed in before, but it was full. Other hotels he tried were also full up. It was the tourist season, which had just got underway after the war. He was getting a bit concerned. Eventually, he found himself behind the church of St-Germain-des-Prés, in Rue Jacob. Here he got a room in l'Hôtel d'Isli. He was lucky.

It was not a large room but adequate and clean. Apart from the bed, there was a small table and a chair, and a washbasin in the corner. On one side, there was a wardrobe and a chest of drawers. He unpacked and sat on the bed. *What have I done?* he thought to himself. *Perhaps George was right. I was a fool to give up a good job.* He got up and walked to the window. *No! You only have one life, and you have to live it to the best of your ability. I don't want to end up in my old age regretting the experiences I had missed.*

The window looked out on to the street and a window opposite that was not much more than three or four meters away, as the road narrowed at that point. He wondered who lived in that room. *Was it used as a tourist's room, or was it where someone like him lived—someone who had more permanent intentions, who was looking to expand their horizons?*

How permanent am I going to be? he thought. *I have a healthy bank balance, but will it last? And I will have to find somewhere to paint. I can't paint in such a small room. Also, the hotel does not serve food. That will make life more expensive.* For a moment, he again wondered if he had been rash, but the doubt did not last long. *I have to make the most of my time on earth. I have to take risks.*

He went to the toilet at the end of the corridor, and, turning the corner, he nearly bumped into a fellow resident. He stepped back and realised he was looking into a large, full-length mirror and confronting himself. For the moment, he was taken aback, but he quickly recovered his equilibrium. He saw a young man in his early twenties, of average height, of average build, of average looks, but exuding excessive ambition. The experience engendered a self-examination.

I have done with school, National Service, short-term jobs, and one good permanent job at the BBC. Now I am going to build on those experiences.

School was boring. I was a bad pupil, I know, but most of the teachers had already retired once and were not very good. They had been recruited during the war to replace the men who had gone off to fight. They kept repeating things to help goody-goody girls to keep up. Thank goodness school is all over.

He stared at his image for some time. *Whatever has gone before, I am now going to start living, and I am going to live dangerously.*

As he walked away and continued his thoughts, Michael realised he was not being wholly honest with himself, and he could not avoid honesty now he had started. The eagerness to get out and sample life had sapped Michael's diligence at school, and he had replaced it with pleasure-seeking. He had been a bit of a loner. He played truant a lot. When he arrived at the station to go to school, instead of boarding the train, he often turned off down the towpath and went for long walks around the countryside. Or when he did board the train and arrived at Finsbury Park, he walked into town and spent the day exploring London.

There had been a few scrapes in the school playground. He was slow to anger, but he had to admit once roused, he had a temper and a powerful aggressive streak. *I must now sublimate the parts of my nature I do not relish. I will have to watch my temper.* People tended to be frightened of him. It made him laugh inwardly. *Yes! I can look after myself,* and it gave him self-confidence. Women seemed to like that, but he had formed no romantic liaisons so far. *Perhaps I am too fussy. Perhaps I have a superiority complex, or perhaps I just have a tendency to look for perfection—not always a good characteristic, and certainly not one that endeared me to a lot of others—or myself. It makes me a bit arrogant.* However, he had to accept himself as he was. *Whatever has gone before, I am now going to start living, and I am going to live dangerously.*

That evening he went out and walked around to get the atmosphere of the district. It was full of small businesses, which gave it a feeling of local cohesion in contrast to the district at its edge, bordered by the Boulevard St-Michel, which was even then showing signs of tourism.

A small restaurant in one of the backstreets displayed an appetising menu on a chalk board outside. It looked a good price, so he went in. As he had not eaten all day, he ordered the set menu, thinking it would be quickest, and he was so hungry. He was right. It came almost immediately.

The food occupied his attention to start with. There was rillettes d'oie, followed by ragoût de boeuf and tarte tatin with cream. *Why is England still in a state of austerity?* he asked himself. *France experienced the war as we did.*

After eating, he looked around. It was obviously a very local restaurant. On the cream-painted walls hung some paintings of various quality. *I could do better than that*, he thought, but then he admonished himself for being arrogant again. Blue plastic cloths covered about a dozen tables, some of which were pulled together to allow for larger groups. The clientele appeared to be mostly regulars, as most seemed to know each other.

One of the men on the next table, with a cheerful smile, addressed him. "You sound English. There's no way you can disguise that accent. What are you doing here? Tourists don't get into this part of town very often."

Michael drummed up his creaky French. "You're right. I am English but not a tourist. I hope to settle here for I while. I intend to paint."

"Oh, so you're a painter?" The man grinned. "Monique over there is a painter."

At the sound of her name, Monique looked up, breaking off her conversation with the rest of those at her table.

"This chap here is a painter."

Monique rattled out French questions like a machine gun.

Michael held up his hand. "Slowly! I have not got my French into gear yet."

She broke into surprisingly good English, but with a mixture of a French and an upper-class English accent.

"I'm sorry. So you're a painter. Where's your studio?"

"I've not got one yet. I only arrived today. Look, you can speak French to me, but slowly. I have to improve my French."

She reverted to her own language with considered precision.

"Studios are a bit difficult to find. You might have trouble, but there just happens to be a couple that have been vacated recently in the block where I have mine. It's a bit far from here, in the 14th District, but it is a great place. You should try for one."

"That would be wonderful. How would I go about that?"

"If you come round tomorrow morning, not too early, I will introduce you to the concierge."

She called the waiter over, cadged one of the bills from his pad, and wrote down the address of her studio on the back. She came across to Michael's table and handed it to him.

He's cute, she thought, *and adventurous. It's his first day, and he has not stayed locked up in the touristy parts of town—and a painter—with blond hair and blue eyes—mm.*

"Thank you. I'll be there."

Michael looked at his benefactor. She was an attractive girl, in probably the first half of her twenties, slightly shorter than him, with a slim but curvaceous figure, an oval face, and strawberry blond hair, pulled back in a fashionable ponytail. She moved towards Michael with precision, forming smooth curves with her arms and giving her a slightly undulating gait as she walked.

She had obviously been in the sun somewhere, perhaps on a recent holiday, but it had not burnt her brown, only given her a honey-coloured complexion. She wore a smock that looked like a dress, but beneath the hem showed the legs of her jeans. It was unusual for a French girl to be wearing jeans. She was obviously not someone that pandered to fashion.

She returned to her table and continued her conversation with a crowd that looked mostly a bit older than her.

She's attractive, Michael thought. *I hope I see her again.*

The next morning Michael found his way to the address she had given him. His mind raced. *That had been a lucky break, meeting that girl yesterday. Fancy getting the possibility of a studio so quickly. She is very striking, very attractive. It would be nice to get to know her.*

He went through a large archway, past the concierge's cubby-hole, and into a ramshackle courtyard. *She probably has a boyfriend. All the best-looking girls do have.* He looked around at the numerous glass walls. *Where could my beautiful benefactor be? It could have been just talk. There are probably no free studios. She just wanted to impress. But she did seem very sincere.*

Nevertheless, he called, "Hallo!" He was just wondering where to start looking when a head popped out from behind the door in the corner. It was Monique. She waved.

"You made it."

"Of course. I couldn't miss such an opportunity or ignore your kindness."

"Let's go and see the concierge then."

They went back to the entrance and rattled on the concierge's shutter. A woman opened it.

"This Englishman is interested in taking one of the empty studios."

"I'll get my husband. He is just having his morning coffee."

A short, heavily built, middle-aged man emerged. "So, hallo! You want a studio? I'll just get my jacket and show you. English, are you?" He spoke with a guttural accent. He probably came from Marseille.

"Yes."

"And you're a friend of Monique?"

Michael looked at Monique for permission. "Yes."

"Nice girl!" the concierge mumbled in an undertone as he gave an appreciative glance at her.

Then, louder, "There used to be a lot Englishmen here just after the Liberation, but there don't seem to be so many these days. It's all Americans."

Then he shuffled his way in front of Monique and Michael, across the flagstoned courtyard, into a corridor, and then into the first empty studio. Michael gave a good look around. *A possibility,* he thought. They then carried on to the second. Michael immediately felt at home. It was larger, and even in its untidy state, he felt comfortable. Monique gave him a conspiratorial smile, and his pulse jumped a beat.

It would be nice if she hasn't got a boyfriend, he thought.

Michael chose the second, the better of the two studios that were vacant. It was about seven metres square and very tall. Windows stretched up from waist height to a glass roof that sloped to the brick wall at the back of the studios. That formed part of the main building behind. Michael could see two or three flats above. Some old curtains hung from half way up the studio windows to give privacy from the courtyard, and blinds, suspended on runners, hung from the glass roof which could be pulled down to give privacy from the flats. They all needed a wash. The floor was wooden, with exceptionally wide boards. In the corner was a large black wood-burning stove. A wide pipe, an exhaust flue, led from it up the wall and diagonally across the upper part, where it joined other flues, presumably from other studios, and up again to the top of the building where it exhaled its fumes. *Other people's wood burners are going to help to heat my studio,* he thought—*useful.* The place was very dusty. There was a sink in the corner, with a small table beside it, and two rather old-looking chairs. Someone had cleaned brushes on parts of the wall next to the sink. Michael was reminded of a Kandinsky abstract. He had never been very keen on Kandinsky's paintings, and Serendipity obviously could do as well. Anyway, it helped to break up the grimy cream walls that obviously had not been decorated for many years and had fade marks where things had been leant against them.

He paid the first month's rent, surveyed his new domain, and then, with Monique's instructions, immediately set off for an artist's suppliers, where he purchased canvas, stretchers, brushes, linseed oil, turpentine, and pigments. It cost more than he had expected, but then, as George Collins had said, he had had a very well-paid job for two years and could afford it. He did not smoke, was not a heavy drinker, and had refrained from getting a smart car, so he had saved quite a bit.

Monique watched him go, *He is just about the right height, and muscularly built, what you might call an athletic figure. He looks able to look after himself, has confidence, and willing to try his French. I like that.*

On his return to the studio, Michael sat on one of the chairs for a while. Looking around, he could not help but be excited. *I have a studio of my own. This is the first step towards being a serious, or even a great painter.* He was elated. He immediately set to work to stretch and prime a canvas with a diluted blue wash. Then, while it was drying, he started to clean the place, with the help of some rags he found in the corner, and a bucket that was under the table.

It was too big a task for one session, so he stopped after an hour or so, and as the primed canvas was dry, started to paint.

It was late on that first afternoon that Monique came to his studio.

"I see you've settled in quickly."

"Yes. I came here to paint, so I had better get on with it." Michael had started to paint the view out of the studio's larger window.

"You can't paint with your canvas propped up on a chair like that. I'll lend you an easel. I have a couple spare." She paused. "You are much more diligent than I am. I should be getting on with painting as well, but I have a problem."

Michael knew only too well, when you have a painting problem, there is always a tendency to pause and do something else.

Monique continued, "I need to paint a man's hand but it keeps looking very feminine."

"It could be an effeminate man," said Michael with an impish grin.

"No. He has to be strong and masculine." She smiled, echoing his demeanour. Then her expression changed as though she had just had a bright idea, but then, changing again, with an air of reticence. "You wouldn't pose your hand for me would you?"

"So you think my hands look strong and masculine?"

She gave him a sidelong look.

He ignored it and continued, "After you have got me this studio, how could I refuse?"

"I have just put some water on for coffee. Come and have a cup, and we can take it from there."

They went to Monique's studio, which was only two doors away. It was bigger than his, also with a high ceiling, but as it was a corner studio, it had windows on two sides, curtained off half way up, like his. There was a sloping glass roof, again like his. In the corner, by the wood-burning stove like the one in Michael's, was a pile of logs. There was a couch, a table, and paintings stacked against the wall with their faces turned in. The only picture visible was on one of the two easels. Her studio, not surprisingly, looked cleaner and more lived-in than his.

"Where would you like me to put my hand?"

"Let's have some coffee first. How do you like it?"

"However it comes."

"I like mine strong but with plenty of milk."

"That sounds alright for me."

She poured the coffee and came and sat on the seat opposite him.

"Well, what do you think of Paris?"

"I love it."

"Is this your first time here?"

"No. I have been here once before, but as a tourist. I spent most of my time going to museums and art galleries."

"That's only part of Paris. There's more—the cafés, the back streets, the ordinary shops where you can buy groceries and hardware."

"I noticed some of that before, from a distance; down side streets. That's what interested me enough to want to come back and explore properly." He adjusted his chair. "That and the reputation that Paris has for the art being created here."

She sugared her coffee. "That's the Paris I love. Shops where you can get sugar, bread, cotton, and buckets. You only saw half of Paris—the grand part, with galleries and boulevards."

"I was very impressed by the galleries and the monumental buildings," protested Michael.

"Quite probably," said Monique thoughtfully, then more decisively, "but Paris has two types of beauty: the formal grandeur of the theatres, fountains, and monuments, which you saw on your first visit, and the intimate beauty of the small streets and alleyways, where life goes on at a pace, and the real people live. Once you get into that, you will realise that that is where its heart beats. However, it's these two things in close proximity that inspires the art."

She quickly picked up her cup. "Oo! That's hot." Monique put her cup down immediately. She realised her excitement led to impatience and she had to control it. She must not let her current enjoyment carry her away, nor her desire to impress. Michael cause her to make mistakes. The prospect of painting Michael's hand must not hurry her. "I've got some biscuits here somewhere. Would you like one?"

Finding the biscuits allowed the coffee and her blood to cool, and she relaxed.

After coffee, Michael placed his hand on the table. Monique arranged it and quickly painted it into the canvas she was working on. Michael went round to have a look.

He was surprised. It was a figurative painting, a bit surrealist, obviously influenced by Dali, but it also had strange perspective, the result of probably having seen Escher. This shocked Michael, as he thought he was one of the few people who had seen and been impressed by Escher's work. Escher appealed more to graphic designers or mathematicians than people interested in fine art. And he was Dutch. One of the engineers he had worked with at the BBC had brought back a poster of Escher from a trip to Amsterdam. That was Michael's first contact with distorted perspective. Monique's painting had the head of a young Muslim woman at the centre of interest, with dismembered parts of men around her. The colours were strong. The technique was more Renaissance than contemporary. Brush strokes were not shown, and the paint surface was smooth, not at all in the current fashion. But Michael immediately empathised with it. His own paintings were figurative, but did not have the immaculate finish of Monique's.

"That's a very vivid red," he observed.

"Yes. I get it by under painting with Indian red and then glazing over it with vermillion."

"I must try that." *I could learn from this girl. She has more than good looks.* "I see you are not taken by abstract art."

"No. I could not paint abstracts even if I wanted to, and what I want to say could not be said in abstracts."

"Abstract expressionism is all the rage these days. Don't you want to be successful?" said Michael, slightly provocatively.

"Fashion is the nose-ring of fools." She put down her brush and continued. "Most young artists make a mistake in following fashion. Because one person becomes successful by painting abstracts, they think they will attain fame the same way. They are not encouraged to be original. Art colleges do them a disservice. They all end up painting like their tutors." She had to be careful and avoided being too critical of art education. She did not know Michael had never been to art school. "No, we have to think what we have to say and then find the best way to say it, and a lot of my contemporaries are neglecting that."

"Perhaps they have nothing to say."

"That could be." She felt she had a sympathetic, receptive audience, so she continued. "There's not much intellect or ideas needed in painting organic abstract surfaces. You can get away with murder. That's another reason they're all doing it. They think it's easy. They talk about their ideas all the time, instead of expressing what they have to say through their paintings." She turned and looked him straight in the eye. She had developed her own strong views about art. "You should find what you have to say and put it on the canvas," she said. "Then I think that paintings should be a balance between content and technique."

"I'm so glad to hear you say that," Michael said loudly, and then in a more subdued voice, "I have tried my hand at abstracts, but I find them limiting. I can't say what I need to say."

Encouraged, she continued. "Abstracts are limiting, and figurative paintings are more difficult. You can't hide any inability. If you are painting figuratively, you have to get things right. Even if you have a stylised version of an object, it has to be convincing. You can't fake it. Everyone has eyes and knows what things look like. The abstract content of a person's soul is a mystery to us all, so even if the painter got it wrong, and it is not what they were intending to say, we will never know." Then turning to Michael with a confident air, "I never tolerate anything on my canvases that isn't convincing."

While Michael inspected the painting up close, she had another great idea. "My current problem is that I cannot afford models. I would like to paint men, but I like to get things right, and imagination cannot substitute for the real thing." She had a captive, appreciative audience, so she continued. "Painting is looking at things intently, as much as standing in front of the easel and wielding a paint brush. It is only when you have absorbed the detail and the meaning, that you can put it on canvas. I have no problem with inanimate objects. They are all around us. I absorb their form every day, but when painting the human figure, I need a model to study, and that costs money. When I was at art school, we had models, but they were always women, mostly students themselves earning extra cash. But we only ever had one man, and he was very old."

I am not surprised, thought Michael. He knew why. *Young men have to retain their dignity. What could be less dignifying than standing in front of an array of young women who are inspecting your naked body?*

Monique continued. She could see Michael was impressed. "I have nothing against old people, but I have no idea how to paint a beautiful, virile young man."

She went and pulled a folder full of sketches from behind the couch. As she spread them out, Michael observed them carefully. They were mostly of young girls, but some drawings had later been gone over. She had tried to make the figures more masculine, to turn them into men. However, her attempts had failed miserably. The waists were always too narrow, and the hips too wide, and they did not stand like a man.

Monique could not understand why young men, perhaps art students, would not act as models, even when they could do with the money. Women had no objections. *Some of my women friends enjoy posing. They are only too pleased to show off their bodies, especially if they have a good one.*

Michael knew. *Men's standing depends on their gravitas—their knowledge, their social standing, their wisdom, their power—and they think that posing their bodies is demeaning. Their appearance is regarded as only of secondary importance in society. You could even be physically disgusting, like Rasputin, and still be attractive to women.*

Monique suddenly and brightly exclaimed, as though she had only just thought of it, "I say, you wouldn't pose for me, would you?"

"What, me?"

"Yes, you."

"But I've never posed before. I don't know how to."

"You just have to stand there."

"Like the girls? With nothing on?"

"Of course. In the nude."

"I'd be embarrassed."

"Don't be silly."

"But I'm English."

"I won't hold that against you."

"I might not be able to control my reactions."

"What do you mean?"

Michael did not quite know how to explain himself. He stuttered and was embarrassed.

"What if I get an erection?" he said with defiant confidence.

"What would cause that?"

"You might."

She laughed. "Come on. I won't be nude, and you've seen nude women before."

"Not many. I never went to art school."

"But you've seen and been seen by your lovers?"

"The light was always out."

"So it is true what they say about the English."

With this, she doubled up with laughter. "Well, consider this your art university—your finishing school."

"The trouble is, it might finish me."

"Come on. You pose for me, and I'll pose for you."

It was at this point that Michael regarded her body very carefully. So far, he had been impressed by her friendliness and her liveliness. That always seemed to attract him in women. He liked women's company, but he had been brought up to think that lust was evil, and he had not yet cast off that conditioning. Nice women could not possibly be interested in sex. Consequently, he had always concentrated on a girl's face, where character is mostly expressed. He had been taught to regard it as rude to stare at a woman's body. As one gets older, one becomes more interested in the beauty of the body, and more lustful. However, he had not started on that journey quite yet, and was not even aware that that journey existed. Nevertheless, as he looked at her, he started to imagine her with her clothes off.

"Think about it," she said, with a smile that gave away her sudden self-confidence. She knew she had him hooked. "Will I see you at the café this evening?"

"Yes. Of course."

With that, she picked up a brush and continued her painting, so Michael left.

When Michael had gone, she chuckled to herself. *How sweet. I do believe he is shy. How English. I am going to have fun shocking him out of his conventions. I bet he has a lot of preconceived ideas about women. He is quite good-looking. I might have an enjoyable journey enlightening him. Yes, he will be a great addition to the studios.*

Michael had not intended to eat out every day. He had to watch his expenditure, especially so early in his stay, but he was already a bit smitten with Monique and could not resist the temptation of her company. So, after a quick clean-up at his hotel, he went revealingly early to the restaurant. It was not long, however, before she turned up.

He thoroughly enjoyed the meal that evening. Monique came and sat with him, and introduced him to a lot of her friends. They were mostly painters or writers, a very intellectual bohemian crowd. It explained a lot of the paintings on the walls. There seemed to be no special man that Monique referred to. *Perhaps I have a chance,* thought Michael.

The company announced that they were all going to see Georges Brassens, the singer, the next night at another café.

"Would you like to join us?" one of them asked.

He said yes, but he was beginning to wonder how long his funds would last if he lived life up at such a speedy level. *Bohemians are supposed to be poor. How do they afford it?*

Quite late, Monique said she must go home.

"May I accompany you?"

"If you like." She smiled, and not only on the outside.

They left together.

As they walked out of the restaurant, Monique started singing "Le Banc Public."

"So, you can sing as well as paint."

"That's one of the songs we'll probably hear tomorrow night. It's one of my favourites." They walked along, discussing their tastes in music.

Very soon, they arrived at the Metro station.

"I'll see you home. Where do you live?"

"Oh, it doesn't matter. I'm going by Metro. I live near a Metro station at the other end."

Michael watched her walk down the steps and then walked back to his hotel. *Perhaps I had better get in touch with those people whose address George has given me,* he thought to himself. *Otherwise, I am going to have to go back to England, just as the future looks so bright.*

The next morning, Michael was up early. He went for a bath at the end of the corridor, just in case Monique was serious about him posing for her. He also put on clean underwear. It was as his grandmother had advocated, in case one got hit by a bus. He felt as if he had been hit by a bus, albeit not in a literary manner. *Why did I give her my word? I can't go back on that now.* He took a quick inspection of himself in the mirror at the bend in the corridor. Then he went to his studio.

Not long after his arrival, Monique came in.

"Are you ready?"

"Are you sure you want me to pose?"

"Certainly! You're not funking it, are you?"

"Of course not, but I am English, after all. We don't normally do this sort of thing."

"Well, now's your chance to become a man of the world."

They went into Monique's studio. Michael got undressed and stood there feeling very silly.

What am I doing? he thought to himself. *I came here to paint, not to be painted. I do hope I will not get an erection. That would be unbearable. I must think of very unsexy things. I must not think of her. How can I do that with her right in front of me? What is she going to think of my body? Perhaps she will think I am a bit skinny. I have not got very big muscles. I might be spoiling my future chances by pandering to her whim. I have a bit of a hairy stomach. That must look terrible. I wonder what sort of men she likes. Oh dear, she is coming towards me.* He felt his blood pressure rise. *I must concentrate on something else, mathematics or music. No. Music can be very sensual.*

Monique came and set him into a pose, and he felt even sillier. She lifted his arm and put it to one side with his hand twisted in, and the knuckles resting on his hip. The other arm was placed slightly back with his torso twisted slightly. He could smell her body. She was so near. He felt an irresistible stirring. He hoped he was not going to embarrass himself. He forced himself to think of the cleaning he did the day before.

"Open your legs slightly, and the pose will be easier to hold."

He did as he was told, and he calmed down, luckily.

"Now raise your head slightly. Imagine you're Alexander the Great or Napoleon. Look powerful."

"Napoleon was short and stooped slightly."

"None of us are perfect." She smiled.

She then went to the other side of the easel and started to paint. She chuckled to herself.

He's really quite sweet, she thought. *He's really shy. He's like a caricature of an Englishman, just as we French like to see them. Well, we'll soon change his ways and make him into a European. I bet once roused there'll be a sexual monster waiting to jump out. I'll have to manage that—to my tastes.*

She started to mix her skin tones on the palette; white, yellow ochre, fake vermillion, and just a touch of French ultramarine to give it a cool feeling, varying the amount in different mixes to build up a transparent effect to the skin. She arranged them in a semicircle around her pallet. She would use them by glazing them, one layer upon another—the most opaque first and then with less turps and more linseed oil to give them more transparency. She held them up on her palette knife against her distant model. *That'll do,* she thought. *You know, he is just as good-looking with his clothes off as with them on. Mmm! I have a very presentable model. He is intelligent, too. He is obviously not attached, or he would not have come to Paris. On the other hand, he is very keen on painting, and as I know myself, that can far outweigh any but the strongest romantic attachments.*

She squeezed out some more yellow ochre on to her pallet to use to get the curve of the arm. *That was a lucky break in the café the other evening. I am sure we are going to have some interesting fun together.*

Romantic and erotic visions came into her head as she carefully observed his body and transferred the form to her canvas. In her imagination, she could feel his hands caressing her as they lay on a bed sinking into warm, soft covers, and her blood tingled. Her upbringing then got the better of her, and she felt guilty. She was a modern woman and demanded freedom, but education by her father and that Swiss finishing school, had taught her to be modest. And as the Jesuits had understood, the power of early training is difficult to discard.

They broke for lunch, and Monique lent Michael her dressing gown. The warmth of his body drew out her scent from its soft, feminine folds. She made coffee and a sandwich for them both.

"I have to adjust my skin tones when I paint a man's body like yours. I must not add so much blue, and more ochre. Women's flesh tones are much cooler. Their skin is more transparent."

Something had been worrying Michael about Monique's choice of pigments. "Tell me, aren't you worried about using vermillion? It's very fugitive. If it comes into contact with flake white, it turns green after a few years."

"Oh, I use zinc white, and there's an ever more permanent white now, titanium white, but I haven't tried it yet. Zinc white is a bit transparent. They say that titanium has more body."

They finished their sandwiches, then back to work again.

At the end of the day, Michael felt that it had not been as bad as he had expected. He dressed, went back to his studio to sort things out, lock up, and then, as it was too late to start anything else, they left the studios together and went to get a breath of fresh air before dinner. They got a bus down to the Seine. This time they both hung out over the balcony at the back. Monique admitted that, like Michael, it was the way she liked to travel on buses, unless of course it was raining. It was mostly workmen on the back platform, but that did not worry her. She regarded old men with sympathy, not fear. Anyway, she liked living dangerously. Monique had developed the same tastes as Michael, and he was pleased she enjoyed the bus balcony like him. *It is a shame to sit inside and be isolated from the Parisian atmosphere.*

On alighting, they crossed the river, and instead of going straight to the restaurant, they walked along the bank for a while, talking all the time about what they liked and disliked. Michael asked her what she thought about the political situation in France.

"Oh, I don't want to know about that. All politicians are either incompetent or corrupt. Leave them alone or you'll get corrupted yourself."

"You must have some view about whether Algeria should get its independence. That seems currently to be the main talking point in French politics; indeed in French society."

"What I think will not make any difference. They say that General Salan and General Massu have sided with the Pieds-noirs and are going to bring their armies across from Algeria to invade France. That will be a disaster, but there is nothing I can do to stop them. The Pieds-noirs have always been trouble, and now they are involving us all in their silly squabbles. They are the French who could not make it here, so they went off to the French colonies where they could lord it over the natives."

"Why are they called Pieds-noirs?"

"They got their feet blackened by walking in Africa."

Michael noticed a clock. It was already seven. "We had better be getting back to meet your friends if we are going to see this singer this evening."

They walked briskly back, met the rest of the group outside the usual restaurant, *Mes Amis*, and all together went off to the café where the singer was to perform, *Double Blue*.

Michael liked the music. It was not the type that he usually listened to. He was mainly interested in classical music, although 'classical' was the wrong term. He tended to like modern orchestral music: Stravinsky, Holst, Britten, and Shostakovich. But he found the songs most enjoyable. Monique sat next to him, sometimes humming along with the singer, and he could not have been happier. He could feel her pleasure and excitement bubbling through her body, and it affected his.

Afterwards, he offered to see her home again, but she insisted that she was going home by Metro.

"You should go home and get your beauty sleep. I have an interest in how your body looks now," she said with a chuckle. "I'll see you tomorrow, and if you like, I will pose for you."

He walked home, wondering why she did not want him to see her home, but with expectations and excitement about the prospect of painting her the next day, he put it to one side.

How will I pose her? My pose had been a standing pose, but somehow, although that is appropriate for a man, a woman was better in a horizontal position.

The thought of her naked was almost too much to bear.

He was at his studio before Monique the next morning, but she arrived soon after and came and offered her services. They had coffee, and then she undressed. He could feel his blood pressure rising. He hoped it did not show.

"How do you want me?"

"I've put some cushions and a blanket on this bench. I am sorry I have not got a couch yet. I hope it is not too uncomfortable."

"Don't worry. I'll manage."

She lay down. "Where do you want my arms? Like this?"

"No, put them a bit lower."

"Like this?"

"No. The left arm more to the side."

"Show me."

Michael went across and adjusted the arm. So close to her naked body, he felt overwhelmed. She was so attractive. She grinned. He hoped he was not blushing.

He returned to his safe position behind his easel and started to paint. With the purpose of painting to be concentrated on, he relaxed.

What a beautiful body.

"I know one should not ask a woman, but how old are you?"

"22. Why?"

"Nothing. I just wondered. We had not discussed our ages."

"How old are you?"

"24."

Perfect, she thought.

His thoughts were elsewhere.

I do wonder if she has a regular boyfriend hidden away. She won't let me see her home. No! She can't have, otherwise she would have mentioned him. Girls always mention even half-regular lovers, to keep prospective men at bay. It keeps the men in their place, until they have made up their mind whether to accept them as a friend or a lover.

He squeezed out some ultramarine onto his palate.

It gives a girl freedom. A skilful girl can keep several men on a string at the same time.

He picked up a broader brush.

In nearly every species, it is the female that finally decides the choice of partner, and the human species is no exception. The fact that she has mentioned nobody means I have a chance. I do find her very attractive and would really like to get to know her properly.

He then got down to serious work. He had to closely examine every detail of her body. Her loose strawberry blond hair framed a balanced oval face. She had sparkling eyes of cobalt blue, quite full lips, and a pointed chin. The two dimples either side of her mouth made it look as though she was laughing, and a lot of the time, indeed she was.

She had a happy disposition. That was comforting and stimulating.

A slender neck attached her head to a straight collarbone, which gave her fairly broad shoulders. Her breasts were full but firm, with small nipples of a light pink colour. Her stomach was flat, although with a deeply indented belly button, brought about by firm, shapely muscles either side, and she had a narrow waist. Her legs were long, which is why she was only slightly shorter than him.

There was nothing remarkable about her feet and ankles.

Some men have an obsession about feet, but I have never been able to understand that. Feet are feet. They are there to stand on. There are much more delicious parts of a woman's body than her feet.

After an hour and a half, they had a break, and Michael made some coffee. Monique put on the dressing gown she had lent him the day before. She noticed his added smell.

They chatted and then got back to work. She lay on the bench.

The pose was not quite right.

Michael went across and adjusted her back and arm. As he did so, she brought her hand round to the back of his head. She stretched up and kissed him.

Surprise and excitement competed for his attention.

However, passion overwhelmed all other emotions. They embraced. He stepped back, and very precisely removed his clothes, never taking his eyes off her.

She could feel those eyes. They whipped up her passion even more.

They made love.

Afterwards Monique felt warm and luscious inside. Her heart was still beating fast, and she knew she had found a glorious and exciting future.

Wow! That was great. But I should not get carried away. There were more things to be sought in a long-term partner than a good lover, but the lover will do for the foreseeable future.

They got back to work, and worked hard for the rest of the day. Monique was now definitely Michael's muse.

He felt it had been inevitable that they would end up making love. Never before had a woman affected him so quickly after meeting, and he had subconsciously known that they had to be a couple, as no other woman would ever capture his emotions in the same way.

It was late when they finished painting. The light was fading. He had the basis of a very presentable canvas. His feelings had been poured into the picture for everyone to see. He had technique, he had tools, and now he had inspiration.

"Shall we go straight round to the restaurant?" he enquired.

"No, I have to go and see my parents tonight. I'm sorry. You will have to go alone."

"Don't you live with your parents?"

"No, I have my own apartment. A small apartment," she said as a hurried afterthought.

"Oh well, I'll see you home then."

"No, I'll go by Metro. You go off to the restaurant. I'll see you tomorrow."

He walked her to the Metro and then set off to his room.

On the way, he bought a couple of rolls and some Brie from a grocer that was still open.

There would have to be some changes made to his expenditure if he wanted to stay some time in Paris, and now he really had to.

As he walked home to his room, he wondered again why she never wanted to be escorted home.

He also came to the conclusion that he would have to get into touch with those contacts of George very soon and find a source of income.

Chapter Two

Two middle-aged men sat at a table in the beach-side Mediterranean restaurant, sipping cognac. The sun was setting to their left, lighting the sky with a pink hue, and giving the scene a romantic, peaceful atmosphere. The atmosphere around the two men was anything but peaceful. The younger of the two, Colonel Peynet, broached a delicate subject.

"You have always been a patriot, haven't you?"

"Yes. I have devoted my life to France. That's why I joined the army."

"I've been talking to my commander."

"General Salan?"

"Yes. We think things are getting out of hand."

"Toussaint Rouge demonstrated that. I'm not surprised. Nothing will be the same again," General Massu said, as he shook his head with an expression of despair.

"People massacred in cold blood, and Algeria is supposed to be part of metropolitan France."

Colonel Peynet spoke with the confidence of an idealistic young man. "Civilisation is under attack. We must cut out this cancer that is destroying society."

"Chaos is increasing, that's for sure," General Massu nodded his head.

"But luckily the opposition is not yet united. The FLN and the MNA are killing each other."

"What can you expect?" sneered the older man.

"We have to form together to counteract them both, before they see their folly and unite."

"How do you intend to do that?"

"We have formed a society. We call ourselves 'L'Organisation de L'Armée Secrète', OAS."

"I had heard rumours."

"You shouldn't have. Nobody was supposed to know of us yet."

"I sympathise with your position. I would be with you should you decide to do anything."

"We have been talking with Jacques Soustelle."

"The Governor-General?"

"Yes."

"But he's a socialist," the older man said this with an incredulous tone to his voice.

"He was, but since the Philippeville Massacre, he has begun to see the *Pied-Noirs'* point of view."

"You amaze me."

"As part of metropolitan France, Algeria benefits from all the advantages of our civilised country, and yet they behave like savages."

The younger man continued, "Soustelle is going to Paris to try and sort things out, but if he does not succeed, we have to be ready."

"What hope is there in Paris? He is wasting his time. This mess is the fault of those fools in Paris. If the government had given us the resources, we could have put down dissent and finished the job by now," said Massu, thumping the table.

"Yes! And now the socialists want to give Algeria away."

"I can't believe they could think of such a thing. It's ridiculous. Algeria is a province of metropolitan France."

"And a bunch of Muslim fanatics want to steal it from us."

"It's not the Muslim Brotherhood that I'm afraid of. It's the ambitious politicians, like Ben Bella, that use them. There are just a few troublemakers, and the rest follow on. They are hoodwinked by the ambitious scoundrels."

"We have approached some other generals, like-minded patriots, and we all agree something should be done to prevent it happening."

"I agree too!"

"I thought you would."

"What exactly are you thinking of?"

Colonel Peynet leant across the table to be sure nobody could hear. "We are still discussing that, but we need to know who is on our side first. The last thing we want is to get into a quarrel amongst ourselves here in Algeria."

"You can count on me."

"Perhaps you would like to come to a meeting at General Salan's headquarters tomorrow at 4.30."

"Who else is with you?"

"You will see tomorrow. Pretty well everyone."

It was the day after Monique and Michael had made love. Monique was already in her studio when Michael got to his. They greeted each other warmly but then drew back as if nothing had happened. Both went to their own studios and worked until it was time for mid-morning coffee. Both were slightly worried that the day before might have given the impression that their interests were just prurient, whereas they were much deeper. Both were smitten and could not believe that the other could feel the same intensity. They did not want to give the wrong impression. Neither had ever had feelings like that before. Over coffee, they soon realised by looking into each other's face that their feelings were mutual. To hide their disorientation and overwhelming joy, they carried on normally as if nothing had happened. They behaved and spoke formally. It was almost as if they were acting out a 1930s play.

"How were your parents?"

"Fine."

"I have to find this address," said Michael, handing her the piece of paper that George had given him. "Do you know where it is?"

"Yes, it's in a poorer district. Why?"

"A friend in England gave me this contact. He said they might be able to help me find a job."

"Do you need to find a job?"

"Yes, if I want to go on staying in Paris and if I go on spending at my present rate."

"Well, in that case, you had better go and see them. It would be a great pity if you had to leave now. You have only just arrived in Paris." Monique quickly contemplated the thought that Michael might go, and her hopes would be dashed before they had got started. *Most of my friends are too old to be lovers. They are talented and good company, but Michael is something different. He is so young and virile—a nice change.*

She continued in a cool manner, "You can get to that place easily by Metro. Let me show you on the map." *What a horrible surprise. I must make it easy for him to stay. I have never been roused like this by a man before. The future promises much.*

After coffee, Michael set off across Paris. When he came out of the Metro, he quickly found the address and entered a small courtyard, rather like the one where his studio was, but without all the glass.

A group of small children were playing football in the yard. He showed them the paper with the name and address on it and asked if they knew where the people lived.

"That's my Papa," said a small tousle-haired boy. "I'll show you."

He took Michael across the courtyard, with the children traipsing after them, and led the way up open circular stairs, and along a narrow open balcony.

The pale green paint on the inner wall was flaking. It seemed to be a feature of Parisian wall paint that it flaked off, with the exception of the wealthy parts, of course. It gave most of Paris an antique fresco look, which was not unattractive.

The little group stopped in front of a dull red front door. The young lad stretched up and rang the bell, and a middle-aged-looking woman opened the door. They all trooped in: the son, Michael, and all the children.

"Good morning," the woman said with a broad smile. "What can I do for you?"

The woman must have been in her late thirties, younger than her first appearance suggested. She wore a dull grey dress that was mostly hidden by a flowered pinafore. It had a wrinkled border of a dark blue. She was obviously not someone who followed fashion. Her hands were rough from housework. Michael thought, *Probably not from just doing her own housework. She almost certainly does several cleaning jobs for other, more fortunate people.*

"I would like to see M. Raymond."

"What's it about?"

"George Collins sent me."

The woman's expression immediately changed. She was serious. She hustled all the children out of the door.

"Yes?"

"Yes," Michael answered.

"Have you got something for us?"

"What sort of something?"

"An envelope."

"No."

"You can talk to me. My husband trusts me completely. Have you got a message?"

"I'm afraid not. George said you might be able to help me find a job."

"He didn't give you a package?"

"No, I'm sorry."

"I understand." She paused and nodded her head. "I think you need to see my husband. He is not in at the moment. He works hard. The only time to catch him is in the morning, early. Come to breakfast tomorrow, about 6 o' clock."

With that Michael left and went back to his studio. Monique asked how he got on, and he related the slightly puzzling experience.

"I went to them to see about a job, but the woman seemed to think I had a package for them. Presumably, she was the wife of the man I was to see, but she evoked an air of mystery. I wonder what he is like."

The paint on Michael's canvas had dried enough to continue with his nude painting, so he went back to that. With Monique busy on her current work, he turned to the background, and it occupied him all afternoon. The strange experience of the morning was put behind him for the time being.

For the first time, he was pleased that Monique did not want him to see her home after the meal that evening. He had to rise early.

The next morning, he rose at about 5 o'clock, caught the Metro across Paris, and found his way to the Raymonds' flat. His host shook hands, and his wife sat him down and put a plate in front of him. Coffee was poured into a handle-less bowl. He was offered a roll and butter, and M. Raymond addressed him.

"So, George Collins sent you. Did he give you a package for us? You can talk in front of my wife."

"No, I'm afraid not."

M. Raymond looked at his wife and nodded his head slightly.

"O.K., I'll leave you two men to talk." With that, she left.

"Now we're alone, you can say anything you have to say."

"I don't have anything to say."

"And George did not give you anything to give us?"

Michael was confused. There was more to this meeting than he knew about. He felt adrift.

"No, he just said that you might find a job for me. Oh, and yes, he said I was to tell you that I am an expert on mushrooms."

"I presume you are not an expert on mushrooms," said M. Raymond with a smile.

"No."

"Ah! So you're a bit of a lefty are you?"

"George seems to think so."

"Well, I might have a job for you. You travel backwards and forwards to England a lot, do you?"

"Not yet, I don't. I have only been here a few days."

"Well, I might have a job for someone who did go back and forth, but you would have to be discreet. Are you discreet?"

"Yes."

"George obviously seems to think something of you. There won't be a lot of money in it, but all your expenses will be paid, and there will be a small remuneration."

"It sounds interesting."

"It would mean absolute secrecy."

"I can be like a clam if necessary."

"It will mean collecting envelopes from George and bringing them here. There will usually not be much in the other direction for you to carry. Do you know where George lives?"

"No. It's in Wembley somewhere, isn't it?"

"I can give you the address. Where are you staying? Have you got the telephone number?"

"I don't know it, but I happen to have one of the cards of the hotel on me."

"Good. Leave that with me. You will hear from me. Now say nothing to anyone about this, even to your closest friends, even close relations."

Michael finished his coffee and roll and left intrigued and mystified.

He returned to his studio, both bemused and elated.

Monique greeted him. "Well, did they have a job for you?"

"No." Then after a thoughtful pause, "At least not yet. There may be something later."

"Come! Let me show you my painting. I think it's finished." Monique was bubbling. "At the moment, I'm rather pleased with it, and you had a hand in it, as you might say." She radiated self-satisfaction with both her painting and her pun.

Michael was impressed by the fact that she could pun in English. *She really is intelligent*, he thought to himself, and he was pleased she had changed the subject and did not pursue what had gone on at his breakfast meeting. They stood in front of her painting. *It is indeed good,* he thought. He was seriously impressed by her talent.

"No! I don't like that bit," said Monique, jumping forward and picking up a brush. She was about to paint over a section, but Michael stopped her.

"Let it rest a bit. You should never change things in haste. It looks alright to me, and maybe with time, it will seem right to you. I like it." He sat down on a chair, leant back, and preceded in a pontificatory mode, "When you have just created something, you only see the faults and the pieces you have had to struggle with. You don't see the overall effect. It is good that you are self-critical." *Some artists fool themselves that everything they do is great.* "Aren't you being too hard on yourself? *But I suppose that if you were not like that, you would not be* an artist. Society gives artists such a hard time; they have to have a large ego. Give things time to settle down." For a moment, Michael wondered if he was being presumptuous in dictating to her on painting. They had only known each other a few days, and she obviously knew what she was doing. He should be reluctant to criticise her.

She turned and kissed him. He was reassured. *She really is quite mature,* he thought. *A lot of girls would have been offended by me lecturing them on their paintings. Only the great at heart can take criticism, constructive or otherwise.*

He is not just sexy but wise, Monique said to herself.

"How is your picture going?" she said, smiling.

She gave him a playful nudge. "Now you are my prime adviser and number one critic, would you like me to do the same for you?" Then, as an afterthought, "or would your male ego get in the way?" Her broad smile gave away the fact that she was teasing him. But she then had an afterthought. *Have I gone too far?*

"I would be delighted with your advice. I hope I will keep my male ego well under control," he said turning to lead into his studio, "but it's not in a state to be criticised yet. I can see too much to be done myself. That done, and I would appreciate some criticism. Give me a couple of days."

"You are a fast worker," she grinned, "like me."

"In more ways than one." They gave each other a mutual smile. He pulled across and hugged her to his chest.

Nevertheless, they went into Michael's studio, and Monique remarked on the use of perhaps too much red. Michael toned it down. *She is right*, he thought. *She really does know what she is talking about.*

They looked at each other and smiled yet again. At that point, they both realised that the other's perspectives nearly always matched their own. Not just in regards to painting, but in emotions. They could feel each other's empathy. They felt so lucky. They relaxed and were filled with joy.

Michael spoke. "Do you think our two consciousnesses are aware of each other?"

"What do you mean? Of course, they are." She was puzzled.

"Well I feel the substance of my mind is closer to yours than it is to the substance of my own body."

She gave him a quizzical look.

"Although I am aware of my body, of my leg, for example, is my body aware of me? How could he explain such a difficult thought?"

"What on earth do you mean?"

"I know that my leg is part of me, whoever 'me' is, but does my leg know that it is part of 'me'? Your brain and my brain know or feel each other's existence. We are aware of each other. We feel the hurts to each other when they arise. Such relationship with my leg goes only one way. My leg is never aware of my mental or emotional hurts."

"You think too much," Monique laughed, "You silly old thing."

However, Michael could not drop the idea. *Monique's and my brain constantly communicate and experience the existence of each other. Is this love?*

The next few weeks flew by. Michael thought it was the closest to paradise he would ever get. His painting was going well, and he and Monique made love nearly every afternoon on a battered but clean chaise-longue he had picked up from a local junk shop. It was a bit too narrow for comfort, but neither of them noticed.

Only three things worried him: how long was his money going to last, why was the prospective job for George so secretive, and why would Monique never let him see her home? *She has been to see my room. Why is she so cagey about where she lives? Does she have a man hidden away there? If she does, she cannot be getting along with him, or she would not have wanted to make love every afternoon and would not have stayed behind at Mes Amis every evening. Maybe it is in a real slum, and she is ashamed of it.*

Two of his problems soon showed signs of an early resolution. A day or so later, after a particularly messy painting session, he went back to the hotel to clean himself up before going to the restaurant. The concierge handed him an envelope.

"A man left this for you."

"Thank you." He looked down at it. "Was he a big man?"

"No, he was quite small and dark, a bit creepy."

Michael read the note as he walked up the stairs. As he suspected, it was from M. Raymond, who wanted Michael to come the next day, and gave a phone number to contact if he could not make it.

At the restaurant that night, there was some political discussion. Monique's friends were worried. They had heard that the socialist government wanted to grant Algeria independence. The various opinions amongst the group came so quickly that Michael had difficulty in keeping up with them.

"Of course you've got to give a country self-government. It's everybody's right."

"But they are part of metropolitan France. It is part of our country."

"That's the trouble. As part of our country, they get all the social benefits that we do," another proffered.

"They can come and go to and from France, and we have no control over them."

"Theirs is a completely different culture. Even the Pieds-noirs do not think as we do."

"Who are the Pieds-noirs?" Michael whispered in Monique's ear.

"They are the French who could not make it here, so they migrated to North Africa."

"It's the cost of their French status. That's why the government wants to get rid of them."

"The state cannot afford it. An Arab woman can have a child every year and a half, and the whole family can live on the income that brings."

"The benefits are too high."

"The child benefits are certainly too high. That's the problem."

"They had to make them high after the war. Don't forget we lost so many men in two world wars, and even in the Franco-Prussian War, that there is a lack of potential husbands, marriages have decreased, and the population has dropped dramatically. We had to do something to encourage childbirth."

"Do away with marriage!" one of the more esteem members said with a broad grin.

That was ignored.

"Yes, the real reason for granting them independence is to cut down the social security budget, not love of democracy. There's no philanthropy in it."

"There are a lot of them that don't want to separate."

"Those are mainly the Pieds-noirs. Of course they want to stay within France. They are French, but have a much better living there than they would have here. They have all that cheap labour."

"The Pieds-noirs can lord it over the Arabs in Africa."

"It's not just dissatisfied Frenchmen who don't want us to go. A lot of Arabs don't as well. Those are descendants from those who fled there from the Inquisition, centuries ago. They like French administration and stability."

"It's not only ethnic Europeans that don't want independence. There are a lot of ethnic Arabs that don't want to separate. They are bitterly opposed to the FLN."

"Algeria was part of European civilisation in Carthaginian times before the Islamic conquest. It was ethnic Berber not Arab."

"Well, whatever the reasons, good or bad, they should have a choice. They should get their independence if they want it."

Michael walked Monique to the Metro station quietly afterwards. Their cocoon of romance insulated them from uncomfortable affairs of the world. They left their restaurant friends to sort out such things.

"They are a very pleasant lot, your friends," said Michael.

"Yes. I like them. They are really the only group of friends I have ever had. I have always been an outsider. Our family has always been separate somehow."

The couple arrived at the Metro.

"Shouldn't I see you right home?" Michael said half-heartedly, knowing the answer.

"No. I promise I'll show you where I live one day, but not yet. Be patient. I want us to know each other very thoroughly first."

So she does live in a slum that she wants to hide from me, he thought to himself.

I can't keep putting him off if I want to keep him, she thought as she made her way on to the train. *I'll have to come clean soon.*

As Michael walked back to his hotel, he contemplated his relationship with Monique. *She wants us to get to know each other thoroughly. That's good. Although I have not known all that many women, and very few intimately, I have known enough to know what I like and don't like, and she fits my tastes completely. I like the way she makes decisions carefully. She has her feet on the ground. I can't stand women who are acting all the time; those giggly women who try to dangle you on a string. I like her directness. She is strong. She makes no secret of the fact that she likes me, so I can be open about my feelings towards her. We are so suited, and not just in emotional and social matters. It's sexually as well. So many women pretend they don't enjoy sex, in case you think they are a slut, but she makes no secret of her appetite. I can therefore relax and indulge myself. I don't have to feel shame... What a relief! And we like the same food and wine. I don't need to hide the fact that I am a bit of a hedonist. I wonder if she indulges in any sport. She has an athletic build and plenty of energy, but she has not mentioned any sporting interest.*

He paused for a minute to think. *She walks at the same pace as I do. It may be silly, but it does get annoying if you are always waiting for someone to catch up. Her tastes in music seem different to mine, but I will enjoy introducing her to what I like... Maybe I will find pleasure in her tastes. At least she appreciates the arts. I know there are things I am going to learn from her. Although completely balanced and calm in her personality, there is an overpowering life within her bursting to get out. That's great! What a woman!*

He walked on and then, with a sudden jerk, *but she has a secret. Why does she not want me to see her home?*

The next morning Michael went into his studio early and worked on the nude until lunchtime, filling in the background with large impulsive brush strokes. They expressed his feelings, and he needed to have a hazy background to focus attention on the central figure. He could express what he thought about her and her body with the brush strokes and the colour behind.

What he was doing was not something that Monique would ever have done. *She was much more precise in all her painting. She has a Renaissance technique. Luckily, she is not so precise in her behaviour as a person. Not stiff, just formal enough to make her company civilised.* Michael liked a casual approach to life. *Is there a contradiction here? Perhaps women, unlike men, when they get down to doing or making things, as opposed to their general approach to life, are more precise.*

He went and said goodbye to Monique, before he set off for his appointment at M. Raymond's flat. The door was opened by Madame Raymond, and he was led into the kitchen, where there were four men standing around the kitchen table, looking at some maps. He was very surprised to see that one of them was George Collins.

"Hallo! What are you doing here?" asked Michael with surprise.

"I've come to inspect you," George gave a chuckle.

A dark man, probably the one who had delivered the note, spoke. "Come along, let's get started."

There was something about this man that Michael immediately found off-putting. He had a sinister air, as the concierge had observed. There was nothing particular that caused Michael to distrust him, just a subconscious feeling. The company sat down round the table, apart from M. Raymond, who was attending to things on the sideboard. The new fourth man was big like M. Raymond, but with tattoos all over his arms.

"You know George here, who says you are to be trusted," said the dark man.

"Certainly," George confirmed.

"He cannot keep travelling backwards and forwards to Paris as he has done. That's why we might be interested in you. As you know, he has a full-time job with responsibility, and our needs are growing."

George grinned. Michael caught his expression out of the corner of his eye.

The dark man continued. "And you are sympathetic to the proletariat?"

"I come from the working class myself, and I disapprove of privilege." Michael was proud of his working class credentials.

The fourth man interrupted with feeling. "Coming from the working class does not always mean that you sympathise with them. People are diverted by religion or a false sense of patriotism."

Disregarding the comment, the dark man continued. He had his own preconceived agenda and was someone not to be diverted. "Good. We need someone we can trust to carry documents for us from England to France. As you know, France is in a spot of bother right now. If we don't do something, we will end up as a dictatorship like Spain. We are getting prepared. Of course, if some people find out what we are doing, we could all be in trouble, including you, even though you are English, so secrecy is of the essence."

"I realise that," said Michael confidently, although he was not feeling so confident.

The dark man continued, and some of his darkness entered his voice. "There are some people who are very much against us—the privileged, the greedy, organising for their own ends, and with a lot of power and money behind them. Secrecy might be a matter of life or death."

Michael felt a bit uneasy. Secrecy was one thing but nobody had mentioned death. However, he had always advocated living dangerously. Here, he might be getting into something exciting.

The dark man continued pompously, "We have to defend democracy. We have to defend the people." He continued with a more declamatory tone. It was if he was getting up on a soap-box. "Now is the time for the proletariat to exert itself."

Michael interrupted. "I am all for democracy. I have always been on the left." He did not want the monologue to go on too long.

The dark man's oratorical tone subsided a little. "You are in a privileged position. As an Englishman, you will arouse less suspicion than any of us. We need a courier. Are you willing to be that courier?"

Michael had always been proud of being English. His grandmother had shown him how much of the world map was pink, but it seemed it had practical benefits as well. As an Englishman, he was above suspicion. He liked that. And it might make him some money.

"Whether you take up our offer or not, nothing of these proceedings must ever be spoken about. Are you willing to help us?" This was said with a bit of a threat in his voice.

"Most definitely." *Why does he keep asking the same question?*

As his inquisitor rambled on, Michael's thoughts wandered. He thought to himself that it might be difficult to say "No" now, even if he wanted to. *They look a serious lot. Not to be crossed.*

"This will be a labour of conscience. You will receive only a little for your work," Michael's attention came back with a bang. After all, he was here to acquire some money. "But all your expenses—fares, food, and anything else—will be covered. Do you agree?"

"Yes." *A little is better than nothing, and it might be exciting.*

"We have a deal then?"

"Yes."

"Has anyone else got any questions to ask him?" said the dark man, turning to the other members. "No?" They all shook their heads. "Let's have a drink to celebrate our new recruit. We call ourselves 'The Sinister Port.' Welcome to the group."

Well named? I think not! Hardly secretive. Michael thought as he chuckled to himself.

Bottles of wine, Pastis, and brandy were put on the table, and liberal quantities were served. Michael went for the wine, which was a bit dry for him, but quite tasty. Madame Raymond brought in some cheese, pâté, and bread, and they all relaxed.

This gave Michael a chance to survey the apartment—or at least the kitchen of the apartment. He was probably never going to see any more of it. He doubted that it was very large. The kitchen was small. The most distinguishing feature was the smell. It was a mixture of appetising cooking smells, Gauloises, and stale wine. The fact that M. Raymond was a smoker was reinforced by the brown hue of the ceiling and a brown stain between his fingers. Copper-bottomed saucepans hung from one wall, taking up even more of the available space. With that, and the range, a sideboard, and a large wooden table with chairs in the centre, there was hardly room for the assembled company, although only five.

Sinister Port, Michael thought. *Left handed, the left side of a ship, the red of port wine... that's not much of a coded title.*

"Here we all use a pseudonym. This is Claude," said the dark man, pointing to M. Raymond. "This is the Spaniard," he said, pointing to the other big man with the tattoos. "I am Bertrand, as I said, and you already know George, although here he is known as Marcel."

Michael regarded the motley company. *Am I to take them seriously?* George looked out of place. His appearance was that of a middle-class Englishman, but with a touch of the boffin about him. One could suspect that he was some sort of engineer, and could easily believe he was an electronics engineer. Bertrand was a small, swarthy man with a bald head, a beard, and a precise way of speaking in a Parisian accent. Michael could not but be reminded of Lenin. He probably encouraged that impression. He was obviously an organiser and enjoyed power.

The others deferred to his leadership. *Such ability, one is born with. It cannot be acquired.*

The other two, Claude and the Spaniard, were so big Michael was pleased he was on the same side. He would not like to tangle with them. They were obviously both working-class—good proletarians. The Spaniard, however, added to his dangerous appearance not only with arms that were covered in tattoos, but a nasty scar on the left side of his face.

Eventually, after a long afternoon, Michael announced he had to go. It was seven, and he was thinking of Monique again, so he made his excuses and found his way back to Mes Amis.

He arrived at the same time as Monique.

"You've been drinking," she said with a smile.

"Yes, I have had a wine or two."

"Or three or four. We'll make a Frenchman of you yet."

They went in, ordered their meal—the set menu—and relaxed. Michael was very thoughtful. He was only just digesting what had happened in the afternoon.

What have I let myself in for? How extraordinary that George should be part of it.

Monique noticed that he was quieter than usual. "How did you get on this afternoon? I presume you went to see about a job."

"Yes."

"And?"

"Well, I've got a casual job, an occasional courier's job. There won't be much money in it, but it might make just that difference to my financial situation." He was not going to give her any details, but he was going to have to explain his occasional absences. *If you are going to lie, it is always better to keep as close to the truth as possible.* He had learnt that lesson at school when dealing with inquisitive teachers. Monique seemed to be satisfied with his explanation.

He sat thinking about his life. It really had suddenly taken some strange turns. *If he meant it when he told people that he believed in living dangerously, here was his chance.*

Monique noticed his silence. "You are very quiet tonight. What are you thinking about?"

"My life."

"You've never told me much about it. Where in England do you come from? You have only told me that you used to work in London for the BBC."

"I was born and brought up in Hastings."

"Where's that?"

"You should know. It's where you invaded us; William the Conqueror and all that."

"Aah! We beat you," she smiled.

"That was the last time you beat us." He smiled.

"Oh, yes?" she said with an inquisitive tone. "Your kings claimed half of France at one time. If you then won all the battles: Crécy, Agincourt, Poitiers, how come you don't own it now?"

Michael was shaken by this thought. *They had never told him about that in school.* He ignored her comment and changed the subject back.

"Hastings is on the south coast. It is one of the Cinque Ports that used to export wool to Flanders in medieval times and then became an important fishing town, but the lawyers and estate agents who have wormed their way on to the local council neglect fishing. They don't understand the local population."

"You do?"

"My mother comes from one of the fishing families, but not my father. That's why I have an unusual surname. Most of the fishermen have the same one or two names: White or Adams. They are all related. The Old Town, where they all live, is a record of the past, with lots of 16th-century cottages, not on roads but *twittens*. I was born there, but when the war started, I went with my parents to London so that my father could work in an arms factory. I do go back there quite often, though. I have a lot of distant relations there. Because of my mother, they regard me as one of them. They wanted me to put a gold earring in my left ear. That's how you know that someone comes from a fishing family. It is supposed to give you some negotiable capital if you are shipwrecked. All the little boys in Hastings Old Town have one. But it would look very silly in London."

"Have you ever been fishing?"

"I have been out with the fishermen, but it's all too smelly for me."

"How did you come to be working for the BBC?"

"After I did my National Service, I did a whole load of casual jobs. I was working in a sub-post office, and one of the regular customers used to chat. One day, he asked me why I was doing a dead-end job. I told him it was the best I could get. He said he worked for the BBC, and they were looking for trainee engineers. The next week, he brought me an application form and his engineering manual to study. I did as he said, and I was invited to an interview. I had to sit an examination on electronics—the stuff I had read up in the manual—and then I went in for an interview. To my surprise, the post office customer was on the board of examiners. I got the job."

"It sounds like a form of nepotism to me."

"It was. I am ashamed of it, but that's how English society works. I did not realise how things worked like that, until I did my National Service. We had an idiot as our adjutant. His only qualification for the job was that he had been to a minor public school. At one point we were threatened with going to fight in the Korean War. He was in charge of our lives and a complete incompetent. It was then that I realised how unjust our society was. I started reading, and I could see the sense in the left-wing philosophers, especially the Utilitarians, Rousseau, and the Marxists."

"You're not a Marxist, are you?"

"Not a real one. The Utilitarians most interested me. 'The greatest good for the greatest number' seemed to be the most sensible attitude to society, and this, unfortunately, is not the basis of Marxism."

"Everybody cannot have all they want. There is not enough to go round." Her father had pointed that out to Monique.

"True, but I agree with Tressell. I think the working classes are exploited. They don't get their share. They are the real creators of wealth. I am a sort of democratic socialist, a Fabian. Robert Tressell lived in Hastings. His book, *The Ragged-Trousered Philanthropists*, showed how the working classes were exploited. The working men are philanthropists because they give away their labour cheaply so that others can become rich. That book really had an effect on me."

The food came, and then Monique took up the conversation again. "So that's how you came to work for the BBC. I have heard you criticising the organisation, but you had a good job with them, didn't you?"

"Yes. I recognise I owe them a lot. They gave me a very good engineering training. That will always be with me. The technical part of the BBC looks after its people very well and trains its own operatives to a high standard, without relying on other institutions or other companies, to do its work for it. In some respects, I will always be grateful. It's the administration and the management that I've got a gripe with," he paused, "and it's the preciousness of some of the programme departments. The music department and the drama department are full of "Darlings," fashionable sycophants."

Life dropped into a sort of routine after that. Both Michael and Monique got a lot of painting done and ate at Mes Amis nearly every evening. It was almost like their lounge.

A group of senior officers assembled at General Salan's headquarters in Algeria. Three officers, including the two gentlemen who had been drinking cognac by the sea, entered.

The younger officer, Colonel Peynet, was apologetic. "I'm sorry we're late."

"No problem," replied General Salan.

"I had to pick up General Maurice, and there was a disturbance on the way. Someone had shot a couple of people in the bazaar."

"Things are definitely getting worse," added General Maurice.

"You can certainly say that. There was another attempt to assassinate me the other day." General Salan gave a fatalistic grin. "Well, you're here now." Then after a pause, "We have heard back from Paris. The government is not willing to compromise, so we will have to go ahead with our plans."

The assembly broke into a hubbub, all speaking at once.

"The fools."

"How can they give away part of France?"

"Do they not love France?"

"This would not have happened in De Gaulle's time."

General Salan brought the meeting to order. "We are thinking of taking over Corsica, as a sort of rehearsal and to test the Paris government's resolve." He paused. "It will also show who really is on our side." Salan nodded in the direction of Massu. "General Massu is going to use the 10th Paratroop Division, but we are not expecting any opposition."

"What is the situation with the CIA? Have your contacts agreed to back us?"

General Challe spoke up. "I intend to go to the United States to speak to my friends."

"As long as they are not against us. Look what happened over Suez," a worried voice contributed.

"Suez is another thing. We should not have been drawn in by the British. The Egyptians were not helping the FLN anyway, and the British just wanted us to help them get their canal back."

The younger officer put in his observation. "In some ways, it is probably a good thing that General De Gaulle is not in charge here. If he were, we might never get the Americans' backing."

"No. The Americans certainly do not like De Gaulle."

"If he had been in charge in Paris earlier, things would never have got to this state. He would not be throwing away part of France. He is a man of honour," insisted Salan.

"He is a soldier," agreed Massu.

"We will offer him the presidency when we succeed. He was always popular with the general populace. They will respect him. He can be our figurehead."

"Has anyone approached him?" enquired Colonel Peynet.

"Not yet. It is far too early, but he must know what is going on, and he must sympathise with us," said Maurice.

"He was a darling of the left as well as the rest of us after the war. They respected the way he stood up for France against the Germans. Most people will listen to him."

"His general popularity will be a great asset. He will unite the country." General Salan was a great admirer of his past boss. He had served in his entourage in England during the war.

"Yes. A soldier; a man of honour. We can rely on him." For Massu, "Soldier" and "Honour" were synonymous. It could not be said too often.

The meeting continued, partly with planning and partly with social matters. Eventually, General Salan drew the proceedings to a conclusion.

"Gentlemen, return to your units and complete your detailed planning."

It was three weeks after the meeting at the Raymonds' that Michael got a visit from Claude, who gave him instructions and tickets. He went to England by train and ferry to visit George. He had no difficulty in finding where he lived. It was a typical semi-detached suburban house. No one would ever suspect it of being the abode of somebody engaged in left-wing French politics.

"I must say you fooled me. I had you down for a conservative," remarked Michael when they met.

"I told you there are more ways of achieving a goal than confronting it straight on."

Michael had always liked George. Now he had more respect for him than ever. He was a canny figure. *Who would have believed that behind that upper-crust exterior lurked a revolutionary?*

"So you are a bit of a rebel?" Michael said this with a grin.

"I'd rather see myself as an upholder of justice."

"Through conspiracy?"

"I saw how things went in the '30s. One country after another fell to dictators—Italy, Germany, Spain—and the democracies did nothing about it. We can't let that happen again. Look what a mess that would land us in if France succumbed. It is even closer to us than Germany. Imagine a military dictatorship in France. No, we can't let that happen." Then with a quick change of tone, "Will you stay and have some lunch?"

After a relaxed lunch, talking about the BBC and updates about Michael's old workmates, they got down to business again.

"Here is a package. Put it in your luggage and don't let anybody see it. Nobody will be interested in you anyway, so don't worry too much. I know you can play things cool. I have seen you with your fellow technicians at coffee breaks."

"I wasn't playing cool. I just think that some of them were naïve."

"As you will. How did you come here?"

"By ferry."

"Are you going back the same way?"

"Yes."

"Well you should try and vary your methods of travel. You don't want a keen customs official recognising you through familiarity and becoming interested in what you're up to."

"Next time I'll come by air."

"Yes, and travel through different airports."

"I could also get some of my fishing friends to give me a lift. They often land fish at Ostend or Boulogne where they can get a better price."

"That would be a very good idea. It could be useful, particularly if it's unofficial." George then thought for a moment. "If you land unofficially, that does run the danger of you being an illegal entry. Then, if they saw you and arrested you, they might take a very great interest in you, so don't do that too often."

"The fishermen often stay overnight to eat at a French restaurant and have a look around. They have no trouble. I'll pass as one of them. Some are my personal relations. I even look a bit like some of them."

"But look at your hands. You'll have to hide those."

"Some wear heavy gloves. I'll do that when there is anyone around."

"Did Bertrand give you money?"

"Yes. He took care of everything."

"Well, here's some more money. Get yourself a good meal on the boat."

"Thanks."

"How is the painting coming on?"

"Very well."

"Have you sold any?"

"Not yet, but hope springs eternal."

"Oh well. I'll see you next time."

The return journey was uneventful, and by the next day, he was back in Paris and in the company of Monique. It was raining gently, giving the streets a soft, mysterious atmosphere. The water crystallised like diamonds on the edge of the canopies of boulevard shops. He felt relaxed. He felt at home.

"So, how was your job? Where did you have to go?" Monique bubbled.

"Oh, I went to northern France by train."

"It's nice to have you back. I missed you yesterday evening. My dinner didn't taste as good."

Michael smiled. He hated deceiving her, but he had not told her a lie. He had been to northern France. He just had not told her he had gone on to England.

That evening at the restaurant, there was yet another political discussion. It seemed as though the whole of Paris was talking politics.

"I hear the army in Algeria has issued the government an ultimatum. They are threatening to invade if the government grants independence to Algeria."

"They wouldn't dare. Would they?"

"They're threatening it."

"It's blackmail."

"What right have they got to tell the elected government what to do?"

"You don't need right when you've got power."

"Military power is only one sort. There is moral power."

"And political power."

"This incompetent government has lost all political power."

"Well, the generals have none."

"The French people have moral power on their side."

"Well, that won't help them if the generals, Salan and Massu, get their way and invade France. We'll have a civil war."

"It will be just like Franco in Spain. It will be worse than when the Germans were here."

"Nothing could be worse than that."

"You wait and see."

"If it comes to that, I'm getting out. I'll go to England. You'd have me in England, wouldn't you, Michael?"

Michael smiled and nodded. Monique tugged his arm tight to her chest. She said nothing. She found politics boring. She knew what she thought, and she had been brought up not to discuss such things. Michael was restrained by knowing more than he was willing to divulge. Talking politics might give him away.

After dinner that evening, they left the restaurant early and went for a walk down by the Seine.

Clochards were curling up under the bridges. Michael was shocked.

"This is terrible. Nobody should have to sleep in the open like this. It isn't Africa. Shouldn't they be taken care of?"

"It's every Frenchman's right to be able to sleep on the street."

"What sort of right is that? We would never allow that to happen in England. We have a welfare state."

"But we were occupied by the Germans. Money is scarce."

"We suffered just as much as you. We may not have been occupied, but our whole infrastructure was destroyed."

"Things like your underground system and your telephone service came out of the war intact. England was a rich country in the '20s and '30s. There was plenty of investment in spite of the depression. Such facilities were buried and safe. We had a series of useless governments between the wars, who never put any money into our infrastructure. The Metro is no better than when it was first built; our telephones are archaic, and our electricity is always breaking down. We need to invest in those things, or France will never get back on its feet and take its rightful place in the world."

"You may be right, but I can't ever imagine a British government allowing people to become so poor and homeless that they have to sleep on the streets."

"Let's not talk politics. I really missed you when you were away." She turned and looked at him with a loving expression. She felt that for all the pleasure it gave her, her love for Michael had weakened her somehow. "I am serious about us. I have realised I want our affair to go on for a long time. Do you feel the same?"

"Yes. In all sincerity, you are the best thing that has happened to me for ages. That stupid BBC manager I told you about did me a favour."

She was excited and reassured.

"My parents are coming to see me next week. I have mentioned you to them on the phone, and they want to meet you." She looked intensely into his eyes to gauge his reaction.

"I'm honoured. I would be delighted to meet them."

Chapter Three

The day had arrived when Michael was due to meet Monique's parents. He took extra care with his shaving and brushed his teeth very hard. He put on a collar and tie and wore his sports jacket. Monique had refused to talk about her parents, so he did not know how to prepare for them. Therefore, he had reverted to the kind of clothes he thought English parents would like to see on a daughter's new boyfriend, or how he would dress for a BBC interview, which was pretty much the same thing.

He caught the Metro to Étoile, as he had been instructed to do by Monique. He thought that was a strange place to meet. Perhaps the parents were staying at a posh hotel near there. On arrival, he got out and looked at the signs indicating the various exits.

"Go out at the exit to the Champs-Élysées," she had said, "and I'll be waiting for you there."

As he mounted the steps he saw her standing at the top, radiating a gorgeous smile and dressed in a very smart blue suit, not at all like her usual working clothes. They kissed, and she grabbed his arm very tightly and led him off down the Champs-Élysées.

"Now promise me whatever happens, it will make no difference to us," she said in a slightly worried tone.

"Of course I promise. It won't change a thing. It's you I'm interested in, not your parents."

"Here we are then."

They had stopped in front of some large green doors, with a small door set within them. Monique unlocked the small door, and they stepped in. The concierge greeted her with a jovial smile, and they passed through a small courtyard and into a hall opposite, where they got into a cage-like lift. Michael was a bit confused.

"Are your parents renting an apartment for a few days then?"

"No. This is where I live."

"In the Champs-Élysées?"

"In the Champs-Élysées." She grinned but then quickly changed her expression.

She enjoyed his confusion, but she realised he might get the impression she wanted to avoid. What Michael did not know, and she needed to impress on him, was that she herself hated rich girls who did nothing all day but went shopping or made up their faces. She had suffered them at school. They were mostly stupid and very boring. She hoped Michael would not take her as one of them.

"You won't hold that against me, will you?" she said.

"I couldn't hold anything against you. But—"

Before Michael had a chance to explain, they arrived, with a clank, at the second floor, and Monique opened her front door. They walked through a small lobby and into a spacious lounge filled with antique Empire furniture. It was hung with paintings. The tall windows were framed by golden curtains, and the wallpaper was panelled and of a subdued red.

A middle-aged man, probably in his sixties, got up from a gilded chair and presented his hand. He was a big man and seemed to have a slight limp.

"This is my father, M. Foch, and this is Michael."

"You're an Englishman, I believe."

"Yes."

"Well, I won't hold that against you. Most of your country's bad behaviour happened before you were born. I suppose you have been on our side for the last two wars."

Monique interrupted, "Three wars. We were together in the Crimean War."

M. Foch ignored his daughter's comment. *Did I make a mistake in ensuring my daughter's education?* Then with a slight scowl, he shook his finger as he leant his head to one side and carried on.

"But before that, you caused a lot of trouble. You always chose the wrong side in any war. French history has time and again been complicated by English interference. Perfidious Albion—well named. However, that's not your fault."

His protestation subsided to a mumble.

Luckily, before Michael could think of an answer, Mme Foch came and presented her hand. Monique also quickly stepped in.

"Can I offer anyone an apéritif? Papa is taking us all to lunch," she said, turning to Michael, "but we do have time for a drink."

Mme Foch, Claire, stepped forward—a small woman with a quiet voice and dressed to match. Hers had been an arranged marriage in order to unite their two smallholdings in the village. But she was lucky. M. Foch had been a good husband: kind, able, and foresighted, so they had lived comfortably. In spite of many setbacks, he had been very successful, and she admired him greatly. Early on, she had decided that he was better suited to making decisions, so she left those to him.

They had produced two daughters. Monique was like her father: strong-willed and self-confident, but Angelique was quieter and a great comfort to her mother.

Mme Foch addressed Monique, "I have put out some glasses and an apéritif on a tray in the kitchen. Shall I get it?"

"No, Mama. I will. Sit and put your feet up."

"I believe you're a painter," said M. Foch, before Michael had a chance to answer Monique's offer of a drink.

"Yes."

"And you used to work for the BBC?"

"Yes."

"Why did you give that up? It was a good job, wasn't it?"

"A very good job."

"And well paid?"

"Very well paid. That's how I could afford to come to Paris and do what I really want to do."

"Painting, eh?"

Then he mumbled something Michael could not hear, but he quickly brought his voice up again.

"Monique tells me that painting is what she wants to do. I let her do what she wants, I'm afraid. In her case, it does not really matter. Eventually, she will find a young blood and settle down, and then he will have to keep her. She does not have to earn her own living, so it isn't a problem."

The end of his sentence faded off into a mumble again. *This is obviously a feature of M. Foch's speech*, Michael noted. Then his verbal vigour returned as he leant back expansively in his chair.

"I have two children, both girls. We have her younger sister, Angelique, at home. She is much less trouble, more feminine, not so strong-willed."

His voice had subsided but then rose again.

"Monique is tough, so she always gets her way. I have no son, so Monique is more like a son to me. I know I shouldn't, but I do let her get away with a lot more than is good for her. I let her indulge herself in painting, for example."

Monique brought in the drinks. She had heard what her father had said. She thought her sister was a bit vacuous. She was not stupid, but she had no gumption. *It's a good job that she is lovely; beautiful and of a sweet nature. Father will no doubt find her a rich husband. Thank God father treats me differently.*

As M. Foch used Monique as a substitute for a son, it gave her a chance to live a proper life and have some influence on the world. *I am not going to be just decorative. The world is going to know I am here. What is life worth if it is empty?*

As she offered her father his drink, she smiled knowingly.

M. Foch took his drink and then continued, with an authoritative air, "You must want to paint a lot if you give up a good, well-paid job. Don't you want to get married and settle down?"

"Yes, but there's time for that, and anyway, the girl I settle down with will understand my passion and go along with it."

"She might! But when women get broody, they start looking for the luxuries in life."

Before Michael could think of a suitable answer, M. Foch had sipped his drink and continued in a louder voice. "The BBC is not a bad organisation. We used to listen to it during the war, although we were not supposed to." The volume of his voice rose again. "Not all English institutions are friendly. Not the RAF, for example. That's very unfriendly. They kept destroying my lorries."

Monique quickly stepped in. "Papa, what time are we supposed to be at the restaurant?"

"We've got plenty of time."

"Not with your gammy leg, we haven't. And not if you want to walk there."

"Don't worry. Everything is under control."

Twenty minutes later, they strolled to the restaurant, Michael and M. Foch in front, mostly discussing the type of trees that were best suited to city planting, with Monique and her mother following on behind. M. Foch was a man of strong opinions, even in the matter of trees.

I can see where Monique gets her self-confidence, thought Michael.

The restaurant was very grand, not like Mes Amis, the one Monique and Michael usually ate in. The head waiter rushed up. "We have your table ready for you, M. Foch. Would you like your usual apéritif?"

"Yes, and you can bring one for my two guests. My wife won't have one. She doesn't like them, but she will have some sparkling water, won't you, Claire?"

Mme Foch grunted a barely audible "Yes."

They were shown to a table in the corner, and the waiter brought the menu.

"Shall I order for us all?" M. Foch asked, anticipating the answer. "There's nothing you don't like, is there, Michael?"

"Oh no."

"That's good."

Without consulting the menu, M. Foch ordered the complete meal and then took the wine list.

"We'll have a Vaudésir with the fish, and Château Pétrus with the main course. And have you got any of that '47 Vouvray left?"

"Just a few bottles, M. Foch."

"Right. We'll have one of them with the dessert."

Then, with an authoritative air, he turned his attention back to Michael, who was feeling a bit ineffectual. "The most important thing in life is the family," he said, wagging his finger again. "With a good family life, you can do anything. People don't appreciate that anymore."

Michael just nodded his head.

"Families cost money. You cannot bring up a family properly without cash."

Michael felt like saying that you cannot bring up a family properly if you are unhappy, and to be happy, you had to do something worthwhile, but discretion got the better part of his valour. He was not a coward, but he remembered what George had said: "There are more ways of achieving your goal than tackling it head–on."

It was a long and slightly painful lunch, but the food was delicious, and the wine excellent. Michael wondered if, once you had tasted the best cuisine, there would ever be any pleasure left in any other food. He hoped there was, as he would never be able to keep up such a gastronomic standard.

After the lunch, Monique walked back to the Metro with Michael. "Don't take too much notice of my father. He is not as bad as he seems at first."

"Your mother doesn't say much."

"She doesn't have a chance to. She adores my father, and she now suffers with arthritis. She has to take life easy."

"Where did your father get that limp? Is that arthritis?"

"No! He was wounded in the First World War. He was badly wounded in his leg, and gassed."

"Mm."

"Listen, I am not coming back with you today. I have to look after my parents. They are not in Paris for long."

"Where do they live then?"

"My father likes to stay in Tours now. He comes from near there, and there are a lot of his childhood friends nearby. It is a reasonably sized town and moves at a slower pace than Paris. He says that the life there is in better keeping with his age. He is slowing up. He used to enjoy living in that flat he has given me, but that was when he was younger; not anymore."

"Your father doesn't approve of me painting. What does he do for a living? Is he retired?"

"My father will never retire. He will go on until he drops. He is indestructible. He has several garages, with a particularly large one here in Paris. He is the Ford main agent for northern France. He also has a lorry business, and he owns quite a lot of land in the Loire valley."

"Gosh! He's a rich man."

"I suppose he is," then added, "but he made all the money himself."

"He said that the RAF destroyed his lorries. During the war? How come?"

"What you have to realise about my father is that he is an opportunist. His only loyalty is to his family, and he will do anything to see they are alright. He started a garage when he was very young, before driving became common. He was ahead of the rest of society and was becoming very successful when the army called him up to fight in The Great War. As a result, he lost everything. Wounded, he was invalided out of the army, a cripple and a pauper, but he started up again and built up several thriving businesses in the '20s and '30s, including garages and a transport company, only to lose them again when the Germans invaded in 1940. He is never one to be defeated, so he co-operated with the Germans and set up another successful lorry business, so helping them, which of course gained him many enemies. It was then that his lorries were targeted by the RAF.

"We had several German officers staying with us when I was a child. One I remember very well. He played Beethoven and Chopin on the piano and knew all about paintings and literature. It was he who taught me to play the piano."

"I didn't know you played the piano."

"There are several things you still don't know about me, not only that I live in a posh flat." She grinned. "But you will. Meeting my parents is only the first step, and it has not put you off, has it?"

"Of course not!"

Monique thought for a minute. "It's strange that such a cultured society as the Germans should have done such terrible things during the war."

"Yes! But don't forget that their culture also contains Wagner, Bismarck, Barbarossa, and Nietzsche; all with a far-right philosophy."

Monique became a bit thoughtful again. "I didn't think my background would worry you, but I admit I was a bit worried that you might see me as a rich young dilettante. I am serious about my painting." She had a second thought. "And I wanted you to be interested in me, not my money."

"I can see that you're a serious painter. I never doubted that. But tell me more about your father."

"Of course, he lost everything again when the Americans came. There was a big move against collaborators, and my father had built up a lot of enemies. However, he courted the Americans and soon he had another transport business. Then it was a lot of Americans that came to our house. They were much louder, and not half as cultured as the Germans, but they were much more friendly. Life was much freer and better. They also had chocolate and silk scarves for my mother. Father was not really a collaborator. He just wanted to do the best for his family. He had served his country and suffered for it. He had done his bit."

"Well, here we are: the Metro," Michael said as he pulled to a halt.

"You will get to like my father when you know him better. He must not put you off me." She stretched up and kissed him. "I'll see you tomorrow. Perhaps a bit late, as I will see my parents to the station first."

Michael had a lot to think about as he made his way back to his room. He was pleased she had said there were things he did not know about her. It eased his conscience. It did worry him that he was keeping *Sinister Port* a secret, and her secrets, if there were any, helped to rebalance the situation.

The next morning, as he was in no hurry to get to his studio—Monique would not be there—and as he had a little cash left from his trip to England, he decided to have breakfast in the café round the corner, opposite St-Germain-des-Prés. He had often noticed it as he walked to the Metro. It was a rather old-fashioned looking café, with tables on the boulevard and lots of polished wood and brass inside. The waiters were traditionally dressed in black with long white aprons. They could have come straight out of a Toulouse-Lautrec painting.

He went in and sat down. The waiter took his order of two croissants and a coffee. A rather pinched-looking man was holding court to an attractive woman and a couple of men friends sitting at the next table. Michael could not hear all he was saying, but suddenly the words, "'I think, therefore I am,' is not enough! We can only start from there,'" emerged out of the hubbub, as the man slapped his hand on the table. "What am I? Who am I? What is 'I'? What do we mean by 'am'?"

At this point, the waiter brought his order and some extra coffee for the noisy group next to him, so Michael took the opportunity to ask the woman to pass the sugar. As the group sipped their coffee, their French subsided to a mumble again, until one of the men leant back on the seat and exclaimed, "Other people are the trouble. They can make life hell."

Michael would have liked to have heard more, but the conversation subsided again. Michael ate his croissants with relish. They were so different to the farmhouse rolls he had had at the Raymond's flat. If there were not class differences in France, there were certainly sophistication and gastronomical differences. He ate his croissants with butter and apricot jam. It had to be apricot jam with croissants, as it had to be strawberry jam with scones and cream in England. Different cultures were not dictated by mere whim but moulded by taste and tradition.

He could hear no more from his articulate neighbours, so he finished his coffee, went up, paid his bill, and left for his studio.

Monique arrived at the studios in the afternoon.

"My mother really liked you."

"What about your father?"

"Oh, he takes longer to make up his mind about people. He is more suspicious. He didn't dislike you, although he thought you ought to get a proper job. Give him time."

She came and snuggled up to him. "But it's not what they think. It's what I think."

Michael started to kiss her neck and whispered a Shakespearian sonnet in her ear. "Shall I compare thee to a summer's day? Thou art more lovely and more temperate…"

It was altogether a tender lovemaking that day. Monique had an indentation under her collarbone, and Michael delighted in exploring it with his tongue. He was then suddenly aware of how beautiful her back was.

Monique delighted in the variety of different moods in their lovemaking. It never got boring. This time there were long, lingering kisses, which she very much enjoyed, and Michael stroked her hair a lot. Birds in the courtyard seemed to have sensed the mood and added their song to enhance the atmosphere, while the sun speckled the floor of the studio with golden afternoon rays.

There always seemed to be new avenues of sensuality to explore, and they all ended in ecstasy. Monique considered herself a very lucky person. She was not aware that Michael felt exactly the same. Young lovers are always a bit shy; usually too shy to express themselves verbally and compare notes.

They had some coffee and then both went to their studios and worked hard, inspired by their relationship. Monique gave Michael enough inspiration to last him for the rest of his life. Again, for the reasons of shyness, neither told they were each other's muse. Monique did not tell Michael that he was her muse also.

They finished work for the day early and went down to the Seine again for fresh air. Their studios engendered passion; their walks by the Seine engendered humanity and friendship. Michael played with the idea that everybody has two distinct parts to their existence, particularly when it comes to how they evolve a friendship with someone of the opposite sex.

There is humanity and gender. One person may be attractive as a human being, evoking sympathy by their intellect, their knowledge, their understanding, and appreciation of others. With another person, it may be pure primeval animal attraction. The balance varies. Usually, it is one or the other of these groups of qualities that seals a friendship, but with Monique and Michael, it was both. Their feelings were perfectly balanced.

They passed a man curled up on one of the grills that allowed warm air from the Metro to escape. It was still early enough in the year for there to be odd cool spells. A pained expression crossed Michael's face. Monique noticed and felt she had to say something.

"He is keeping warm."

"I find it very disturbing. Society should look after its disadvantaged."

"At least he is free. He is not liable to be carted off to a concentration camp."

"Maybe, but we would never let that happen in England, even if times were financially hard."

They carried on.

It was becoming a habit to walk along the lower bank of the river, but on this occasion, they crossed the bridge to Île Saint-Louis and walked through the small garden to the end. There they sat on a bench and cuddled up in each other's arms, watching the boats and the world go by. They did not need a Metro grill to combat the chill in the air. Monique felt things could never get better, and Michael quite separately had come to the same conclusion, although they still never discussed the matter.

When it became time to eat, sensing the moment together, they roused themselves and made off to the restaurant.

A heated conversation was well underway when they arrived at Mes Amis.

"Jacques Soustelle is trying to tie up with the Gaullists."

"Who is Soustelle?" Michael asked Monique in a whisper.

"He used to be the Governor-General of Algeria. He has sided with the Pieds-noirs, the long-standing French immigrant families that have exploited Algeria for several generations."

Michael smiled. "I thought you were not interested in politics?"

"I'm not, but that is common knowledge. Soustelle wants to stop the government granting independence to Algeria. It is currently part of metropolitan France, and most people think it should stay so."

"Most people?"

"Well, a lot of people. I don't know much about these things. I do know that this government does not know what it is doing most of the time. It was much better when De Gaulle was in charge just after the war."

Michael grinned. "Churchill thought he was a very difficult and stubborn man."

"He is, but very often people's biggest weaknesses are their greatest strengths."

"And stubbornness is his greatest strength?"

"That quality helped to put France back on its feet after the war. Otherwise, we would have been swamped by the Americans, and you British."

Most of their group of friends continued with animated political arguments, but Monique and Michael kept quiet and just stared into each other's eyes as they ate their meal. Love can be very debilitating.

"Don't go home. Come back to my hotel with me tonight," Michael pleaded.

"What will the receptionist say?"

"I am on good terms with him. I am sure he will make a concession."

"O.K."

The next morning, they went to have breakfast at the café on the corner together. Michael really liked that café, so he wanted to share it with Monique.

"Les Deux Magots," Monique exclaimed. "I have always wanted to come here but never made it."

"You've heard of it?"

"Yes, of course. Some of my friends come here."

The group of the previous day was there, engaged in hectic conversation as it had been the day before. Michael chose a seat on a bench the other side of the café this time. He did not want his time with Monique interrupted. She agreed with his approval of the place.

"It has a really nice atmosphere."

They had their breakfast and then went to their studios.

As they entered the courtyard, the concierge stopped Michael and gave him a note.

Michael read it. "Where did this come from?" he asked.

"A swarthy dark-haired man delivered it."

Michael was perplexed. *How does Sinister Port know how to contact me here?* It worried him slightly. Nevertheless, he was pleased, as it said that there was more work. It asked him to go to Claude's flat. They had been generous the last time, although they had said the work was to be a labour of love. Money is always useful, and now he was determined to woo Monique, he had to show M. Foch that he was not just a penniless artist.

Monique was curious. "What was the note about?"

"Oh, they want me to do another delivery job."

"Well, that's good."

"I'll have to go and see about it this evening."

"I was thinking of going back to my flat this evening anyway. I need some fresh clothes. I won't go to the restaurant."

This time Michael arrived at the Raymonds' flat to find Claude, the Spaniard, Bertrand, and a new man there. He was smartly dressed and had a suave air about him. He was probably in his early forties but had a very youthful look, evoked by a mop of blond hair.

"This is Pierre."

"So this is our young English courier."

"Michael. How do you do?" said Michael, holding out his hand. Pierre shook it with a surprisingly firm grip.

"This time we want you to take something to England as well as bring something back."

Bertrand took a small package from a drawer and gave it to Michael.

"How did you travel last time?"

"By train and ferry boat."

"Perhaps you had now better go by air, and come back a different route. Try another airport," Bertrand said as he took another package from a drawer, this time a bundle of francs.

"They tell me you're a painter," said Pierre.

"Yes." *Obviously, they know more about me than I realise.* Then, turning to Bertrand, "How did you know where my studio was?"

"It's our business to know these things," Bertrand explained.

Pierre continued. "I am very interested in art. I must come and look at your work."

"You can, with pleasure. Bertrand obviously knows where I am." *I hope that did not sound too petulant.* "He'll give you directions. I am there every day."

"A conscientious painter. A somewhat rare individual."

"If you have an urge to do something, you had best get on with it. I have no time to waste."

"Well, I look forward to seeing you and your work."

Bertrand interrupted. "Here's money for your trip." With a stern expression, he glanced at Pierre and handed Michael a nice thick wodge of francs.

"Good luck," said Pierre, "I'll see you."

The next morning, Michael went again to the café opposite St. Germain for his breakfast. He was going to be in the money now, much larger than before, but with the same people as the centre of attention. Other members of the group, though, were doing most of the talking, mainly directing it at the pinched-faced man, who sat and nodded his approval. Although he was ugly, he was obviously someone who demanded respect. The woman sometimes interjected, and the thin-faced man would approvingly tap her wrist. She would turn and give him a smile. There was obviously something between them, but it was not the same as that between Monique and himself.

The woman was somehow submissive. Monique is not submissive. That is what I like about her. She is strong. She is a person in her own right, not just a sex object.

He sipped his coffee. Then another thought hit him. *How ephemeral is her love, I wonder? She says she loves me, but will it quickly wear off? A woman like her must have had a lot of suitors and have high expectations. I hope I can compete.*

Monique was waiting for him when he arrived at the studio. She had been contemplating how she felt helpless and weak in Michael's presence, when she knew she was a strong woman really.

I know I am strong, but love makes me so weak. Women suffer from being in love.

Michael knew he was mentally strong so why did he feel so weak in Monique's presence?

"I have to go on a trip again tomorrow. I'll be away for a couple of days, but I will be earning money," explained Michael.

"Don't worry. I wouldn't ever want to get in your way." She had remembered what Michael had said to her father. "And, if it ever looks as if I do, tell me."

"You are my inspiration. I can't imagine you ever getting in my way." *Am I sounding pompous? I hope not.*

She giggled, uncharacteristically. "Are you as serious as I am about our affair?" she said, shaking her head as if in doubt. "We have only known each other for a short while, but I feel as though I have known you forever."

"Yes! Of course! You are just the woman I have been looking for without me knowing it." *If I was pompous, it has not worried her.* "I did not realise that there could be someone as ideal as you. You cast off my winter and make spring and summer glorious. I want to spend the rest of my life with you."

She blushed, again uncharacteristically.

"Could we make it a more formal relationship?" She could feel her blood tingling with excitement and fear.

"Why not!?"

She jumped up and kissed him, holding him in a tight embrace.

"Shall I tell my father?"

"What is he going to say?"

"Oh, it does not matter what he thinks." She kissed him again. "But I have to tell him anyway. With time, he will get to like you. He did not disapprove of you, and that is something. I can handle him." She then added as an afterthought, "and my mother likes you."

Michael went out that afternoon and got an airline ticket, Air France, as he had been told they had the best food. He had time to have a coffee at the café on the corner before he went to the airport.

The trip to George's was uneventful. He had lunch with George, and George gave him a package. "How are you travelling?"

"I came by Air France, and Bertrand suggested I should go back by another airline, but I thought I would go down to Hastings and negotiate an unofficial trip this time. I want to try it out, and see if it works."

"That's very good, but come back here another time unofficially as well; otherwise, the stamps in your passport might get out of sync. You could end up with too many entries and not enough exits."

The next day, Michael was in Hastings. He had not been there for some time. The walk from the station to the Old Town along George Street brought back memories. There seemed to be a few cafés, where once there had been hat shops and butchers, but the smell and the noise were the same. He had forgotten how the net huts at Rock-a-Nore looked so forbidding when you first saw them. They now evoked an altogether different feel. He felt a warm familiarity. He regretted he did not have enough time to wander through all the twittens, with their 16th-century cottages and their endless steps, but returning to Paris was the priority. Speed was essential.

He went into the 'Nelly,' The Lord Nelson. It had a reputation for being a rough pub, but he had never had any trouble there, and he had been going there since he was an underage drinker in his teens. It was frequented mostly by fishermen, and occasionally their wives or girlfriends. It was a place where you could buy contraband cognac or illicit Swiss wristwatches—all very cheaply.

As he went in, up the steps came his second cousin, Charley, a six-foot muscular chunk with a gold earring, gold beard, slightly thinning gold hair, and a red face.

"Hallo, Mike, we haven't seen you here for a while. What have you been up to?"

"All sorts of things, which is what I would like to talk to you about."

"So, you've got a proposition for me?"

"Yes."

"Right. Let's go into the back bar. It's quieter there. We'll get a drink on the way."

They pushed in through the crowd to the bar, and ordered two pints.

"Let me pay for this," said Michael, whipping out his wallet.

"That's nice of you. It must be something bloody serious you want to talk about."

Michael smiled. They collected their drinks and walked through the front bar, where the noise was deafening. Chrissie, a notorious local lesbian, was stripped to the waist and dancing on a table. There was pandemonium.

"Hey. Charley! Don't go away. It'll be your bloody round soon." A fellow fisherman was intent on taking his celebrations to the limit.

"Right. I'll be back." He turned to Michael. "The lads have had a record catch. Now they are going to drink it all away. They'll never be bloody rich. Fish are fetching a hell of a good price at the moment, and there's plenty of it about, but they won't have any bloody money left when the market turns down, as it will do." Charley dodged a body as it staggered back and fell on the floor in front of them. It was John Maridadi—not his real name. Charley ignored him, stepped over, and carried on. "Adolf Hitler was no bloody good for the human race, but he did a great service to the fish and fishermen. Without the boats being able to go out so regularly, the bloody stocks recovered."

They sat down in the quieter back bar.

"Well, what can I do for you? Do you need a new watch?"

"No. I believe you sometimes put into Ostend or Boulogne."

"Yes, we can often get a better price in their market."

"How do you feel about giving me a lift there? No questions asked. I'll make it worth your while."

"You cunning old sod! What are you up to? You're supposed to be one of the respectable members of the family." Charley had a wide grin.

"Sh--! It's just a little job I am doing. It has to be hush-hush."

"Well, in our line of business, you learn to keep your bloody mouth shut." He nodded his head and, looking at Michael, said, "But if you're coming with us, you can't bloody well look like that. Go and get some old clothes and a hat. The customs would take one look at you and know you're no bloody fisherman. They are easy with us. We did things for them during the bloody war, but they have to be tough on everyone else to make up for it."

"Old clothes should not be hard to find."

"Go and see Maggie. My clothes will be too big for you. We were meant to go with the high tide at 5.30 tomorrow morning, but I think this lot will have bloody thick heads. We might not make it."

"I'll be here at 5.30 anyway. Thanks. This is quite important to me."

"Not here. On the stade. You know my boat."

"I really appreciate this."

"Well, it's bloody family, isn't it? I like to help out a family member if he's in trouble."

"Oh, I'm not in trouble."

"As you say." Charley gave a sceptical grin.

A loud voice suddenly came from the front bar. "Come on, Charley. It's your bloody round."

Michael left.

After having spent the night at Maggie's, his aunt's, Michael was there at 5.30 in the morning in his newly acquired old clothes, and his better stuff wrapped up very tightly in a bundle and stuffed in a canvas bag.

Charley greeted him. "Just waiting for Jim to come back from the Ice House."

When Jim arrived, Michael helped push the boat off down the shingle, and they were away.

The sun was just rising. There came a glow across the grey horizon. A golden line etched its way along the edge of the world, and then, as a cork out of a bottle, it suddenly plopped up in all its glory, golden and warming.

"The gods are with us. It's going to be a bloody nice day," said Charley as he coiled a rope. "This is Jim, and this is Brian." Jim was at the bow checking on the winding gear, and Brian was at the wheel in the small half-cabin. They both raised their hands in recognition. "You can help them shoot the trawl when we start fishing. I told the coast-guards that we might put into Ostend if the prices were good, so the Belgian customs won't be surprised at our appearance. They are all in cahoots with each other, the British, French, and Belgian customs, so they will be expecting us. There is a good ground on the way to Ostend, which fits in with our plan very well. It's a bit bloody close to the shipping lanes, but perhaps because of that, it usually has plenty of fish. It's good for young brill and turbot. They're easing their way up to the North Sea this time of year."

Charley set a course east by south. He had consulted the tide charts. "If we do a bit of fishing, it should bring us back just right." The engine was noisy and smelly. Michael sat in the bow, where he was away from the fumes, and the loudest noise was the ripple of the water against the hull. They passed Fairlight, Rye, Dungeness, Dover, and out into the North Sea. Once past Dover, Charley got out his hand-bearing compass and made some sightings. He then looked at the charts. "Right. I'll take the helm. You can help the others shoot the trawl. They will show you what to do. Here's some industrial gloves; otherwise, your nice hands will be ripped to bloody shreds." He grinned.

Once all the nets had gone over the stern, the crew relaxed a bit. There was nothing to do until the first catch came in. A breeze was coming up, and the sea was becoming choppy. Charley steered the boat in a straight and steady line, not too fast. Eventually, it was time to haul in. As the net was coming over the side, Brian was releasing the fish from the net on to the deck, while Jim was being sick over it.

"I thought you were a fisherman. How come you are seasick?" enquired Michael.

"Being a fisherman doesn't stop you being fucking seasick. Did you know that even Lord Nelson was seasick and had to stay in his cabin for the first fucking week at sea?"

It was a good haul. Fish were flopping all over the deck.

"Leave that," said Charley. "Brian and Jim can do the gutting. You won't be quick enough. I've got another job for you. Come with me." Charley secured the helm with a short piece of rope, and they went round to the foredeck, where Charley opened a hatch. Michael then helped him get up a canister, rather like the ones that Michael had seen on the newsreels with supplies for paratroopers.

"Attach it to this drift net, and with that rope to that orange marker buoy, and then it will be time to shoot again, so go back and help the others." With fish still all over the deck, Michael helped Jim and Brian get the tackle over the side. At sea, nothing is happening, or everything is happening. Charley swung the boat into a 180-degree turn, then called them all together to ease the canister and a small drift net over the back, and when it had sunk, he pushed over the orange marker buoy.

With that done, Charley got on the radio. "Hallo. This is Motor Fishing Vessel Carey calling Le Corbeau. Are you receiving me? Over."

There was loud crackling and static.

"This is Le Corbeau receiving you loud and clear. How are you, my friend? Over." This was said in a very strong French accent, or so Michael thought.

"Fine. It's good to hear from you, my dear Loik. We have a bloody good catch, and I wondered what the prices were like in Ostend today. Over."

"They are very good. Worth a visit. Fish is very popular at the moment. You British prevented us from getting any during the war, so the housewives are making up for lost time, and meat is still in short supply and expensive. Tell me, where did you say you did so well? I am looking forward to a good catch myself. Over."

Charley spoke in a very clear and precise tone. "As a good friend, let me share my luck with you. At 51° 17.2' N and 2 ° 22.5' E, you should be in for a good haul."

"Thank you. I will follow your suggestion. All the best. Out."

Charley turned again to Michael. "These new ships' radios are so bloody good. They make life so much bloody easier."

"The French have the same as well?"

"Yes, but he's not French. Loik's a Breton. I speak French as well as him. Didn't you hear his bloody terrible accent?"

They were putting into Ostend harbour—the fishing boat section—just as the sun was going down. It had been an exhilarating day. Michael felt tired but healthy. He would like to do that more often. The fresh air! The excitement! Then he realised that the dangerous part had just begun.

They tied up and unloaded the boxes of fish on to the quay, while Brian went off to get a trolley. A customs official came down the dock. "I'm sure you won't have anything you shouldn't on board, will you?" he said with a big smile.

"Hallo, Coos," replied Charley, with an air of innocence. "Come on board and have a drink."

The official sauntered down the gangplank, gave a cursory look around, and sat down to a small cognac.

"Oh, by the way, here is some English tea for your wife," Charley presented a small package, "and perhaps you would like a couple of Dover soles for your supper tomorrow."

When the official had gone, Jim and Brian got the fish on to a trolley and round to the market, then came back to change into cleaner clothes in order to go out to the restaurant they knew. While they were away, Michael took his money from his wallet. "How much do I owe you?"

"Oh, nothing. Consider it part of the family business."

"No. Come on. I said I would pay you, and I will. Will this do?" He handed over a wad of francs. "This is what I can comfortably afford."

"That's fine. More than fine. Anytime you want a lift, just let me know." He radiated a broad smile.

"I'm sorry it's in francs."

"Oh, that's alright. It's not just the bloody government that has a foreign balance of payments problem. Francs are fine."

"I might want a lift back one day. How can I contact you?"

"I'll give you a phone number. Say you want to make a special order for fish. Give the time you want to be picked up by the number of kettles or half kettles you want. So, if it is 5.30, say, 'Five and a half kettles of mixed fish to be delivered in the morning or afternoon,' and the place by 'Down the End' for Ostend, 'Queen Mary's Head' for Calais—because she lost the place to the French—or 'The Bread Shop' for Boulogne."

"That's not a very sophisticated code. Won't the customs be able to quickly work that out?"

"Oh, they're not that intelligent, and they're even less bloody professional than we are. More than that, they owe us one. One of their bloody cutters had broken down off Dover the other day. We took it in tow and made for Rye. We took it up the Channel and left it at Rye Harbour, tied up to the harbourmaster's quay to repair their engine."

He chuckled. He always liked to recount a good story. "We nearly came a bloody cropper, though, on their behalf. It had only left just enough tide to get out over the bloody bar. The tide was out by the time we got to Hastings, so we couldn't beach and had to stand off for a tide."

He stuffed the money into his tackle bag and continued, "However, that turned out alright in the end. We were surrounded by a large shoal of bloody mackerel, so we shot our nets and made a bloody good haul."

He was looking very happy as he put on a sports jacket. "You see, King Neptune loves us more than the bloody customs. He looks after his own."

Michael left his old clothes in a locker and went with the crew to eat.

At dinner, Michael tackled Charley. "You seem to be on very good terms with the customs."

"At sea, we all have to help each other. Neptune is a stern and sometimes cruel master. Either you help each other, or you sink, one by one."

The meal was so good, and the conversation and drink so enjoyable, that Michael stayed longer than he intended and had to rush to get the late train to Paris.

He slept on the train. Rather blearily, the next morning, he went straight away and delivered the package to Claude.

Monique was waiting for him at his studio. "Did it all go alright?"
"Yes. Fine."
"Where did you have to go this time?"
"Oh, I went to Belgium." Michael was pleased it was not a lie.
"I have thought a lot about what we said the other day," said Monique. "You have not changed your mind, have you? If you are still serious, I would like to tell my father."
"No. I am serious about our future. By all means, tell your father. I want to marry you."

Chapter Four

A rather prosperous-looking group had assembled at Albert Renier's large, luxurious house in the Loire Valley, across the river from Courtay. There was Madame Muson, a well-known socialite; Hubert Gamon, the racing driver; General Duchamp, who had retired directly after the war; and M. Dubret.

The French did not usually entertain at home. Food was an art, and therefore had to be worshipped in a place devoted to it. A restaurant was usually preferred, but on this occasion, there was a very delicate matter they wanted to discuss, and one for which they needed complete privacy.

"If the army do stage a coup, the populace is not going to take kindly to it. We are going to have civil war." Albert Renier, as host, was acting as a kind of chairman.

There was chaos as everybody started talking at once.

"We don't know which side will win in that situation. It could be very nasty and go on for a long time."

"Civil wars are always the worst kind."

"Most of the small farmers around here are members of the Communist Party."

"It's not those I'm worried about. It's the rabble."

"The rabble? The riff-raff? Aren't the communists the rabble?"

"No! The Communist Party is usually very well-organised. They will let things develop and then step in. We only need to worry about them in the long run."

"Yes! Communist Party members are disciplined. They will act on orders when their hierarchy see which way things are going."

"They will only be a problem and try to take over when chaos reigns. It is later that they will come into their own and try and sort things out to their own advantage."

"I'm worried about the townies, the jealous rabble-rousers. It's people that resent success. They are our real enemies."

"So what are we going to do about it?"

M. Renier resumed his chairmanship duties and brought the conversation to the point. He had gravitas. "We have to be prepared."

They all looked to him for a suggestion.

"It will be impossible to defend ourselves around here, so we have to make sure we have somewhere to go until things blow over. Now is the time to plan in case we have to leave in a hurry."

"What do you suggest?"

"It will be safest abroad," M. Dubret put in.

"Exactly! That is what I was coming to. In which case, we will need funds abroad. We need to deposit capital safely waiting for us in foreign banks. We don't want to depend on charity."

"Certainly not! You're right. We might have to get out of the country fast if things get too bad. We need to prepare."

"That is going to be difficult," General Duchamp added. "The government has already stopped any transfers of capital abroad."

"I have no desire to leave France," Madame Muson protested.

"You might have no choice," came a reply.

"Don't you spend most of your time abroad anyway?"

"Only on business."

"But you must have contacts, and surely you have some credit there."

"They are only business contacts."

"For whatever reason, you have contacts. You will be alright. Not like the rest of us. You must have money stashed away in foreign bank accounts somewhere."

"No, I never thought things would come to this."

"None of us expected things would be so badly managed as to come to this."

Albert Renier decided he must concentrate the company's thoughts. "We should make arrangements now. We should decide where to go, and set things up there. Between us, we must have considerable resources. It will be easier to organise if we combine forces and shift funds there together. The size of our joint funds will tempt somebody and attract help. Someone or some organisation will be very interested."

There was a murmur of agreement.

"So, if it is agreed, I will look into it."

It was about a week later that Pierre turned up at Michael's studio one afternoon.

"I've come to see how well our courier can paint."

"Come in. It's nice to see you. Would you like something to drink: tea, or coffee? Or wine?"

"A glass of wine would be welcome."

"Monique has some decent wine. Let me get her."

Michael disappeared to get Monique and wine and, if he was honest to himself, to get some moral support.

It does not matter how confident I feel about my paintings. When it comes to showing them to others, I am hesitant. When looking at a picture with another person, the faults seem to jump off the canvas at me. I see problems that I had not noticed before.

While Michael was away, Pierre looked round the studio. He studied the canvas on the easel and then looked at the pictures that were leant face-in against the wall. He picked out a couple, including the nude of Monique.

Monique and Michael entered.

"I can see this is the young lady. That explains the beautiful picture. With a model like that, one could not fail to paint a masterpiece."

Michael blushed. "It's not a masterpiece."

"It is, or very nearly," insisted Monique.

"I am sure it means something special to you, and I would not deprive you of it. It really is a good picture. I like the way that it is not just the body that is important. You have shown character in the face."

He turns to the young couple. "We have to thank Giotto for that, you know." Pierre felt more people should know the history of art. It was one of his mini-crusades. "Giotto put feelings into the faces of his humans. They were no longer just creatures of God—anonymous creations—but beings in their own right. It was probably his paintings that inspired Piero della Francesca, who then developed that idea. His characters are completely human."

Pierre's enthusiasm increased. "You feel as if his figures could step off the wall to meet you. I still feel the excitement of my first visit to Arezzo." He suddenly became self-aware. "However, I digress." He reverted to a more prosaic voice level.

"You are a better painter than I was expecting, so I am interested in purchasing one of your works for my collection."

Michael and Monique were dumbfounded. There was silence while Pierre picked up another one of the pictures from the wall and propped it up on a chair.

Neither Michael nor Monique were expecting Pierre to be a customer. Their pulses quickened with expectation and excitement.

"Yes, they are very good," exclaimed Pierre.

Monique's confidence blossomed. *I knew he was very good.*

Michael was flattered, but then the thought came to him, *Maybe Pierre is humouring me and only interested because he knows me.*

"I like these two very much. Which one do you like?" said Pierre.

Michael wanted to say that the colour was not quite right in the one on the right, and he had not been able to get the perspective correct in the one on the left, but he only said, "I don't know."

Monique butted in. "They are both excellent paintings."

Pierre stepped back and sat down on a chair.

Monique took control of the situation. "Here, have a glass of wine while you think. It's a Chablis Grand Cru." Monique proffered the wine.

Pierre smelt it and then took a sip. "I can see that you have other qualities as well as looks."

"I was brought up to appreciate the good things in life. That's why I admire Michael's paintings."

Pierre was impressed. *She has wit and drive as well as looks.*

Michael felt like jelly. He had nothing to say. His normal confidence was missing when it came to something as close to his heart as his painting. The future would confirm where he stood in the world of art, but so far he had nothing by which to judge his own ability. *I have not been in Paris all that long, and here I am on the verge of a sale; and to a man who obviously knows what he is talking about. Perhaps I have already progressed further along the road to quality than I am aware of.*

"I think I marginally prefer the one on the left," Pierre commented, stroking his chin. "How much would you charge for that?"

Michael stood in confusion. He did not want to lose a sale, but he did not want to sell himself cheap.

Monique looked at Michael, and seeing his confusion turned to Pierre. "We could not accept less than a hundred thousand francs." She put on a defiant air.

Michael was shocked. *I would be willing to take a lot less*, but before he could say, Pierre replied.

"In that case, I will give you a hundred and fifty thousand."

Michael and Monique looked at each other, not knowing whether to laugh or cry.

"Now let us enjoy this excellent wine," Pierre remarked, easing the tension.

Michael and Monique relaxed, and the three of them sat around laughing and joking for the next couple of hours, discussing painting, travel, the weather, Paris, anything but politics.

Eventually, Pierre announced that he had to go. "I have an appointment. It will be difficult to carry the painting. I will pay you now," he said, pulling out his rather fat wallet. "But I will send someone to collect it. Better still, why don't you deliver it? Come to dinner. I live in Montmartre. Here is my card, with my address. When could you make it?"

"As soon as you like. How about tomorrow?" suggested Monique.

"Tomorrow it shall be then. Shall we say 7.30? Nothing formal. Just come as you are." Then, as an afterthought with a big smile, "But bring the painting."

They waved as they watched Pierre cross the courtyard, and then they both screamed and flung their arms around one another. They jumped and danced around.

"Wow! How about that! A hundred and fifty thousand francs!"

"You deserve it," exclaimed Monique.

"We should have shown him some of your paintings," said Michael in a more serious tone.

"Oh, never mind. There is plenty of time for that. We might have confused him."

"A hundred and fifty thousand francs!" Michael could not believe his luck. "What shall we do with it?"

"It will be a great meal tonight."

"Where would you like to go?"

"Our usual place. We don't want to change. We must practise for when you become really rich and famous. We must practise at being normal and above temptation."

"IF we become rich and famous." Michael was more cautious about success. "We must not get carried away."

They did have a big meal that night, and instead of the house red, they ordered a couple of bottles of the best wine for their friends. They announced that Michael had sold a painting, but not how much he had sold it for. Their friends were very pleased and celebrated with them.

The next afternoon they went up to Montmartre. They left early, not only spurred on with excitement, but to take their time to enjoy the view. From the Metro, they wound their way up the narrow street and then up the steps, stopping every now and again to look back and see Paris rise above the screen of houses in the foreground. Half way up the steps, they sat on a bench, and Michael put his arm around Monique.

This will be a moment I will remember for the rest of my life. With the most wonderful person in the world next to him, and a view suggesting an animated

French impressionist painting in front of him, he knew he was alive, and he knew he was privileged.

Monique looked sideways at Michael. *He enjoys the view in the same way as I do.* She was suddenly aware that her lover had more to offer than just good company and sex. *He is going to be a great painter; a great success. Kind and understanding, he has soul, and we have so many common interests to talk about and share. What a great partner. I am so lucky.*

There were quite a few tourists around, mostly Americans, but not so many yet as would swamp the place. A man was playing a violin at the top of the steps, where they paused for their final view before entering Sacré-Coeur. Michael put a coin in his hat. He felt that now he suddenly had some money, he ought to think about those less well-off than himself.

Monique was a bit sceptical. *Should beggars be encouraged?* she thought.

Inside, the church was cool and had a very mystical air. Although he accepted Marx's view of religion as the opiate of the people, Michael had to admit the great church was impressive. *If it was their belief in God that had inspired those two soldiers, facing certain death in the Franco-Prussian War, that made them vow to create this beautiful building, then religion has a function,* he reluctantly thought. *The truth does not matter. Myths have their place in the world. Religion, the greatest myth of all, should be tolerated for that reason alone.*

They sat for a few minutes. Michael could see that Monique was also impressed, although he knew that she had been there many times before. Eventually, however, they came out, bursting into the glorious late afternoon sunlight, and their newfound expectations. They both of them, in their own way, looked forward to a future of artistic success and domestic bliss.

"Shall we go and find this address?" Monique suggested.

"Alright, but it is still a bit too early: 7.30, he said."

"We'll just have a look. We don't want to be rushing around at the last minute, not able to find it, and then turn up late."

"But we don't want to interrupt him by turning up early."

"I have been taught that one should always turn up five minutes after the stated invitation."

They walked round the corner, seeking out the address. Its entrance was not so imposing, but you could see that the other side obviously looked out over Paris. *What a grand place to live*, Michael thought. *It must have a view as good as that outside Sacré-Coeur.*

"Let's go and get a cup of coffee in the square."

They sat in the square for some time, looking every so often at their watches. The canopy under which they sat gave a diffused light, making Monique's face glow. *She must be one of the most beautiful women in the world,* Michael thought. *And intelligent, and gifted. What have I done to deserve this?* He kept returning to this same thought to the point of monotony.

Monique's head was backlit, receiving reflected light from the white tablecloth beneath. This made all her features even more delicate and beautiful than they were usually.

"Is this the face that launched a thousand ships and burnt the topless towers of Ilium? Monique, make me immortal with a kiss." Marlowe's words did more justice to how Michael felt than any he could conjure up himself.

Monique just laughed and changed the subject. "Your friend Pierre must be very wealthy."

"It looks like it. I don't know him very well. I can't call him a friend. He is more of an acquaintance. He is one of the group that employ me to deliver messages."

"What do they do, these men? Are they businessmen?"

"Sort of."

"What sort of business?"

"Ooh. Supply. Transport."

"Then my father will probably know them."

"I don't think so. They work in a completely different area."

Michael was shocked by how silly he had been to let the conversation move in the direction of his job. *It must not happen again. I must be on my guard. That was a close-run thing. I must be more careful.*

Monique speculated, "Yes, he must be quite rich to live in such a beautiful place."

"But I know he is very sympathetic to those less fortunate than himself, in spite of his wealth. He has expressed worry about most people's state of existence, and the lack of equality in society. I think he must be a socialist."

What on earth am I saying? he thought, and he kicked himself for again being so off his guard. *It's stupid to let the conversation go in the direction of politics.* He gave himself a harsh mental admonition. *I must learn.*

They went back to sipping their coffee.

Eventually, the time came to go to dinner. They were so intent on gazing into each other's eyes that they nearly forgot the painting, and had moved several metres away before they both screamed and rushed to retrieve it.

Standing outside Pierre's front door, they adjusted their dress.

"Do I look alright?"

"Perfect."

The door was opened by a tall man; not Pierre. "Ah! The young guests. M. Pierre is expecting you."

They were shown into a spacious lounge, richly furnished, but Michael hardly noticed the Empire furnishings. He was struck by the large windows down one side of the room that looked out on to a panoramic view of Paris. Monique was also taken by the view. She would not have noticed the furniture anyway, as she had lived with such stuff all her life.

"Wonderful, isn't it?" Pierre stepped forward, but instead of proffering his hand, he turned and stood beside the couple admiring the view. "It is the most beautiful picture in my collection."

"But I forget myself," he continued "That's what beauty does to you."

He held out his hand and greeted the guests. "Welcome!"

The man who opened the door entered carrying a tray of drinks.

"I took the liberty of getting you an apéritif—San Raphaël," said Pierre. "You must have seen it advertised on the back of all the buses. I rather like it, but if you don't, Guillaume will get you something else."

They sipped it.

"It's great," exclaimed Michael.

"I have decided that I am going to cook for you myself this evening. We are having confit de canard. It is easy to do. I have it shipped from a friend of mine in Cognac. His wife makes the best confit I have ever had—probably the best in France—maybe because she puts plenty of Rémy Martin in it. I thought we would start with some lobster as the fish course. Neither of you are allergic to it, are you?"

"Oh no."

"We will eat in the kitchen so that we can talk as I cook. But before that, let us have a look at the painting."

It was unwrapped and put on an easel that Pierre took from a cupboard.

"Yes, you are a good painter, and there should be a bright future for you."

Monique, who was sitting opposite Michael, gave him a big smile and winked. She really was as pleased as he was.

After a pause, "Perhaps you would like to look at some of my other pictures?" offered Pierre.

"Yes, please!"

Pierre led them into the hall.

"This is my Braque."

"A Braque!"

"It's glorious. One of the best I've seen."

There was a canvas about one foot six by two foot of a still-life. It had wood graining—a feature of which the artist was very proud. Pierre pointed this out.

"Braque was able to do this because he had been a house painter before he met the artistic crowd. Picasso was jealous of this ability, and it was said that that was the impetus towards collage. Not able to emulate Braque, Picasso just stuck pieces of wood or photos on his canvas."

Michael was not usually keen on still-lives, but in this case, the colours were so harmonious that he would accept any subject matter, even still-lives.

Pierre continued, "Yes. I wasn't so lucky with my Picassos, but they are not bad, even though they are not his masterpieces."

Michael's eyebrows went up in amazement.

Pierre led them into a small bedroom, and there, sure enough, were two Picassos.

"I think they are fantastic," said Michael.

"But they are not inspired. The thing about Picasso is that he is an inspirational painter. He goes along turning out adequate work, based on the odd visual thing that interests him intellectually, but it is when something affects his emotions that he really comes to life. Look at that beautiful head of his lover, Marie-Therese Walters—that one with the ponytail. There his feelings were disturbed. He saw her in the street, you know. He was immediately smitten. He went up to her and is supposed to have said, 'I want to paint you. I feel we have a great future together.' Within a week they were in bed. She was seventeen, and he was forty-five. That gives me hope," Pierre said this with a big smile. He went on.

"It was the same when he painted *Guernica*. There, a different emotion roused him but just as strongly. On these occasions, his paintings were injected with fire. Art should always be a subtle balance between the intellectual and the emotional."

"That's what I think," interrupted Monique with great glee.

Pierre's face lit up at finding a like mind. He continued, "With these two paintings and his other great works, his emotions were disturbed, and being a great artist, he was able to balance his inspiration with technical know-how and aesthetics. Picasso is always intellectually interesting, but it is when he injects his emotions that he becomes great."

"Well, I think they are fantastic," said Michael again, turning away towards Pierre, "even if they are not his best."

"Picasso is a bit of a joker," Pierre continued. "He does not always take his own painting seriously. This is both an advantage and a disadvantage. It allows him to inject wit and humour."

As they turned to go, Pierre continued, "Now let me show you a painter that goes in the other direction—the opposite of Picasso."

He led them into another bedroom and pointed to a picture over the bed.

"It's a Modigliani!" exclaimed Monique.

One of Modigliani's nudes—one with the pose created by Goya—held the place of honour, looking down on the bed.

"Yes, and I love it. It is perhaps a bit too emotional and contradicts what I have just been saying about balance, but given the choice of only hanging on to one picture, if I ever went bankrupt, I would choose this. He is a painter whose work is always full of emotion, but does not always come up to scratch in visual theory."

Pierre stepped back to pontificate, a habit of his of which his friends chided him. "There are some painters, who are not the greatest, that just appeal to you." He continued with a slightly apologetic look. "Cézanne, for example, is a much greater painter than Modigliani, but I have no desire to own a Cézanne, although I can appreciate his greatness." He paused. "Perhaps I'm just a sentimentalist."

"There's nothing wrong in that," protested Monique.

"Maybe." A wistful expression momentarily overcame Pierre's face, and then vanished. "Come. Let's go and start the cooking."

Michael interrupted, "Who painted this?"

"You would not believe it, but that's a Gauguin. You know he exhibited in all but one of the Impressionist exhibitions before he discovered the style that we recognise as his... He was a man who was always torn in many directions. He felt as though he should be a successful businessman, but was drawn by a creative urge. Mythology has him down as a tough, uncouth rebel. That's nonsense. But he was always teetering between bourgeois respectability and bohemian artistry. He was a successful stockbroker in his early life. His Danish wife married him thinking she would have a comfortable future, not realising he had already been bitten by the painting bug. For a long period in his life, he could not decide between being respectable and being an artist. In the end, the artist won, for which we should be grateful. For him, however, the final judgement might be different. It destroyed him socially, emotionally, and probably mentally."

Michael was still young. He did not understand what Pierre was talking about. He could not yet see how there could ever be such a conflict.

As Pierre spoke, they passed into the large kitchen-cum-dining room, and he went behind a cooking island, with gas rings, and a copper extractor hood above. Neither Monique nor Michael had ever seen anything like that in a domestic kitchen before, but Pierre occasionally liked to cook for his guests, and having such an arrangement allowed him to face his friends and participate in the conversation while he worked. Pierre was an excellent cook. Michael had never had confit before. He liked it. The lobster did not impress him so much. Having lived in Hastings, he had had it often.

They went back to Monique's flat that night after a long and entertaining evening. Michael was very impressed by the luxury they had enjoyed. Pierre had organised his life beautifully. Michael could easily get used to such living.

Monique was interested in a different aspect of Pierre. *Why is there no evidence of a woman around, and what business is he in?*

"What is it that you deliver for Pierre and his company?" inquired Monique when they were alone.

"Oh, letters mainly, or small packages that need to be delivered quickly and safely."

"Couldn't they be sent by post?"

"Yes, but you know what the post is like. Things get lost or take ages to arrive."

"They must be valuable or important to make it worth their while to pay you and cover your expenses."

It was several days later that Monique came in with the news that she had been in contact with her father, and told him that they wanted to get married.

"How did your father take it?"

"He scoffed, but he brightened up a bit when I told him how much you had sold your painting for."

"That's not so surprising." Michael had him down as a materialist who did not have much time for artists, only money.

"Oh, come on. He is not so bad. He will get used to you," said Monique, nodding her head.

"Let's hope so."

"He has invited us next weekend to a house he has in the Loire Valley."

———

Le Manoir d'Espérance was not a chateau but an 11th-century manor house just outside Courtay, a small village on the River Loire, not far from Amboise. It predated those great buildings by a couple of centuries, but it was fairly large. It was a fortified manor house. The cream-white stone walls were six feet thick at the base and had few windows, except for arrow slits in the upper stories. On one corner, it had a round tower, topped in blue-grey slate. At the bottom of this tower, there was an unimpressive small door through which you entered into the hallway. From there, a circular staircase took you to the upper floors, and another small door to the left took you into a large high-ceilinged hall, which was used as a lounge. Although the front of the house was still in its original defensive state, the back had been altered, and now French windows led on to the garden. This garden had been neglected and become a bit overgrown, but the gravel area along the south-facing elevation gave a perfect space for sitting in the sun, perhaps under a parasol, whilst sampling wine and eating olives.

M. Foch was not at the house when they arrived.

Mme Foch and the housekeeper produced a tasty meal for the four of them. Mme Foch said very little at dinner, so the conversation was mainly between the young couple and the housekeeper, who explained a lot of the history of the house. She was a local and quite proud of it. Mme Foch, although of few words, smiled and nodded as points were made. She enjoyed listening. She had been taught to be seen and not heard by her parents.

After dinner, Michael was shown to a large bedroom, with a black-and-white stone floor and a high vaulted ceiling. There were several large tapestries hung on the walls. This gave the room a medieval look, which was enhanced by a grand, heavily carved, four-poster bed.

Michael's curiosity, always practical, was roused. *I wonder how they got such a big bed into the room, when all the doors are so small? It was not built with the house; the style is several centuries later, so it must have been brought in pieces and assembled here... or perhaps carved here. That's a nice thought.*

M. Foch arrived the next morning by chauffeur-driven car while Michael and Monique were out in the grounds. Monique was showing Michael the vineyards. A local farmer kept them under control, although Monique complained that they were neglected. The boundaries were unkempt, and it was difficult to know where the family's land ended and other people's began. Even Monique could not tell. Michael was struck by how hard and practical Monique was in worldly things, while so soft with him.

They made their way back to the kitchen for lunch. M. Foch was there, sitting at the end of a long oak table. He did not beat about the bush. Directly, everyone was seated; he came straight to the point. "So you want to marry my daughter."

"Yes, we do love each other," said Michael, staring at Monique.

"Well, there's more to marriage than love. Love only lasts a couple of years. At least what you youngsters call love." He gave a small smile to his wife.

"Yes, I know,"

"I call that infatuation."

Monique interrupted. "We are more than infatuated. Our characters fit perfectly together."

M. Foch scoffed and turned again to Michael. "You are stealing away my prize possession, my daughter, so how do you intend to keep her?"

"I'll earn a living."

"Selling paintings?" M. Foch scoffed again. "Mind you, she tells me you just sold one for a tidy sum."

"Yes. I was lucky."

"Luck does not last forever, you know." M. Foch tucked into his grilled ham. "Monique should show you round the estate this afternoon. I have a few jobs to do. We'll talk about this again at dinner."

Monique jumped in. "I have already shown him the vineyards."

"Well, show him the house and the cellars."

Mme Foch had drifted away. She mused over all the different people she had entertained over the years: French, Germans, and Americans. *And what was it all about?*

The afternoon was spent firstly exploring the house. Michael was again struck by how small all the doorways were. That was probably for defensive purposes, but it meant that you had to duck your head a lot, and Michael did not succeed every time. Monique took the opportunity to 'rub it better.' The house was extensive, and Michael wondered how you could heat it. It must get cold in the winter. Even in summer, it was cool. Then they went down into the cellars beneath the house.

"We've got about 200,000 bottles here," offered Monique.

"It does not look that many."

"No, all the valuable wines are buried beneath the floor. That keeps them at the right temperature and also prevents theft. They are worth a lot of money, you know. The '47 would already sell for 700 francs a bottle in Paris, and the price is going up all the time."

"Wow. We are talking about big money."

"Yes, but my father is not interested in the wine business, except for his own consumption," she said with a smile on her face. "He bought this place on a whim, and has been wondering what to do with it ever since."

Eventually, the dinner gong sounded. The young couple were embracing each other at the time, in a haystack behind the barn next to the house. They spent a lot of time embracing each other. However, they heard the gong quite clearly, so adjusted their dress as they made their way back to the house. Michael flicked a piece of straw that they had missed from Monique's hair just as they entered the dining room.

M. Foch was slow to come to the point this time, concentrating on his food, but eventually he brought up the subject that was dominating his mind.

"I've been thinking. I have no son, as you know. I have two daughters. Monique is much more businesslike than her sister, Angelique. I had hoped she would take over the family businesses from me, although I always feared she would go off and marry some wealthy young man rather than continue the business I have built up. However, I now have a better plan. You have no profession to speak of, so how does this sound – If you marry my daughter, that you and she take over this place?"

Monique and Michael looked at each other in astonishment.

"You could run it as a business. I have to admit I have neglected it, which is a pity as it is a wasted asset."

Monique gave a little laugh. "Papa always likes to see his capital working."

"You see. She knows. She has a good business brain in her head."

"This comes as a bit of a shock," exclaimed Michael.

For the first time, M. Foch gave a broad smile. "I'll have to talk to my lawyers. I'll get them to draw up a contract. We must do it all businesslike." He paused. "Monique has a dowry of 3000 bottles of the '47. If I pass over the house to you, that can be her dowry instead, and I'll keep all the '47." His smile seemed bigger than ever.

"We'll have to talk about this," said Michael as he caught Monique's eye. He was not going to be stampeded into anything he did not fancy.

"Of course, you have to think about it, but it would solve all our problems," said M. Foch, easing back in his chair, and sipping his wine.

Over the next couple of weeks, the couple discussed the matter frequently.

"It's a marvellous offer, and something I would never have expected," Michael observed.

"I never expected it either."

"But what about the painting? I must be able to paint."

"Once we have got things sorted out, and the business is running properly, we could employ local labour to do the work, build a studio somewhere in that vast house, and you could spend some of your time painting."

"What about your painting?"

"I could do that as well."

"The commercial world needs a lot of attention. It would demand one of us to attend to it full time. Look how your father has devoted his life to building a fortune."

"And done it very well."

"And done it very well. He obviously has a feel for it. I am not so sure I have the same talents."

"I am sure I can make up for any deficiency on your part." She gave a big grin. "As if you could have any deficiency."

"And I don't know anything about wine."

"I could teach you."

"It really is a marvellous offer."

"And one I think we should take."

"I agree."

It was not long before Michael went off again to collect another package from George. As Monique and Michael had decided to accept her father's offer, it was planned that she would go and take him the news while Michael was away.

It did cross her mind, *Michael is going away too much for this firm he works for, but presumably that will stop when we start our wine business, and we have other money coming in.*

Michael went by ferry from Boulogne this time. He felt his travels were becoming routine. No customs official had even asked him what he was carrying. When asked if he had anything to declare, he had said "No," untempted by Oscar Wilde's answer, and they had just waved him on. It all seemed too easy.

Michael was in high spirits when he got back to Paris. It had been another pleasant trip, with no hitches. As ever, Monique was happy to see him.

"My father was pleased that we accepted his proposal, and he wants to see us again. I think he has got a job for you, but he wouldn't tell me what it was."

"Fine! Whatever it is, and whenever he likes, I'm available."

Two days later, two train tickets arrived by post to take them to Tours the following day. A car would be waiting for them there, outside the station.

That was a bit quick, Michael thought. *I might have been busy and unavailable. I know I had said any time, but he could have asked if we could make it. Will he expect me to be always at his beck and call? I hope not. However, one of the advantages of being a painter, I suppose, is that you are free to do what you want, when you want. So fine!*

It was Michael's first sight of the Foch's home in Tours, more modern than the Paris flat, and certainly the Manoire d'Espérance. It was nevertheless spacious and comfortably furnished in an art deco style this time.

"Make yourself at home and refresh yourselves first, then we will have dinner, and I have got a rather delicate matter to talk to you about after," said M. Foch as he greeted them.

Michael spent the meal wondering what could be so important that it could not be brought straight out. *M. Foch broached the subject of a marriage straight away. What could be more important or delicate than that? Has he had second thoughts about us taking over the wine business?* Eventually, the food was finished and the plates and glasses all cleared away.

"Monique tells me you often go to England."

"Yes."

"Well, you are almost part of the family now, so I thought you might be interested in helping us out." M. Foch lit himself a cigar. "Would you like one?"

"No, thanks. I don't smoke."

"Clever fellow! Well, as you know, these are troubled times in France."

"It's difficult not to hear about it."

"I have a lot of enemies, silly people who are jealous of any success. If the shooting starts, I will be in trouble, and so will my family."

Michael was about to say something, but M. Foch raised his hand, preventing an interruption. "We French are prevented from taking any money or anything of value out of the country at the moment, but as an Englishman, that law does not apply to you."

Monique could see where he was going and interrupted, "Doesn't the rule apply to any French currency?"

"They won't bother to question an Englishman leaving the country." M. Foch looked a bit irritated by the interruption, but he continued. "Anyway, how do you feel about carrying some francs and perhaps Mme Foch's jewellery out of the country for us, and opening an account in London, in case we have to flee in a hurry?"

"I would be pleased to help in any way I can, but I don't see it coming to that. Do you?"

"Isn't that going to be dangerous?" interrupted Monique, looking a bit worried.

"I certainly do," said M. Foch, answering Michael.

"O.K.," said Michael in reply, "If I can help, I will, and I am not averse to a little danger." He smiled to himself.

"Good chap. I will organise a package for you to carry," said M. Foch with a certain gusto.

"Any time. I am at your service."

The young couple returned to Paris that evening. M. Foch handed Michael a package as they left Tours. "Just let me know the account number."

"Well, that was a surprise," said Michael as they settled down in their seats on the train.

"You see. I said that my father would like you. He obviously trusts you."

"He must do. I don't know how much cash there is in the package, but it must be quite substantial."

"He told me. 50,000,000 francs."

"Wow."

Michael did not go to England immediately. He thought it expedient to wait until the leftist group, Sinister Port, also had an errand for him. A lot of trips, one after another, not only might arouse suspicion, but they had made him want a rest, to enjoy Monique's company, and perhaps catch up on his painting. He could do two projects together. He hid the money, but nevertheless, all that money in his possession worried him a bit. The sooner he could get rid of it into a bank, the better. Luckily, he did not have to wait long. George called.

When he did get to London, before he went to George's, he went and opened an account at the London and Provincial Bank, in the name of James Grey. He invented a signature and had a brief interview with the manager, explaining that he had just returned from abroad—which of course was true—and wanted to deposit his wealth until he could sort himself out. *I will take out the money when the time comes, and give it physically to M. Foch to deposit it wherever he likes.*

He then went on to George's, where they discussed the previous operation. They celebrated the success with a bottle of good whisky.

George had some bad news. "There are some worrying developments in Algeria. Colonel Biaggi has pledged the 10th Parachute Regiment to the generals. I wonder how many others will jump on the generals' bandwagon." George was obviously very worried.

The travelling had become almost a routine now, so Michael was not even nervous going back into France this time.

He took the first opportunity to visit his leftist group.

Monique phoned her father, and told him things had gone well. The money had been deposited, and the jewellery put in a safe deposit box. "We will come and see you later with the details."

Two days later, another two train tickets to Tours arrived in the post, so at the first opportunity, they went again to the Fochs' abode and reported to M. Foch. He was very pleased. Michael gave him the account number, and a key to the safe deposit box.

"If the worst comes to the worst, and you have to flee to England, I will withdraw the money and hand it to you to do what you like with it," explained Michael.

"I have another package for you. Have you thought of going to another country, if we can't cross the Chanel, Belgium perhaps, or Switzerland?"

"Belgium would be alright. I often go there, but Switzerland is a different matter. I don't know the Swiss frontier, and the Swiss are very efficient. It would increase the hazard."

"I know Switzerland from my finishing school days," offered Monique. "The border crossings are a bit intimidating, but you should be able to cope with Swiss bureaucracy. Swiss banks; the gnomes of Zurich, are only too keen to accept money without asking questions."

"Think about it," said M. Foch.

"We'll think about it, Father," replied Monique quickly. Not only did she have a sharp mind that could sum up problems, but she had a sense of diplomacy.

On the way back to Paris Monique pleaded with Michael. "Couldn't I come with you if you go to Belgium?"

"But then my advantage as an Englishman would be lost."

"Oh, the Belgians aren't all that efficient."

Michael spoke slowly as he thought through the problem, "We could cross the frontier separately and meet up afterwards. Perhaps stand in different queues to go through the customs. It will be as we leave France that the main trouble will exist."

"That's a good idea. Different queues should be enough. I'll carry just enough money for my fares."

"We could go on to see Bruges or somewhere like that after, and have a little holiday."

"I'll have a word with my father and see if he will finance the trip."

"Should we ask him for more than he is already offering us?"

"Of course. As he said, 'You are almost one of the family now.'"

Michael smiled. He felt so secure. He felt so warm. He felt like one of a family.

"Don't go back to your hotel tonight. Come and stay at my place."

Chapter Five

Both Monique and Michael found themselves emotionally in uncharted waters. Both searched to understand what was happening to them, unbeknown to each other.

Michael thought long about his feelings, but at a distance. He tried to understand the nature of love. *In the early or mid-twenties, we are probably a third of the way through our prospective life, and a responsible thinking adult, so we should not get carried away by emotion. Yet we all are.*

Monique was disturbed by the physical effect that Michael had on her. *Love has a sizeable element of sexual attraction in it. That is undeniable. There is a tingling in the presence of the desired other. You feel it physically, but one can be attracted physically without love. That is lust. What I feel, however, is more than that. That must be love!*

Michael continued speculating: *When in love, all other interests are pushed long-term to one side. There is a constant desire to enjoy the other's presence. Separation gives a feeling of incompleteness. That must be love!*

Monique was speculating the same way: *Time spent apart is only time to collect experiences to tell your loved one about. Life is shared. The other becomes a part of oneself. For the other to be absent is to feel a limb missing.*

Nevertheless, both simultaneously had the same doubts: *Could these feelings be just the result of sex?*

Michael had no trouble at the Belgian border, but the French police asked Monique how much money she was carrying, just as Michael had expected. He watched from a distance, very worried. He felt physical pain.

"I just have a thousand francs," said Monique.

"A thousand francs? That is not going to get you far."

"It will get me to Brussels."

"And then what?"

Monique put on an indignant air. "I have a cousin there, married to a Walloon." She could feel her pulse rising and enjoyed the sensation. This was exciting. This was living.

"Let's have a look at your bag."

She felt a bit short of breath. This was a new sensation. They took her bag and emptied it out on the table. "Is this your purse?"

"Yes." She flicked her head back. *How dare they?*

They opened it. "One five hundred, three more hundreds and another one hundred, and thirty francs… and a few cents. Less than a thousand." The sergeant turned to her. "Is this all?"

Michael was getting anxious, although he knew she had no money of consequence on her, but they might not let her through. He felt his pulse increasing, however.

"Yes!" she said with her voice rising.

"O.K., then you can go."

Monique was flabbergasted. She must not let it show. She walked on past Michael, not even giving him a glance. Michael felt a great weight lift, as his pulse and blood pressure returned to normal.

They met up on the Belgian train, halfway to Brussels. Monique was triumphant. "It was so exciting." *I am very good at this*, she thought.

Michael was relieved. *I am glad she enjoyed it*, he thought. *I did not!*

He had gone through so many emotions during the previous hour that he questioned what emotions were. He was confronted by a part of life he had never considered before. *I have been worried, happy, relieved, elated, and all at a distance. I have seen Monique excited, indignant, and joyful. All these emotions are of a different flavour, but they have the common factor that they are felt internally and physically. I can see Monique felt her emotions in the same way. But how did we feel them and where? Mine physically affected my body. It was not in my head. My brain was taken up with reasoning—thinking how to control my emotions and solve the problems should Monique get into real trouble. But where are my emotions felt? Is it in my gut? It somehow feels a bit like that, but it is a more universal sensation, especially with those stronger feelings. Most of those are probably remnants of our primeval past, animal feelings, needed for protection, but we are civilised now—I think.* He looked intensely at Monique. *Compassion and love are emotion only present in the higher sentient animals, and only occasionally are they elevated to sophisticated levels as in humans. Perhaps we shouldn't try to explain. We just have to accept them. There is no point in trying to explain the inexplicable.*

His love for Monique was definitely overpowering. He was never going to be able to explain it, but he knew it, and felt it, and was resigned to it.

'Living Dangerously' certainly expands emotion and life as a human being.

Michael and Monique had never thought of Belgium as a place to visit, and they had never associated it with romance, but their two days' stay in Bruges changed that forever. Once on neutral ground, the couple clung closer to each other than ever before. For them, there were only two categories in the world of feelings: those they felt in their own relationship, and those they left to the rest of the world for other people to feel. They were in a warm capsule of love, flying through space, through the whole universe, experiencing sensual pleasures, amusing ideas, and intellectual stimuli, as one after another flashed past them.

They enjoyed cultural experiences as well, but that was at a distance. They went to an art gallery, to the cathedral, wandered through the medieval streets, ate delicious food in tiny restaurants, went on a boat trip round the town's canals, and of course, they made love. Every experience was there for the picking, and they picked. There was no way either of them would ever forget this period in their lives.

This time Michael suggested that Monique opened the account for her father, as she was her father's daughter. She had a bit of trouble proving that she was Brigitte Martel, back from Martinique, but the bank manager was as keen for her to open the account as she was. He was coming up for promotion. Her new-minted signature looked a bit feeble, but that would strengthen with practice. Convincing the bank manager added to her conspiratorial self that she had recently discovered, and relished.

They decided to celebrate this new-found identity in a bar.
"Why don't you try a beer?" Michael suggested.
"I don't like beer."
"Have you tried?"
"Yes. My father gave me a taste once. He doesn't like it either."
"Was it French beer?"
"Yes. Of course!"
"Well, that explains it. France is a wine-growing country. They don't know how to make good beer. We are in Belgium now. They make very good beer."
"That's going to be no better than French beer. I'm sure I won't like it."
"Try some. If you don't like it, I will finish it off."
"I'm sure I won't like it." She mumbled in a low tone, as she shook her head from side to side.

"You won't know until you've tried."

At his point, the waiter approached. "Can I help you, sir?"

"Yes, what beer do you recommend?"

"That's up to you, sir. Do you want a dark beer or a light beer?"

"We want a beer with a lot of flavour, not too strong, not too bitter, and something that could appeal to someone who is used to wine."

The waiter smiled. "You are trying to convert the young lady here?"

"Yes. I want her to gain new experiences."

"Leave it to me, sir. I can be an evangelist for our Belgian beer. The Czechs, the German, and even the English make interesting beers, but the Belgians make the best."

As the waiter went away, Michael turned with sympathy to Monique. "You see. There are a great number of flavours to be discovered." Then, with understanding in his voice, "If you don't like it, nothing is lost, but you should not go to your grave without trying every experience that is available. We only have one life, and we must make the most of it. Devour as many experiences as possible."

"If you say it's good, I will try."

The waiter returned with a tray containing two beers and some nibbles. He poured the drinks and stood back to see the effect. He was a patriotic man and he wanted his country's products to be appreciated. She lifted the glass gently to her lips. She took a sip, then a bigger sip.

"It's quite nice. Better than expected," she exclaimed, as her face radiated a mild pleasure.

"Here's to Brigitte Martel," Michael exclaimed.

She picked up the bottle and looked at the label: Palm, it said. Michael laughed with satisfaction as he leant across and kissed her. The waiter laughed with the same feeling of satisfaction as he turned and walked away.

Eventually, it was time for the couple to travel home to Paris. Going into France, Monique's nationality did not matter. She carried no money or contraband, so they travelled together. Most of the time in the train, they travelled very much together, in each other's arms.

Monique reported to her father by phone what they had done, which pleased him considerably, and he invited them to come to Tours for the next weekend. He said he had some friends he wanted them to meet.

They accepted the invitation, though not without a bit of hesitation on Michael's part. He wanted to get back to painting. *I have not touched a brush for a couple of weeks.*

When he did get to his studio and start a new picture, he immediately felt at home. He luxuriated in the smell of linseed oil and turpentine, and the blue and red pigments. The picture flowed from his soul, which was currently vibrant, stimulated by Monique and an exciting life. His passion was exposed on the canvas for all to see.

They arrived in Tours late afternoon. M. Foch was in his office in town and had not yet arrived home at the flat. After dropping their overnight bags at the Foch's apartment, they took the opportunity and had just enough time to look around the town. It was obviously very prosperous, and Michael could see why M. Foch enjoyed living there. It was not Paris, but Michael felt he could get to like it if it became the nearest urban life, when they had to spend a lot of time at Le Manoir d'Espérance.

On returning to the Foch's flat, they were surprised to be met by six prosperous-looking people chatting to M. Foch, who stepped forward to present them.

"This is General Duchamp, retired now, of course. This is M. Dubret, a business associate with whom I have a lot of dealings. This is Albert Renier. He has the large vineyard the other side of the valley from Le Manoir d'Espérance. You can see it from the terrace. This is Hubert Gaman. You may have heard of him. He races cars. This is Jean le Clerc. He used to be the French ambassador in Austria, but he has retired now, like the general, and this is Madame Muson, the most successful businesswoman in France."

"Oh. Nonsense." She blushed.

"Truly. Don't be too modest."

Monique turned away with a haughty expression on her face. Michael wondered why.

M. Foch turned to Michael with one of his rare grins on his face. "After dinner, we want to have a talk with you."

"Fine." Michael wondered what on earth it could be about. *This is the second time M. Foch has delayed a subject till after dinner. It must be something important. His associates all look pretty wealthy. They haven't found out about my left-wing activities, have they? Are they going to confront me? No. If that was the case, they would not wait until after dinner.* He followed his host to the table. *Time will tell,* he said to himself. *There is no point in speculating.* He was becoming more of a fatalist.

Monique was not so fatalistic. *I have never liked this lot; Papa's business associates. What is Papa up to? I have tried to get away from this bourgeois atmosphere.*

The dinner was of the usual high standard and obviously appreciated by M. Foch's guests. They discussed each dish as it came and offered their approval. Albert Renier was interested in the wine served, and particularly the wine that had been produced by M. Foch himself. Monique turned to Michael and gave a wink.

Afterwards, General Duchamp got out a notebook and seemed to call the assembly to order. He had an authoritative air, acquired through years of giving orders that nobody dare question. The polite conversation dropped, and he had everyone's attention.

"Now, young Michael. I may address you as such. May I not?"

"Yes. Of course." Secretly he objected to the 'young.'

"We know you have been doing a few favours for the Fochs. Well, we could do with a similar service. However, none of us have anyone in the family we can rely on like you, to do the same for us. We wondered how you feel about extending your services. For the Fochs, it was a family affair, and we would not expect you to do the same for us for nothing. It would be business. You would be well paid. Putting it bluntly, we would like you to deposit some funds for us outside the country, in case of emergencies. You would be paid a percentage of the value of what you carried. With cash, it would be easy to agree on the sum, and other goods could be valued at the place of receipt."

"What sort of percentage?" Monique asked.

"How does ten per cent sound to you?"

"How about fifteen per cent?" Monique chipped back.

"Fifteen percent if you pay your own expenses."

"What sort of figure are we talking of?"

"Well, we have immediately accumulated 30,000,000 francs. There will be more when we have had time to liquefy our assets."

Wow! thought Michael. He tried to work out the payoff, but it was a bit complicated and the whole idea had come as such a surprise that he was excited and felt disorientated. Monique realised immediately that it was 4,500,000 francs, with more to come.

"O.K. We'll pay our expenses. Done!" She had no hesitation.

"Done!" said a relieved General. "Of course, we cannot have a formal contract, but M. Foch tells me that you are a trustworthy couple. Monique is his own daughter, whom he must know, and he seems to have a very high opinion of you, Michael. We of course are men of our word," then with a quick afterthought, "and women of our word as well, of course." He gave a quick bow to Madame Muson. "I think we can seal the agreement with a handshake."

The business having been concluded, a whole series of very good wines were brought out from the cellar and sampled. Eventually, it was time for the party to break up. Everyone seemed happy and relaxed, as they all felt they had done a deal that was very much in their interests.

"I'll meet you in Paris, in the bar of Hôtel Regina next Monday," said General Duchamp. "Unless you can't make it," he paused, "and I will entrust to you the consignment. You know where the hotel is, by the statue of Jeanne d'Arc; next to the Louvre, 5.30!"

"I'll be there."

The rest of the weekend, the young couple spent wandering through the countryside surrounding their prospective new home in Courtay, walking down to the Loire, and exploring the villages along its banks. It was an attractive part of France, mostly inhabited by a population of small farmers of left-wing leanings. The large estates that had belonged to the chateaus had been broken up by the revolution, 150 years earlier.

Michael was very uneasy, excited by the financial prospects, but worried by the political implications. Living dangerously was no longer a joke. *I now have to take life more seriously. I am involved with two groups who are diametrically opposed to each other. If I am going to survive, I have to be serious and cool. Anything else is going to give me away.* Then his conscience felt a prick. *And should I be helping these people? I doubt that they have the same sympathies as I do. I do not know their political leanings... almost certainly not mine... but the money will be useful.*

Monique was very excited. The trip to Bruges had given her an appetite for adventure. She looked forward to a trip to England, and challenging authority once again. *All that money. It will more than finance the wine business.*

Michael was not excited. He could not confide in Monique and look to her for support. *She might well not sympathise, and I have given my word to Sinister Port.* He could see she was excited by the prospect of more adventure and did not want to corrupt her pleasure. *I will be a piggy in the middle, between two groups, and should either group find out about the other, there will be real trouble.*

There were also the authorities in two countries to worry about. A cool, detached attitude to life was the only option. *Feelings will have to wait!*

Back in Paris, Monique pleaded with him to let her come on the trip.

"It worked alright last time!"

"Yes, but England will be different. The customs are sure to question me. With you accompanying me, they will be very suspicious."

"I won't be with you. It will be like last time, when we went to Belgium."

Eventually, he gave in. They would cross on the same boat but separately and meet up on the train to London.

All the arrangements went well. Michael met the General at the hotel and collected the money. It was a smaller packet than he had visualised. The General bought him a drink and tried to question him about his life and background. Michael gave nothing away. He avoided any discussion of politics, even though his companion returned to the subject several times. *I used to be honest and straight with people. Now I have to censor everything I say.*

Michael was fascinated by the hotel. He thought it a bit posh. It had the air of the Paris of about 1900. He would have liked to have explored it. There were potted palms, mahogany furniture, and a pianist playing gently in the bar. However, he dropped the package into the bag he had brought for the purpose and left as soon as it seemed polite.

For the journey to England, he put most of the money in a money belt and carried only a reasonable amount in his wallet. Luckily, his youth still allowed him a small waist. This time Michael would not open the bank account himself, but pass it over to the group's contact in London, who would pay him his percentage and deal with things from then on. Michael was more comfortable with that arrangement.

The couple went by train to Calais, parting before they entered the port, and travelled across the Channel separately. Michael got into conversation with some lorry drivers on the boat, and as it was calm, Monique spent most of the time sunning herself on deck, reading, and watching the white cliffs heave into sight.

There was no trouble at all for either of them leaving France or entering England. *We must look honest,* Michael thought. He had an explanation for it: *Dame Fortune favours the good,* and Michael knew they were both essentially good.

Everything worked like clockwork. They went immediately to Dolphin Square on arriving in London, found their contact, a middle-aged man with a French accent, and delivered the money. It was counted. Their percentage was paid with no argument, and they left to find a hotel, with their spoils safely tucked into Michael's money belt. They were jubilant.

Their spirits were somewhat dampened when they found the first few hotels they tried were full, but then, as they passed a paper boy, he called out in a loud voice, "Star, News, and Standard!" They bought all three, searched 'the small ads,' and saw an advert for a flat to let in Wilton Street. They phoned and were told that the owner did not want to let it for less than six months at a time. They had a mini conference over a cup of tea.

"We have plenty of money, and we will probably be coming backwards and forwards a lot if what my father's friends say is true. Let's take it," Monique suggested. She had a feeling that it would be fun to set up a home together, albeit temporarily.

"It will mean that we won't have to keep looking for hotels," said Michael slowly and thoughtfully. *We can afford it now*. He could see the wisdom of her idea.

"That will save a lot of time when we could be enjoying ourselves," Monique said as she screwed up her face with delight.

"Alright, but I will have to put these francs in the bank and get some English currency."

"Don't change it all to sterling. We will need some of it back in France."

They phoned the owner again. "Can we come and see the flat?"

"Certainly. We are just behind Buckingham Palace. Victoria will probably be your nearest tube station. Where are you?"

"In Chelsea."

"In that case, I'll expect you here in half an hour."

The flat was on two floors, very comfortably furnished in a 1930s style. They signed an agreement and paid the first month's rent, with an extra month's deposit. The owner was a jovial woman in her forties. She had moved to the country, but did not want to lose possession of the flat she and her husband had lived in before he was killed in the war.

Michael and Monique then went and had a meal at a restaurant the landlady had recommended, 'The Soup Kitchen,' situated between the new flat and the French Embassy. Monique enjoyed the idea that the French Embassy was a neighbour. She always liked to think she had 'got one up' on authority.

"Do you realise we are going to be living next door to the Queen?" observed Michael, but without much of a laugh.

"People of quality should always stick together," said Monique with a great smile.

"You forget I am one of the proletariat."

"Quality supersedes class. At least in France it does, if not in England, and you are nearly half French now."

They spent several days in London, looking at some of the sights, and buying bits and pieces for their flat. Michael did not really like shopping, but he indulged

Monique. Her company was worth any discomfort on his part. During one morning's expedition, they had coffee in an expensive café in Bond Street, and on the pretext of going to get a magazine, Michael left her in the café, rushed into a jewellers shop next door, and purchased a ring with a solitaire diamond. In the context of the tray he was shown, it looked quite modest, but it was big to Michael's eyes. He had not yet got used to the idea that their newfound occupation was going to produce big money. The shop assistant was surprised and pleased by the speed of the transaction. Michael had chosen straight away, from the first tray. She was not used to that. Most of her customers liked to be indulged. On the way back into the café, he quickly purchased a magazine on cars from a kerbside stall, as a cover. He did not mention the ring to Monique. The appropriate moment was going to be important.

They spent another two days in London, mostly rearranging their flat, but of all their London activities, they most enjoyed just sitting on the grass in the parks and feeding the birds, or on the embankment watching the boats go by, as they often did in Paris.

They had been back in Paris only two days when Michael got calls from Sinister Port and General Duchamp. Both wanted him to go on another trip to England. He was to pick up papers from George and take stuff for M. Foch's friends. He went to the Hôtel Regina again, and the General gave him an even larger amount of money than last time. Michael did not tell Monique about the George mission, but he let her check General Duchamp's cash that was to be taken. There were 200,000,000 francs. She was very excited.

"Let's go by air this time," suggested Monique. "I have never been on an aeroplane."

"If we do, we should go on different flights. I'll take the bulk of the money, and you can use the excuse for the small amount that you carry, as you are going to stay with friends, and give our Wilton Street address. If asked, tell them that you have been invited to stay with a distant cousin."

"Alright. I'll see you at the flat."

Michael flew to Heathrow by BEA this time and went into the terminal on the Cromwell Road by coach. It was not far from their new flat, only a short taxi ride. He had not been in the habit of taking taxis and was about to walk, but he felt he ought to get used to dealing with his newfound riches. This left Monique to travel by Air France. Michael insisted that she take a taxi all the way from Heathrow. As she could not carry too much money, he would pay the taxi driver when she arrived at the flat. He would be waiting for her.

As Monique approached the airport north of Paris, her blood pressure rose, but she liked that. It was a sensation close to that of lovemaking, and she relished it. Having passed the French customs with no trouble whatsoever, she walked out to the plane and was refreshed by the draft from the turbo props as she mounted the steps. She had become very hot without realising it. She was not doing anything illegal, but being part of the bigger project made her identify with it. Danger, or the perception of it, was a drug to which she could become addicted. Her first flight was also an exciting project. Never having flown before, she had got a seat next to the window. Luckily it was a clear day, so she could see the French countryside pass below her. When the Normandy fields gave way to the sea, it was even more exciting. She could not swim. The Channel is not all that wide, however, and they were soon touching down in Heathrow Airport. Other travellers hardly existed. They were a blurred background on her journey to see Michael. She arrived in the airport hall with a heightened awareness. English customs were not interested in her. That caused her a certain amount of disappointment. She quickly found a taxi and took the precaution of negotiating the fee. In Wilton Street, Michael paid the driver.

They closed the door and looked silently at each other. Without saying a word, Michael stepped across and caressed her hair with the outside of his hand. She moved her head to the right slightly, and he kissed her neck. Staying deliberately apart, he walked around her, covering her neck with a hail of kisses. She stood and appreciated it. She felt the heat of his passion without the heat of his body. Her heartbeat increased. As she turned and kissed him, he brought his hands into play and clasped her round the waist. A motor bike clattered down the street outside. They did not hear it. He lifted her up. He did not notice her weight either. He carried her to the couch and laid her down. He lay down beside her and slowly removed her jacket, then her blouse, and then her bra. They looked at each other. They had made love many times before, but this time it seemed more poignant. He kissed her on the lips, on the eyes, and the forehead, and then on the neck again. He worked his way, kissing down across her shoulders into the dip beneath her collarbone and on to the soft flesh that led down to her breasts. He did not kiss her breast immediately but descended through the centre of her cleavage to snuggle into her lower ribs. From under her right breast, he started to kiss circles, up and around it, starting at the outside and progressing towards the centre. Her nipples were proud and firm and deliciously pink. She longed for him to kiss them, and the anticipation heightened her desire. But he pulled his head back in order to see the whole of her upper body, those shapely shoulders, her gorgeous breasts, her intelligent face, those eyes that promised paradise, warmth, compassion, and love.

She undid her belt and eased her skirt over her hips. He continued its progress down over her knees and ankles. She slipped off her panties and stockings. He stepped back in order to see her whole body. She could feel his eyes boring into her, and she revelled in it. She was beautiful, and she felt it. His gaze stimulated and enhanced her feeling. He could not believe that such a perfect creature would want him to love her. His clothes were very quickly discarded, and he lay down again, this time naked against her naked body. The soft silkiness of her skin thrilled him to newer heights of sensual pleasure. His hands slipped over her skin, enjoying the thrill of its tenderness. Again with kisses, he made circles round her breast, this time more quickly, reaching the centre and taking the nipple between his lips. She felt like screaming, but she just released a moan. He was sucking her passion into his body, and she gave it willingly.

He was so beautiful. He was so lovely. She could eat him up. He could eat her up with pleasure. She could feel his hand creep down over her stomach, exploring the subtle curves around her navel and the ups and downs that curved out to her hips and into the centre of her belly button. She was always a bit self-conscious about the hair that started at the bottom of her torso. It made her feel like an animal, but she was an animal now, primeval and primitive and wicked, and she loved it. All her civilised inhibitions had gone. She was a bundle of sensual desires, and she wanted them satisfied. His hand worked its way down to her clitoris. He massaged it, and it firmed up. His finger entered her, and the fluids flowed. The sensation was unbearable, but she wanted it to go on forever. He touched her G-spot. It made her bend forward, and she let out an uncontrollable scream. Her hands stretched out, and she grabbed his head, massaging it passionately.

She arched her back, spread wide her legs, and he entered her slowly. She felt him inside her. It was lovely. Slowly but surely, he started to move backwards and forwards. Thrills, generated deep within, shot out through her whole body to the tips of her limbs. It was excruciating, but she hoped it would never stop. The thrusts, firm and manly, increased in tempo. She moaned. The pace quickened as he fondled her buttocks and breasts and head until there was an overpowering explosive sensation, and she screamed. They reached a climax together. He mingled his yell with her moan, and they fell back on the couch together.

They lay exhausted in each other's arms, panting and wondering at what had happened. They cuddled in a warm embrace, wanting to say thank you, but without the words to do their feelings justice.

That night, they went out to walk round the district and explore. They walked past the French Embassy into the park, and Monique giggled at their conspiracy that defied the whole French state. The need for food eventually encroached on their consciousness, so they returned to the city streets, intending to find an expensive restaurant to celebrate. Instead, they found themselves in a mews, drawn by an invisible hand. Surrounded by garages, they were taken by a sign announcing 'Luba's Bistro.'

"Let's try that. We don't need to always eat in expensive restaurants."

"Good idea."

They entered. They entered into another world, more like their beloved regular restaurant in Paris. There was a spirit of happiness in the air. It was full of people enjoying their dinner at long communal oak tables. On the tables were candles in discarded wine bottles encased in wax. Around the walls were numerous pictures of a rather fat woman, who was present, serving the customers and joking with them in a strong Russian accent. This was obviously Luba.

They ordered borscht. This was a beetroot soup. Beetroots were one of the easiest crops peasants could grow in a harsh climate. It was served with a large dollop of sour cream in the centre. Their neighbour showed them how to break it up with their spoons, stirring it around—not vigorously enough to mix completely with the red soup, making it an opaque pink, but leaving white globules floating on the surface.

Monique and Michael followed this soup with Luba's golubtzi. A Russian peasant could use any sad cabbage leaf to wrap around anything digestible and cook it in the oven. In Luba's case, it was mincemeat, with herbs and mushrooms, served with a thick, tasty brown sauce.

They stayed long after they had finished eating. The atmosphere was one of happiness. It echoed their feeling. They were not the only ones to delay their home-going, for very few of the other customers left after they finished their meal.

Michael surveyed the place. It was little more than a mews garage, sparsely decorated except for the pictures. However, it went to show what Michael had always believed: that if the product is good, people will always beat a path to your door, and if you induce an amiable environment, they will stay.

A tall, scraggy man emerged from the kitchen and took a balalaika from the wall. He started to sing a Russian folk song. Customers who were obviously regulars joined in. The music quickly turned mournful. It then added anger and determination. Michael was struck by a realisation and had to share it with Monique.

"Russian music is often at its best when it portrays the sorrow and disasters that have befallen those people, and it echoes the vast spaces of the steppes. The great Russian composers—Shostakovich, Stravinsky, Prokofiev, Mussorgsky, Rachmaninov, Tchaikovsky—all knew this, and put it to great use in their music."

The current music and singing, however, continued through many different moods and styles, expressing most of the facets of life. Luba, and all the other staff who emerged from the kitchen, sat and joined in the impromptu party. It became late.

Eventually, Monique and Michael retired to their flat and slept very soundly.

The next morning, Michael was up early. He made some tea and took Monique a cup in bed. She had hardly woken, but with tea, she rose, made some toast and coffee, and they sat down to breakfast.

"Close your eyes. I've got a little present for you."

"A present?" Monique was curious.

"Yes. Close your eyes."

Michael took the ring from his pocket, opened the box, and bent down on one knee. "Right, now you can open them."

She opened her eyes, looked at Michael, saw the ring, and screamed with delight.

"Will you marry me?" he whispered.

"Of course."

She grabbed him round the neck, which sent him sprawling on the floor, with her on top of him, smothering him with kisses.

"Of course. Of course. Of course."

"I guessed at your finger size. If the ring doesn't fit, we can take it back and they will adjust it."

"It's perfect, and it's lovely. Thank you." She kissed him again.

They were laughing as they rose, got back to the table, and regained their equilibrium. They settled down to their coffee and toast.

"Have you ever seen the English countryside?"

"I have never been to England before."

"You must see it. It's very beautiful."

"As beautiful as France?"

"Better."

"I don't believe it."

"You wait and see."

"Perhaps we could hire a car and drive out to the country?"

"Better still, why don't we buy one?"

"Why not? We have got plenty of money."

Michael was suddenly reminded of why he was there. "Ah yes. I must first go to Dolphin Square, and then to my bank, and then perhaps we could look at some cars."

Their chores done at the bank, they sat on a bench in the park and looked at adverts in the evening paper for car showrooms. One caught their eye. It was in Bond Street. 'By Appointment to Her Majesty the Queen,' it said.

"That should be good enough for us," Monique suggested. "We have to keep up with the neighbours."

They therefore found themselves walking into H. R. Owen's, probably the most expensive car showrooms in the country.

"We have come to buy a car."

"Yes, sir. What were you thinking of?"

Before Michael could answer, Monique interrupted. Her attention was taken by a beautiful white drop-head Austin-Healey next to the door. "Oh look! This one's lovely."

"A very nice car, sir." The salesman addressed Michael, not Monique.

Michael missed the point, but Monique did not. Her hackles rose.

We are so suited, Michael thought, oblivious to Monique's irritation. *Our tastes are identical. I have always wanted an Austin-Healey.*

"This would be an ideal car for a young couple like yourselves." The salesman continued.

"How much is it?" Monique asked harshly.

"Well, sir, I notice the young lady has a French accent. Do you live here or in France, if I may be so bold?"

"Mostly in France." Monique spat it out. However, the salesman was oblivious.

"Do you have a French address?"

"Yes!" she announced sharply. She was determined to make him notice her.

"In that case sir, we could let you have it on our export quota. That will greatly decrease the cost. That is better for you, and it is better for us, as we do not want to use up our limited domestic quota."

"We all benefit!"

"Exactly."

"So how much is it?"

"I do not know exactly. With the export discount, I will have to go and look it up." He went away.

Michael could see the salesman in a heated conference with someone who was presumably the manager.

"This is our perfect car," said Monique.

"I agree."

"We have to have it—regardless of cost."

The salesman returned. He started to explain. "On the export quota, you will get 20% off the list price. Just over £500 with the extras and delivery charge." Michael interrupted him. "It doesn't matter. We want it anyway. When can we have it? Now?"

"I'm afraid not, sir. We have to register it, and you will need to insure it, but if you come back tomorrow with an insurance certificate, you can drive it away."

"We'll do that." Monique contributed.

"May I ask a slightly delicate question, sir? Are you wanting any finance?"

"Oh no. We'll pay cash. We can even pay in francs if you like."

"That would be very interesting. Perhaps you would like to step into the back office, and we will complete the details for the registration and invoice."

That afternoon, they found an insurance broker and purchased policies for either of them to drive any car. They then went back to the flat, where Michael checked that they had retained enough francs to pay for the car in cash. By the time this was done, it was late, so they decided to stay the rest of the day in town, perhaps going to a film, and go to the country after collecting the car the next morning.

They thought they would try eating at The Soup Kitchen again, where they had been the first night they had got the flat. Whether it was because England was still in a period of austerity, or that it had not caught up with continental cooking yet, most restaurant food was not as adventurous as in France or Belgium, but they had found that it was more than adequate at The Soup Kitchen. The menu was very adventurous.

The manageress, 'Big Molly,' came to their table and asked them if everything was alright. They congratulated her on the food, and they set up a friendly conversation, explaining that they lived nearby. Monique felt quite English. She looked forward to living the part quite often in the future.

As Big Molly walked away, a young, very pretty, very feminine girl came in and approached her with a petulant expression and a submissive demeanour. She snuggled up to Big Molly in what Michael thought was a slightly unnatural way.

"Do you think that she's her daughter?" Michael asked.

"Not at all! That's a lesbian relationship if ever I saw one," answered Monique.

Michael was a bit taken aback. "The waitresses here are all rather good-looking. I thought that was to attract male customers, but perhaps there is another reason."

"Almost certainly."

"Whoever chooses the staff certainly has an eye for feminine beauty. Be careful!" he said with a smile.

The next morning, the couple were up early and at the car showroom soon after it was open.

"Nice to see you, sir. Your car is ready for you."

Michael retired to the back office again to complete the essentials, while Monique inspected the car, caressed the wooden steering wheel, and stroked the leather seats. Such pleasure banished all anger she felt towards the salesman. Michael enjoyed taking out a wodge of French notes and peeling off the required amount as the salesman counted them.

"We have put a small amount of petrol in, but you will have to fill up at the first opportunity if you intend to go any distance. Here are your petrol coupons."

They drove out into the sunshine, down Bond Street, down Piccadilly, past Kensington High Street, and through the suburbs into the Surrey countryside. They filled the petrol tank. Before long, they were on the Hog's Back, with the wind in their hair and excitement in their hearts. They changed drivers, with Monique driving. She was worried at having to drive on the left at first, but soon got used to it. Her biggest problem was when they came up to a roundabout. She was on the edge of panic, but Michael talked her slowly through it, and after the first one, she never had any more trouble.

They went into Guildford for lunch and then took off again in wide circles, up and down the North Downs through narrow sunken lanes, enjoying numerous views. It was dark before they returned to London, but they did not put up the hood. They wanted to be in touch with a world that had become their oyster.

The next morning, they had another mini-conference over breakfast. Michael would have to take the car to France within a certain time to fulfil the regulations with regard to the export quota.

"You could go back by plane, and I will follow on with the car."

"Oh, couldn't I come along with you? I love the driving."

"It's dangerous," and as an afterthought, "Crossing the borders together, I mean, not your driving." He had forgotten he had to be cool.

She ignored the joke.

"So what? We won't be doing anything wrong."

Monique did not know about the package he would be carrying. This caused Michael to stop and think, *What is the point of living dangerously if you don't make the most of it, and enjoy it?*

"O.K. then. We won't have any large amounts of money on us. I suppose at worst, we could end up in gaol together."

"Ooo." She squeezed his arm in her now habitual way of expressing her love and approval.

Michael then spoke more seriously. "I will have to do an errand first. I have to go and see my Uncle George on some family business."

"Don't be away too long."

"I'll be as quick as possible."

Michael collected the papers from George. He told him about the purchase of the car but not how he got the money to pay for it. He did tell him that he had sold a painting to Pierre for a lot of money, and George was pleased and assumed that that was where the funds had come from.

"Don't spend all your money too quickly. Save some for a rainy day." George had another tip. "I believe there is a new service by which you can take cars by plane from Lydd to Le Touquet in France."

"That sounds exciting."

"Yes, and it is another route, and one not so often used. We have to keep your means of travel varied, but be careful that you do not get the stamps in your passport too much out of sync."

"So far my passport will stand up to any logical inspection."

"They tend not to look at the passport too carefully anyway, but if they do have suspicions, it is best if the stamps make sense. They do not usually bother to go through the other stamps. They just stamp it where it falls open and there is a space."

"I am keeping ahead of that problem."

"O.K. then. Good luck."

When Michael got back to Belgravia, there was plenty of time to find a travel agency to book a trip for two days later. Monique was very excited with the idea of flying with the car. And the idea of going in another type of aircraft that was smaller, and not a regular airliner, increased the interest. They went out and did a bit of shopping together. Michael wanted to buy a few English foods that he had been missing in France, like Marmite, and porridge, and Lyle's Golden Syrup, and tea.

The next morning, Michael was intent on having porridge for breakfast. He had not had it for such a long time. Monique did not know anything about it, so Michael cooked the porridge while she prepared the toast and the coffee.

"Would you like some porridge?" he asked her.

"Eer. It looks horrible."

"It's lovely. Try some."

"I don't think so. Oats are what you give to horses."

"This prevents you being hoarse. It makes you fit," said Michael with a smile.

"English puns are worse than the French."

Michael ignored the criticism. "Come on, try some."

He poured a large helping into a bowl and crowned it with a knob of butter, which melted almost immediately. He then added a large spoonful of the golden syrup. That melted also, mixing with the butter and forming a sort of toffee mixture. Finally, he poured milk over the lot.

"That looks extraordinary."

"Come on. Try some."

"I don't fancy it."

"You won't know what it tastes like unless you try. You liked the beer, didn't you?"

"Yes," she said with a reluctant drawl, "but that was different."

"So is this."

However, when Michael offered her a spoonful, she accepted it, and her expression changed.

"It tastes better than it looks."

"You see. You should always trust me." He grinned.

"But you're a man!" She grinned disbelievingly.

The next day they set off early, down through the Kent and Sussex countryside, to Lydd airport. Michael thought it did not look much like an airport. It was, in fact, a fighter aerodrome left over from the war. It consisted mainly of Nissen huts. They booked in and waited in one of them, with two other couples and a young man. They were all given a cup of tea. Their car was inspected by the customs officer, who took the engine and chassis numbers. He inspected the papers and looked in the boot. Michael was about to take their cases out and put them on the trestle table next to it, but the officer waved his hand with a satisfied gesture.

Noticing their deep attachment, he asked if they had just got married. They said they were just about to. He was warmed and livened by their deep regard for one another and waved them through without another glance. Michael drove the car out across the field to the waiting plane and up the ramp into a small hold. There was just enough room for about four cars. It was a twin-boomed transport aircraft, left over from the war, well in keeping with the style of the airfield. He then went round to the small cabin at the front where he joined Monique.

It is a cliché that everybody loves a lover, but it is true. The couple emitted such an aura of mutual affection that customs officers and police just waved them through on most occasions, remembering their own youth. The couple had no trouble at Le Touquet and were soon back in Paris in the Champs-Élysées.

"I think you should stay here tonight," said Monique as they got into the lift. "It seems funny to live together in London and live apart here."

"You're right. I think I'll give up my room at the hotel. It's silly to perpetuate any myth that we are not a couple."

"Go and sort it out tomorrow."

"As we are going to admit to being a couple, I think I should tell you something."

"Let it wait. I'm hungry. Let's just drop our bags and go off and eat."

They wanted to eat at their usual restaurant, Mes Amis, but felt they could not go there in their new flashy car, so they went by Metro.

Chapter Six

Monique was young and beautiful. She evoked an irresistible desire in Michael. This was no more than the way any red-blooded young man would have reacted when confronted by such a beautiful woman. Michael was well aware of this primitive compulsion. However, he was a bit ashamed of it. But he justified himself: *I am an animal. I can't help it, but her physical presence causes a tangible tingle in my blood to the extent that I want to cry.* Then he had second thoughts: *But as a civilised human being, I should be above these primitive instincts.*

He consoled himself by the fact that he was also impressed by her mind. Not only did the way she laughed captivate him, but her conversation that followed held him in awe. Nevertheless, he was disturbed by his primeval feelings.

He excused himself by the fact that, intellectually, her views were so much in tune with his own, he wondered if a carbon copy of his mind had been made and planted in her. *Is it a magic spell, as Pierre suggests? Nothing else could explain his entrapment by her existence.*

Monique often looked at Michael and was completely at ease. He evoked a calm and satisfaction in her. There was no friction. She knew exactly what she wanted in a man, and this man had it. He would never force her to do anything she did not want to, but he often persuaded her to try a new experience, and because of that, her life had expanded. She had enjoyed things she did not know existed. Her life was enriched. Without him, her body was not whole. Their lovemaking reached levels of ecstasy she had not realised existed.

He is a strong man. He is stronger than he realises. He is a brave man. I like that. He is wise beyond his years, confident in himself in a complex world, yet willing to take risks, and so calm and understanding. And he is so talented. I love his paintings. I admire his creativity. They say that a girl chooses a partner that resembles her father, but that could not be true, for Michael is nothing like my father.

She loved her father, but her father had many faults, and she could see no faults in Michael. It was unbelievable that she could have found the ideal partner.

It was magic. She also secretly delighted in the fact that he evoked primitive responses in her.

Yes, Monique and Michael were young and beautiful, talented and intelligent. The whole world was theirs. Nothing was beyond their grasp together. Nothing! Or so they thought.

———

General Massu sat at his desk. On the other side of the desk sat his fellow conspirators. Lorillot was there, the new Governor of Algeria. General Salan, had just arrived from Spain, and General Challe, who had just returned from the United States, were present, along with lesser ranks.

General Massu started the proceedings. "As we know, the honour of France is at stake. We cannot allow these jumped-up politicians to give away parts of our beloved country."

This unleashed a babble of conversation.

"If they had given us enough resources, we would have crushed this revolt long ago. Instead of which, talk of self-determination has encouraged these barbarians."

"Not all of the populace are against us," a young colonel offered. "We must not underestimate the sizeable number of the more sophisticated Muslim population that is on our side. They do not want to be ruled by a load of ignorant peasants."

A hubbub erupted.

"And the Pieds-noirs are wholly with us."

"But things are getting worse."

General Salan cut in with a slightly mournful air, "You don't have to tell me. Someone tried to assassinate me again the other day. A bazooka killed my driver and several bystanders."

"Yes, things are definitely getting worse. We have to take things into our own hands, and quickly."

General Challe addressed General Salan. "How did your trip go? Have you told those lazy politicos in Paris that if they do NOT drop this silly idea of independence for Algeria, we will step in, and redeem the situation?"

General Salan answered with a depressed demeanour. "I have, but to no avail." Then, more optimistically: "However, I went on to Spain and talked at great length with Ramon Suner. The Franco government will of course be very sympathetic to our action, but they are not willing to give us any material support.

They are worried about the Americans. They regret choosing the wrong side during the war."

General Massu wanted the group to keep to material considerations, not sidetracked. Nothing was to be gained by expressing emotional positions and the hope of support that might or might not materialise. They had to get down to the practical arrangements.

"We have to be responsible for ourselves. We can expect nothing from the government in Paris except waffle, and the Americans are the other side of the Atlantic. So! Colonel Argoud, along with myself, have identified all the strategic points to be seized in Paris. With gliders in the Bois de Boulogne and paratroopers dropped in the Tuileries, we should be able to secure all the essential points within the hour. Jacques Soustelle, here, will then broadcast a statement telling the patriotic members of the populace what to do."

"Seizing the radio station is essential. We need to get our message across as soon as possible," the young colonel added.

"That is all taken care of. We do have sympathisers within the radio company, RDF. There are other important locations less easy to secure. I am worried about the Paris garrison. There are a lot of conscripts there. They are not professionals like my paratroopers. They may not see the need to retain French honour."

General Massu then turned to General Challe. "What is the situation with the CIA? Have your contacts agreed to back us?"

"They are certainly with us in principle, but they are a bit concerned with Cuba at the moment."

This caused the babble to start again.

"As long as they are not against us. We don't want another Suez fiasco."

General Salan answered with a subdued laugh, "In some ways it's probably a good thing that De Gaulle is not in charge here." Then, as an afterthought: "At least not as yet. They never liked him. The chances of getting the Americans' sympathy with him in charge would then have been nil."

"No. They don't like De Gaulle."

General Challe turned to some younger officers present and explained, "The Americans wanted Admiral Darlan or General Giraud to take over the French forces after the North African landings. you know. That Vichy traitor, Darlan! Can you imagine!? It was only Churchill's insistence on De Gaulle that persuaded them that they should stick with the man who had been so steadfast."

General Salan, overhearing, leant back in his chair with an air of one who had been proven correct. He had been De Gaulle's assistant during the war and a great admirer of his boss. "I told Charles he should not be so suspicious of

Churchill. Churchill did a lot for him behind the scenes, although they did not get on personally."

"Gentlemen," General Massu said this with great authority. He wanted to keep the meeting short and sharp. The company immediately turned their attention to him. "Destiny is in our hands. Retire to your units and prepare to invade Paris. With Paris in our hands, the rest of the country will fall in behind us."

Colonel Grouchant rose from his chair slowly. He regarded his fellow conspirators carefully for the first time. *They are all getting old. Most have spent all their life in the army. Do they realise what they are doing? Most were professional soldiers before the debacle of 1940. I am the youngest here, and the only one with a current perspective. Unfortunately, they reinforce each other's position without thinking. Do they not question what they are about to do? I was all for getting the government to see reason. I was not for invading France.*

Of course, they are my senior officers, and as such, I have to obey them, but if they are going to invade Paris, people will get killed. Surely they have seen misery enough in the Second World War? There is already a war going on all around us here, and people are losing their lives, but if they invade France, Frenchmen are going to get killed. That is different. Do they think that it is a price worth paying? Where's their humanity? Do they really think they can usurp the government without the populace fighting back?

As he retrieved his briefcase and stepped towards the door, he took another hard look at his fellow conspirators. *Yes, these are old men who back up each other's position, and it is easy for them to be carried along, but they are human. Can they not see? Do they not see their personal responsibility? I am a soldier, and have the duty of a soldier to obey, but I am also human. Do they not see where things are leading? They must know that we Frenchmen value our freedom. The current populace are descendants of the people that swept aside an Ancient Régime. They are not going to take kindly to being told what to do now. As soldiers, we all have a duty to uphold the honour of France, certainly, but as humans, we must value life. Are they so removed from reality that they do not see, or feel, the tragedy that might befall? They are human beings. They must feel.*

Monique loved driving their open two-seater car, particularly round Paris. Michael was a bit surprised that she was so reckless. In her dealings with him, she had become soft and sweet, but behind a wheel, she was a demon. He sat white-knuckled as she blasted her way round the Étoile, cutting in and out at a breakneck speed and driving the other cars off their line. Worse still, he was always sitting in the passenger's seat on the left-hand side of the car, so the other drivers thought he was driving, and they swore at him. Monique and Michael's trips around Paris were a cacophony of car horns and blue language. It was a good job that the standard of driving was exceptionally high, or they might have had endless accidents. *However, we all have faults,* Michael thought, *and this is an easy one for me to put up with.*

Life for Monique had become so embellished and expanded; she laughed her way through the traffic, food tasted better than it had ever done, flowers smelt sweeter, and sunsets were more beautiful. She was now invincible. She could see a bright future ahead, but she knew it could never be more glorious than the present. Maternal feelings had not yet entered her current agenda, but she knew they would one day. For now, she just wanted to enjoy Michael. She luxuriated in his company. He drew out her adventurous spirit. She was alive. Later, she would have to share him with their children.

The fact that the relationship was balanced also greatly pleased her. *I can influence him. Some men do not like to be persuaded by a woman. It interferes with their male ego, but that is not the case with Michael.* There had been the episode with the snails, for example. They had gone to a very expensive restaurant near the Louvre. Surveying the menu, she had suggested he try snails as an hors d'oeuvre, but he had screwed up his face in horror.

"You won't know what they taste like until you've tried. Remember what you said to me about beer and porridge."

"But they're different."

"Exactly."

He tried them. In fact, he liked them so much that they had ordered them several times since.

The couple went on several financially rewarding trips together, mostly to England, but often to Belgium. Most of the time, they were not even stopped, let alone questioned. Michael did not understand why at first, but he reasoned that it could only be that officials on the border posts could see they were in love and sympathised with them. It reminded older men of their own youth, and all but the most cynical and bitter of them did not want to do anything to spoil the couple's obvious happiness. And while Monique and Michael enjoyed these trips, and the places they saw, they grew rich. While Michael's left-wing group supplied only a meagre amount of cash, the right-wing group yielded copious riches that financed their luxurious lifestyle. Both client groups, as well as Monique's father, were pleased that their requirements and correspondence had been taken care of. Everybody seemed happy.

Except Michael.

Of course, he was superficially happy. No! More than that. He enjoyed their life just as much as Monique, but lurking in his subconscious was the worry that he was deceiving Monique all the time. *You cannot keep a secret from someone whom you hold so dearly, from someone who has become part of you, and be at one with yourself.* It worried him that he had to appear strong and cool all the time. He could not now afford the luxury of conspicuous emotions.

He was also missing painting. With so much going on, there was little time to spend in their studios. It was one entertainment after another. They went to the opera. They saw *La Règle du Jeu* in a small cinema in Paris and *Orphée* in a small cinema in London, the Hampstead Everyman. They went to the French theatre, although Michael thought the French theatre could not compare with that in England. The acting was stiff. Monique was coming round to his point of view, so they nearly always went to a play when they were in London. They ate at a series of expensive, and very good restaurants, both in London and Paris. They seldom went now to Mes Amis or met their old friends. When they did, they enjoyed it and intended to go more often, and they were always welcomed by the old company, but they were now so busy. Their friends expressed sorrow that they had not seen much of them of late.

Whilst sitting in the parks or walking through the streets in London, Monique was fascinated by fashionable young men she saw, particularly some in Bond Street, who were wearing curly-brimmed bowlers. She had always thought of a bowler hat as a sort of black pudding basin with a brim, a sign of convention and boredom. This was different. The curl suggested defiance and irresponsibility. She persuaded Michael to get one. He felt such gesture to her whim would not destroy his cool pose—the gravitas he had cultivated—and he wanted to please her. They also went to Simpsons in Piccadilly, where they ordered him a couple of very smart bespoke suits, which they were able to collect one week later after a few fittings. He looked splendid in his new outfit, and she was very proud of him.

She did not stint on herself either. Several dresses were purchased, along with handbags, shoes, and some very chic jewellery. In spite of her intelligence and her rebellious, unconventional nature, she was not immune to feminine things. Michael said she looked a million dollars. Indeed, she felt it.

When back in Paris, dressed in their new outfits, they attended a fashion show. With the death of Dior, Yves Saint Laurent had taken over the position of chief designer at the fashion house, and he had introduced the *Beat Look* to supersede the *New Look,* which had been so successful in raising spirits after the austerity of post-war Europe. There were several catwalk shows to be visited. Michael's bowler caused quite a stir. Monique was proud and amused at the same time. Inwardly, she giggled. People obviously regarded them with interest and respect and made efforts to get to know them, but they were complete in their own company.

They went several times to Le Manoir d'Espérance. It was a nice run in the car, not too long and nor too short. Several different routes were tried. They planned how they would arrange the accommodation: what furniture they needed for the lounge, which of the two large four-poster beds they would use themselves, and which they would use for visitors. Monique wondered where to put the nursery, but she did not mention this to Michael. That was something for the future. One of the old stables would have to be cleaned out and made weatherproof for their beautiful car. A lot of time was spent walking around the vineyards. Monique started to show Michael the different varieties of grape and explain what particular qualities they would bring to their wine. One weekend they started to clear a lot of junk from the cellar, but they did not get very far, as they usually ended up in a pile of straw, making love.

The house had not been regularly lived in for some time; only visited for occasional weekends. It suffered from neglect. A woman from the village came up and acted as housekeeper when the family was expected, but there were no permanent staff, which was really needed for a house of such size.

It was the same with the estate. The vines had been neglected. A farmer from the village had done some essential work on them, but he had his own to attend to, and his vineyards needed his attention at the same crucial times. M. Foch, unusual for him, had bought the place on a whim, thinking romantically that it would be nice to relax in at weekends, not realising the amount of work that was needed to maintain it. With it shut up and empty most of the time, it had started to deteriorate. He had made a little effort some years and had made some surprisingly good wine, with the help of folk from the village, but in small quantities for his own consumption. That excitement was wearing off. Monique and Michael were going to have to put in a big effort to bring the place up to standard and start their wine business commercially. The tremendous amount of work needed had not yet dawned on them.

One warm evening, as they lay in a hammock together outside the kitchen, looking at the stars and dreaming of the future, Michael was thinking how to broach the subject that most caused him discomfort. *If we are to live together, I must come clean and tell her about Sinister Port.* Eventually, he broke the silence.

"You said there were a lot of things I did not know about you, and you were right. I would never have believed that you were so keen on adventure, and that you liked to drive like a valkyrie."

"I did warn you," she said with a big smile.

"You did." He paused. He took a deep breath. He was determined to tell her about his left-wing errands, now she was his partner in the right–wing adventure. It was so difficult to keep such a big secret from her. "There are a lot of things you don't know about me. We have never properly discussed politics."

"Come on. I can read you like a book. I know you're a wicked revolutionary."

"No! Really! I do have dark secrets. I am not sure I should tell you, but I feel the need to. I hope you won't feel less for me as a result."

"I know. You're a vampire." She dug him in the ribs.

"I am not joking. There are things I think you ought to know."

"I know. You murdered your parents."

"Seriously."

"If you are going to tell me that you are a sex maniac, I already know that."

At that, she jumped up and, with a laugh, rushed off into the dark.

Michael gave up. He was partly relieved. He knew he had given his word not divulge his secret to anyone, even to those close to him, so he was happy to just let life drift on, but he realised that not telling her was weakness.

There was a fear at the back of his mind. *Supposing she does disapprove. She claims she is not interested in politics, but scratch the surface, and a conservative comes out. She would certainly not have any sympathy for my left-wing friends and what they are up to. I hope her sympathy for me will make up for that, when I do tell her.*

It was after this idyllic period, when they thought things had become an enchanted routine that it started to turn sour. Like all troubles, they did not come alone. Troubles like company. They are gregarious. Physically, at first, things lost their smooth progress.

They had their first problem with customs. This came as a surprise. On a journey back from England through Le Havre, they separated to go through customs as usual. Michael went straight through, but Monique was stopped. Michael waited for her outside, behind a building, but she did not appear. His breath came in short gulps. He was beginning to get worried.

Inside, a tall, mean-looking official was scrutinising her passport.

"You seem to have a lot of stamps in your passport recently."

"I travel a lot."

"How do you afford that? You are not supposed to take money out of the country."

"I have relations in England and Belgium. They subsidise me."

"Nice relations."

"Very."

"Would you just step around here for a moment."

A policewoman came forward and took her arm, leading her into a small room behind the desk. Here, she was frisked down.

"Have you found anything?" said a sergeant as he entered.

"No. She seems clean."

"We have reason to believe that you have been smuggling." The sergeant stood before her with a very stern face. "Have you anything to tell us that we might take into consideration later on?"

"I have nothing to tell you except that you have made a big mistake." *What do they know? What makes them suspect me?*

"French people cannot afford to travel at the moment. Who is financing you?"

"I have told your colleague, I have a lot of relations that are married to foreigners. They like to see me, so they help me with finance."

"They seem to want to see you a lot."

"Is that a crime?"

"No, but it might lead to a crime."

Monique was determined she was not going to show any weakness. *Huh! I'll show them.* She put on the haughtiest of her expressions. *They are not stronger than me!*

At this point, another official opened the door and called the sergeant away. There were three or four men having a small discussion outside the door, which had been left slightly ajar. Monique could hear nothing of what they were saying except, "There's nothing in her bag."

Two of them then entered.

"We have reason to believe that you have been conspiring with a group of left-wing dissidents."

Monique burst into genuine laughter. "Me? Left-wing? Where do you get that idea? My father is a respectable businessman and landowner."

"That does not say anything about his politics or yours for that matter."

"You don't know my father. Money is his politics."

"Perhaps you are rebelling against him."

"Why should a privileged young woman like me rebel against luxury? Do I look like a rebellious beatnik?"

With this, the sergeant's determination seemed to abate slightly.

Monique caught his hesitation and decided to take advantage and counterattack. "If you don't believe me, you can phone up General Duchamp or Madame Muson, the fashion couturier. They are friends of the family. They will vouch for me. Unless you think that they are left-wing revolutionaries, of course."

The second policeman whispered into the sergeant's ear. Monique decided to press home the attack. "You first of all accuse me of smuggling, and then of plotting. You are just out to get me. You can't make up your mind which holds the best hope of success. Are you misogynists who have to take revenge on an attractive young woman? Do you get a bonus for the amount of disruption you foist upon travellers?"

They ignored her and withdrew to the corridor again. After some mumbling, the sergeant came in. "O.K. You can go."

She picked up her bag and stormed out, with her nose in the air, surprised by their change of attitude but relieved, and not arguing.

For Michael, waiting outside, her detention seemed an eternity, and he was very worried. In fact, no more than half an hour had passed. He was pleased and relieved when she did appear, and his breathing returned to normal. He did not show it in his face. She walked straight past. He waited to see if she was being followed and then, at a suitable distance, followed after her himself. At the station, there was a police car with two policemen standing beside it. She went into the station, and the police got into the car. As Michael went past, he thought that they might have been on the radio. They paid no attention to him.

At the booking clerk's cubby-hole, there was an old lady struggling with her change. Behind her was Monique. She had obviously seen him but gave no gesture of recognition. He was about to join the queue, when a woman with a pram and several children came in and got in the line behind Monique, so he had to join at the back. Up at the window, Monique exclaimed in a loud voice, "A single to Rouen." She paid for her ticket and went out on to the platform. The family was served, and then Michael asked for a single to Rouen as well.

On the platform, Monique was sitting on a bench. Michael went past her, down to the front of the platform, and waited. There were very few other passengers. The family came down to a position near him. The old lady stood opposite the waiting room, and then a middle-aged man in a trilby and a duffle coat came hurrying onto the platform beside her and looked around, just as the train came into the station. Monique got on, and the trilby-hatted man rushed down the platform and got on directly behind her. Michael helped the family up into the carriage with all their paraphernalia. This gave him a chance to see if there were any other travellers at the last minute. There were not, so he jumped on as the guard blew his whistle. He found a seat and settled down.

When the train had got well out into the country, taking his bag, he walked back down the train. He saw Monique sitting about halfway down, and the last man on the platform sitting a few seats behind her on the other side of the aisle. Monique again ignored Michael, and he walked straight past.

Sometime before the train approached the stop before Rouen, Monique got up and went to the ladies toilet, leaving her bag conspicuously on the seat, having taken out everything essential. When she came out of the toilet, she could see the man standing by the seat she had vacated. She went back another coach and stood by the door. The train stopped. Few got off. When the whistle blew, she jumped out at the last minute.

Michael had been standing by another door further back. He had pulled the window down, and was leaning out, watching the few passengers that alighted. He saw Monique get out, and then he too jumped off, after the guard had got on, and the train was picking up speed. As the train sped away, he stood and checked that no one else had got off after him and then followed Monique into the booking hall, where both she and he separately bought a ticket to Paris. Once on that train, they met up and exchanged anecdotes of their trip. They were ecstatic. Monique thoroughly enjoyed the excitement. Michael thought the episode had been a little too close for comfort.

When they were back in Paris, Michael made an effort to visit his studio. It saddened him. He took some pictures that he had stacked with their face against the wall and put them one by one on his easel. He repeated to himself one of the maxims he held most dear: *You should always seek distance from a painting when you think you have finished it, for if you are still too close to the problems you have struggled with, you cannot see the whole.* His observations confirmed his view. *Those areas of intense work stick out like a sore thumb. It's only after you have not seen it for some time that you can see a picture as a stranger would see it. Then you can judge.*

The pictures stimulated his thought. *The subconscious input to the painting is what is most important. What does it say? An artist is more than his technical skill with a paintbrush. It is me as a man that impregnates my work of art. Am I saying anything worthwhile? Perhaps that is why so many artists' last works are their most profound. Close to death, they cannot afford to be anything but honest.*

Michael was pleasantly surprised by what he saw, but he told himself he should not get too complacent. Although he realised that the distance from his pictures had been forced upon him, rather than chosen, the effect was the same.

He could see several improvements that needed to be done. *In that respect, it had been a useful gap in time, but not necessarily so. I could have been getting on with other paintings in that interlude.* He fumed at himself. *Why am I not doing more painting?*

He picked up his brush and added a few carefully selected strokes to several canvases. He had just taken a fresh canvas from the stack in the corner and started to lay on a blue wash when there was a 'Hallo' from outside the studio door. He opened it. There was Pierre.

"Come in. To what do I owe this pleasure?"

"Exactly to that. It's not business. It's pleasure. I have come to see how the artistic production is going."

"Not very well, I'm afraid. Other things keep me busy."

"Well, these look very good," said Pierre, looking at the paintings Michael had recently taken from the wall.

He really likes my work. I have a fan. Michael then had a second thought. *Or perhaps he is just flattering me.*

"I'm tempted to invest in another."

"You flatter me. It's only because we are acquainted."

"I would not waste my money if I did not think you were any good. I would spend it on someone better, but I have not seen anyone better recently. Besides, painting means too much to me to use it as a vehicle of flattery."

"You have never seen Monique's work, have you? She is very good. Wouldn't you like to see some of her paintings?"

"Of course. I did not know she was a serious painter."

"She is! Very serious, and very good!"

Michael took the key from behind his stove, and they went along to Monique's studio. Michael selected a few of his favourite paintings and propped them against the wall.

"Yes, she is good. Two geniuses together." This was said with a twinkle in his eye and in his voice. "What a couple. I particularly like this one. Would she sell it?"

"I'm sure she would be very pleased. I can't tell you how honoured I am to be hanging in the same house as Braque and Picasso."

"I won't do her the dishonour of taking it from her now, without her being here, but ask her if it is for sale and how much she wants for it."

"I will. I have your phone number. We'll give you a ring and perhaps bring it up to you."

"You know it is very dangerous both partners indulging in the same profession, especially when they are both very good. There is liable to be jealousy."

"Oh, I don't think Monique and I could ever be jealous of each other. We never disagree."

"When you get to my age you realise that women are very strange creatures. We think we know them, but their behaviour is wrapped in mystery. They surprise us when we least expect it. One day she will catch you off your guard and disagree."

"Monique and I are completely at one with each other. We have no…" At this point, he stopped for a moment. He felt a sharp pain. "…no secrets from one another."

Pierre gave him a quizzical look. "No secrets?"

"She does not know about our group. That is a secret I guard at great cost."

"I am glad to be reassured, but it was not that sort of secret I was thinking of. How about those black thoughts you have deep down in your subconscious; those things you are reluctant to admit to yourself? Don't be too ashamed, for she will have thoughts and desires that she would not tell you about, even if she admitted them to herself."

"Monique is very straightforward."

"Nobody, man nor woman, is straightforward. We all have thoughts and behaviours of which we are ashamed. We are animals. We certainly would not admit our dark appetites to a partner from whom we would like respect. We concoct an image to guard our prurient thoughts from those we love. I have a theory that men and women are really two different species, but God, who has a warped sense of humour, decided to make them live together. He sits back and watches the fun. I sometimes wonder why he did not invent three sexes necessary to reproduce the species. Then he could have enjoyed even greater chaos."

"I never realised you were so cynical. I am sure you are wrong about Monique, even if you have had bad experiences with lesser women in the past."

"You are young, and I am a bit hesitant to disillusion you, but remember my words when you are in your forties."

"Let's hope things do not go wrong, and we are both alive when I'm forty."

They both laughed, slightly nervously.

"Whatever Monique is like as a woman, she is certainly a good painter, and I am very serious about buying that picture."

"She is going to be thrilled when I tell her."

She was thrilled, and the transaction was completed on the phone. When Michael had sold his picture, it had made a significant contribution to their finances, but with all the treasures coming from their illicit travels, the money was now not so important. Nevertheless, a sale reassures you. You start to think you are on the right lines.

Monique saw a painting as a vehicle for the transmission of ideas and feelings. She, as an artist, put her experiences into a picture. If the viewer drew the same feeling from viewing that picture, it was a success. The idea that Pierre wanted one of her paintings gave her a great thrill. She relished the thought.

Pierre is a connoisseur. He knows the language. He will understand what I am saying. She was very proud. She was very pleased.

They delivered the painting and had another beautifully cooked dinner.

Chapter Seven

A week after they delivered Monique's picture and had enjoyed another pleasant evening in Pierre's home, Michael got a call from Pierre.

"Sinister Port has another job for you."

He found himself in the Raymonds' kitchen once again. As he went in, he met Pierre, who whispered something in his ear. "Things have got worse. There has been a coup in Algeria."

This time the Spaniard did most of the talking.

"If they invade in the south, probably Marseille, it would take them some time to make their way up to Paris. We would have time to prepare." His expression gave light to his concern.

Bertrand butted in. "Things never happen the way you expect. The generals know what they need to do. They are good generals. They would not come in at Marseille. There is a strong left-wing faction there. It might bog them down."

"There is also a large displaced Pieds-noirs population, and they resent having been terrorised into leaving Algiers. They will support the generals," said Claude.

The Spaniard modified his speculations. "True, but wherever they land, it will take time to consolidate and move north."

Pierre added his opinion. "We are not going to be able to take on the whole French army anyway." He paused for a quick thought and, turning to Bertrand, continued, "More importantly, have we made contact with any other like-minded groups yet, to see if we can organise a united front?" Pierre believed in negotiations. "There must be people like us in Marseille and elsewhere."

At this point, the Spaniard broke in again. "It is not as easy as that. Not only do you have to be careful about the police, but you have to know who you are dealing with. Not everybody who is against your enemy is necessarily your friend."

Claude's wife was an idealist. She felt compelled to join the conversation. "We should not wait to see who thinks as we do. We should do our own thing."

"We should do what will prove most useful," Pierre added.

"We should not do what is expedient, but what is right," Bertrand added, who was also an idealist, in spite of his cunning.

"It is no good doing what is right if you're dead." Pierre was adamant.

Michael had said very little up to this point. He felt out of his depth.

Bertrand took over the conversation once more. "Pierre here has arranged for the finance of some weaponry, and it has currently been brought from Russia as far as Hull. We now need to get the shipment across the Channel. This is where you come in, Michael. I believe you don't always travel on public transport."

Now the attention of the group turned to him. He sat transfixed. He could see where the conversation was going. He felt a target, and very uncomfortable.

Although they don't know him, they want me to use Charley. Should I get him involved?

"That's true," Michael said hesitantly.

"So you could bring a shipment to us by clandestine means?"

He had not expected to be put in such a position.

"Why yes! How big a package is it?" he said to Pierre, gaining time to think.

"About two meters, by half a metre square, I believe, though I haven't seen it."

"Hardly something that could be smuggled in a suitcase," said Claude.

"Or I could put in my pocket," offered Michael. "It would need special means of transport." He remembered Charley dropping off a package in the middle of the Channel, but this would be much larger and presumably very heavy. It would sink. The whole project seemed fraught with danger. He was not sure he wanted to tell of his fisherman route, even though he sympathised with the group's predicament.

"Nevertheless, we have to find some way to get it to France," said Pierre. He offered a rational comment. "There are only two reasonably practical ways of getting it here; one is bribing someone to smuggle it across on a cargo ship, but then the port authorities are going to see it and want a manifest for a cargo that size being unloaded. The other is if you could fix up something with your fisherman friends…"

How does Pierre know about them? Michael was shocked.

"…and land it somewhere that is not a port."

He can't know about the way they drop things off things mid-Channel.

Michael felt a bit as though he had been dropped off in mid-Channel. He needed time to think things through.

What is Charley going to say about gun-running? And would Loïk Cuek play ball? He is a Breton after all, and might not have complete sympathy with the French.

Michael needed to play for time. He was committed to these people, and he sympathised with their cause, but...

"I don't promise anything," he exclaimed. "I'll have to make some enquiries, but leave it to me. I'll see what I can do. This will mean a trip to England if I am to sort something out."

I am already in over my head, he thought to himself. *Will an extra step take me too far?*

"Go as soon as you can. Pierre will see to your finances," Bertrand said.

"We will need everything we can get," said the Spaniard. "We rely on you."

Michael could feel the weight of a great responsibility falling on his shoulders.

I am no longer in charge of my destiny. Do I fool myself when I think that I am a strong, decisive, independent person? I have tried to be, but is anyone in the face of fate? Is fate what other people will have you do? If I believe in living dangerously, is that not throwing myself into the arms of powers that I cannot control? I must pull myself together and be strong. Now I have made my decision to get involved with these people, I have to go on with it. Opting out now would be the weak—the cowardly thing to do.

He compelled himself to act like a man.

I have to fulfil the course that fate has dictated—or I have dictated. Too many people are now relying on me. If the army does invade, many people will be crushed. It will become like Spain, or even Nazi Germany. The people must be able to protect themselves.

Eventually, the meeting broke up.

Pierre touched Michael's arm. "Hang on a minute Michael, while I get my bag. I'll walk with you to the Metro, and we can discuss the money you will need on the way."

As they sauntered along, they quickly got the financial arrangements out of the way.

"Don't worry about the money. I'll cover everything. Offer any helpers exactly what they ask. It is essential we get the stuff here quickly. I believe things are much more serious than the others think."

"Surely you have not a bottomless well of money?"

"Not bottomless, of course, but enough."

"It's rude of me to ask, I know, but what business were you in that produced such wealth?"

"Oh, no business. It's inherited wealth, I'm afraid," he paused and chuckled to himself. "And when I was your age, my father gave me money to go and buy some paintings for my future home. Much to his horror, I bought modern pictures. He hated them. He expected me to buy David or at least Impressionists, not the Picassos and Modigliani which I did acquire. He was flabbergasted. It has turned out alright, however. Apart from the money he left me when he died, if I ever get a bit short, I sell a painting. Once you have money, it makes itself."

Pierre's demeanour then quickly brightened. "How is that lovely lady of yours?" he enquired.

"Oh, very well."

Michael was very curious about Pierre. *How can he be so cool?* He instinctively liked him. He admired him. Pierre was a bit younger than the others in the group and intelligent. Not that the others were not, but his intelligence had been educated. He also came from a wealthy background and knew how to spend his money; on the art that he loved and the political ideas that he embraced. *There is no meanness in his makeup. That is what's attractive. So why is there no sign of a woman in his life, although he is quite good-looking? He is certainly not in any way effeminate.* Michael also wondered why he was involved in a group so different to himself. *Is he lonely, perhaps?*

There were some things only time could tell, so Michael snapped out of his chain of thought and returned to the more prosaic. He had another puzzle on his mind. Perhaps Pierre knew the answer.

"Tell me, how the Spaniard comes to speak such good French?"

"Because he is French."

"Then why do you call him The Spaniard?"

"He fought in the Spanish Civil War." Pierre had a little laugh and then became more serious. "He had a terrible time. He was double-crossed by his own side, captured by the Nationalists, escaped, and then, when everything collapsed, and he returned across the French frontier, he was interned."

"Oh."

"That's why he is cautious about who we get involved with. He hates anything military, but his fighting experience is invaluable."

"He does sound as though he knows what he is talking about."

"We are going to rely on him. He has seen it all, and his experience will be invaluable. He is one of those working-class people who are intelligent, but have never been educated."

"I have a friend in England like that: intelligent but badly educated by the school system. However, he has read more than anyone else I know. If you want to know something, on almost any subject, you ask him. He works in a garage where they call him the professor."

They stopped.

"Well, here we are." Pierre lent against the railings. They had arrived at the entrance to the station. "You go on a different Metro line to me, so I'll say goodbye. You have my phone number in an emergency." Then, as a second thought, "Or even if there is not an emergency. We should meet for a drink sometime."

Michael thought deeply on his way back home. *Life is now serious. I can no longer joke about living dangerously. No longer can I act as an overgrown teenager. I am now an adult. If I don't develop gravitas, it will be thrust upon me.*

A few days later, Michael set off for England and George's. He had difficulty in persuading Monique not to go with him. He told her that his Uncle George lived in a home (which he did—his own home) and that he did not want visitors. Michael said this with an apologetic air. Monique accepted that Michael had been called to see a difficult, grumpy old uncle suddenly and that he would not be away long. She would catch up on some shopping.

When Michael got to George's home in Wembley, he found George worried by the news from Algeria, which was being given big coverage on the wireless. They discussed the shipment, and its importance.

"Our friends will have very little to defend themselves, and to stop the military taking over. And like all fascists, the military will not tolerate any criticism, and our friends will be arrested and probably tortured. That is the nature of right-wing thinking. They can only rule by fear."

"What is it we have to get to France?" Michael asked with concern in his voice. "What is in the shipment, and how big is it?"

"It is mainly Kalashnikovs and ammunition. I don't know its size."

"I am going to have to see if my contacts in Hastings are willing and able to transport such a cargo. This is gun-running. They will have to know exactly how big and heavy it is?"

"I'm told it's sizeable, but a couple of strong men could lift it. You will have to offer them good money. Offer them whatever they want. We have no time to haggle."

"When will it all happen?"

"If everyone agrees, I can get the shipment to Hastings on a food lorry from Hull any time they like. It's up to them when."

Michael thought about what Pierre had said, "As soon as possible." Then about getting it on board the boat, "It would be best if the lorry arrives at night—fewer people to see what's going on."

"Won't that arouse suspicion, activity at night?"

"No. Fishermen's lives are ruled by the tides, not by the clock. There is often night activity at Rock-a-Nore."

"I presume your fishermen friends can be trusted."

"Yes, of course."

"This time we are asking them to go further into criminality."

"They probably won't know the contents of the cargo, and won't ask." Michael hesitated for a moment. "Looking the other way is part of their nature. It's not them that the gun-running will worry; it's me! Guns are designed to kill."

"It shouldn't worry you. Tyranny has to be resisted wherever it tries to impose itself. Look what happened in Hungary."

"I took you to be a Communist?"

"Any Communist sympathies I had during the Russian Revolution or the Spanish Civil War were dispelled by the way the Soviets behaved in Hungary. I believe in freedom and democracy, as the least bad of all possible disastrous systems." He dropped his head in despair. "We should have helped the Hungarians, but we were too wrapped up with our own tyranny in the Suez Canal. We have to help the French. They are too close, both politically and geographically, to let them down. Don't be worried about helping ordinary people to arm themselves."

Michael went straight from George's to Hastings. The negotiations with Charley were short and to the point. Michael was completely honest with him. He told him exactly what the cargo contained. Not to, would have been unfair.

"It will be something about the size of a paratroopers' gear container, I think—a bit heavy, but moveable by two strong men."

"I'm sure Loik, my Breton friend, will do it. He is of the left, but he will need to be bloody well paid. Money talks very loudly with Loik Cuek. There will be a problem at the other end. Loik has his own distribution network for the usual cargo, but your stuff will mean trusting bloody outsiders. He will not know the people he is dealing with, and he won't like that. But the money will tempt him. Recognition signals will have to be arranged, and where to collect the bloody shipment—somewhere away from his usual haunts—on the Brittany coast. Yes, Loik will be very worried about working with people he doesn't know. Our bloody business builds paranoia."

"You can tell him that we are all very trustworthy. Our lives and freedom depend on secrecy as well as his."

"I will know by the day after tomorrow if, in principle, Loik accepts a deal, and then, if so, you can set things up at the other end. Get them to suggest several handing-over places for Loik to choose from."

Business done, Michael and Charley had a beer together, and then Michael drove quickly back to Wilton Street to await the result of Charley's negotiations.

Word came through that night, quicker than he expected, that Loik was agreeable. An amount of money had been suggested. On behalf of his group, Michael agreed to it. It was, in fact, pleasantly less than Michael had expected.

On returning to Paris, Michael reported progress to Sinister Port, who were very pleased. They arranged for half a dozen hefty sympathisers and a van to collect the stuff when it arrived in Brittany. They suggested several rendezvous in hidden bays, and Michael informed Charley.

It was a week later that Michael heard from Charley that Loik agreed to a chosen place to pass over the goods. The sum of money would be paid half up front, and the other half when the goods were handed over. Various signals were agreed to identify each other. All was ready to go. Michael was pleased and self-satisfied that all had been arranged so quickly.

Very soon, Michael was again on a ferry with Monique to Dover. This time it was a car ferry. He intended to do a round trip in the Channel with Charley, to watch the valuable cargo dropped off, get quickly back to Wilton Street by car, and return again afterwards with Monique to France. He wanted to see the goods as far as possible on their journey. He took Monique to England, as she was very keen, although ignorant of the real purpose, and he could not keep refusing to take her. They would be taking nothing illegal in the car in either direction, so there was no danger for her.

Michael had thought nothing could be more intense than the first time he had carried messages for the group, but he was wrong. On the ferry, he had plenty of time to think. *Now I am embarking on an altogether more hazardous and illegal arrangement. I am part of an international political conspiracy. It is exciting, but is it moral? This is gun-running. Is gun-running ever justified?*

He went and got a coffee in the café.

How have I come to this position? Not by design, but unplanned short steps. Do I really want to be here? On the other hand, if good people do not stand up for democracy, who will? If the democratic countries had helped the government in Spain, Franco would not have won, and we might not have had the Second World War.

He justified himself with the fact that it was for a cause he really believed in. He had come to this conclusion several times, but his conscience kept returning him to the quandary.

Once they were in Wilton Street, he had the problem of how he was going to get away from Monique while he went on the Channel trip. He had had doubts about telling her of his carrying of letters for people she would disapprove of. Telling her he was gun-running was out of the question.

He persuaded Monique to go and do some shopping for more household goods, and tins for the cupboard while he visited George. Shopping was something he hated, unless it was for cars. Monique knew this, so she was not surprised that he opted out. He then went to see George and Charley all in one day, to ensure for himself that everything was in place. He arrived back home exhausted. Monique was very sympathetic.

"Poor thing. Your uncle must be a great strain."

Michael felt his conscience pricking him. "Well, I have taken on responsibilities. I have to do my duty for my family as we have to do our duty for your family."

Can carrying money be equated with what I am now undertaking?

Michael now used an excuse he had been saving up for some time. He announced that he had arranged to meet up with some old friends from school. They were going to have a lad's night out. Monique had no desire to spend an evening with a group of drunken, overgrown schoolboys, so she offered no protestations.

The go-ahead was given, and the lorry duly delivered its cargo in Hastings without a hitch. Michael arrived at the boat at the same time, just after dark. The lorry driver was a bit gormless. He was not interested in what he was carrying, only the brown envelope. He did not stop to count its contents. He hurried away. His mates would be waiting for him back in the depot.

The cargo was slightly bigger than expected but not unmanageable. In the darkness of the early hours, the canister was carried to Charley's boat. They started to lift it up on to the deck with some difficulty when Allen, another of the fishermen, appeared and offered to help. Charley jumped, and had a very infrequent extra heartbeat. Although all the fishermen were comrades, Charley was not particularly close to Allen.

Eventually, the cargo installed in the bilges, the boat was pushed down the shingle beach. This time they sailed further west, along the Channel, and somewhere opposite Cherbourg, they shot their nets. It took the whole crew to get the canister out of the hold and on deck. As it was much heavier than expected, there was some apprehension in that it would be too heavy for the buoys. However, they took the precaution of using a fairly long drift net, which had a lot of buoys attached, to put over the side with it, and even fixed a giant buoy to the whole to be safe. If it were to sink, all the effort would be lost. Michael hoped that Loik had enough strong men on his boat to haul the net on board. They chose a position where the sea was not too deep just in case.

As they saw their valuable cargo disappear beneath the waves and the marker buoy slip behind the boat, Charley called up Loik on the radio and gave the position, which was by this time somewhere nor-west of the Channel Islands (49° 35'N by 2° 05'W).

"Right. I'm in St Malo now. If, as you say, there's a lot of fish around, I'll come out right away. We did very well with that catch you put us on to last week. Thanks."

"You're very welcome, mate. There's nothing like co-operation. That's how we managed to defeat the bloody Germans. Together we could probably take on any bloody one. I'll be in touch. Out."

Michael went back to Hastings with the boat this time. They intended to do very little fishing on the way back, but the nets came up full. They were all exhausted, but they could not relax. The fish had to be gutted, sorted, and packed into the boxes for the market, or officials might be suspicious. But as they had not crossed the Channel, there was no cause for either customs to suspect smuggling of any kind.

Michael rushed onto an early train to meet up with Monique and his car in Mayfair. He had helped with the fishing on the way home and hoped he did not smell of fish. They only shot the nets once, but there was a lot of it, and he was exhausted by the time he got ashore, much to the amusement of the crew.

"You bloody landlubbers are all the same. You don't know what real work is."

It was now well into the morning. He changed into his clean clothes and caught the train to Charing Cross.

Monique was worried, but when he got home, he had an excuse for her. "I drank too much and had to crash out on Brian's sofa. It took me ages to get up this morning. I had a hangover."

"Poor thing! Oh well. Let that be a lesson to you. I was very worried. How do you feel now?"

"O.K."

"I'll get you some tea."

Michael felt terrible, but not just physically. He hated deceiving Monique.

Later that day, the couple drove down to Dover. Michael let Monique do most of the driving. He dozed. The wind had dropped by the time they crossed the Channel. He was still aching all over when they got back to Paris. He was not used to such physical work as he had been called to do on the fishing boat. *How do they do it day after day? No wonder the expectation of life for fishermen is so short.*

Back in the Champs–Élysées, Monique phoned her father. "My father has another job for us," she said to Michael with renewed excitement.

"I was hoping to get in some painting, but never mind. Whenever he likes, I'm available."

He had a need to placate his conscience and do something for Monique.

Two days later two train tickets arrived by post to take them to Tours. A car would be waiting for them there outside the station the following day. *I might have been busy and unavailable. It is a bit presumptuous on her father's part to expect me to be always available, even though I have said so. I hope he does not always expect me to be at his beck and call when we are married. I need to paint. My conscience only stretches so far.* At that moment however, he could hardly call himself a painter. He longed to get back to his easel.

As expected the consortium of the right had another parcel for Michael and Monique.

"It's bigger than ever. I'm told there are 200,000,000 francs in here," said Monique with a sparkle in her eyes.

"With so much money in our possession, I am worried about burglars."

"Well, there's nothing we can do about it. We can hardly insure it."

"I suppose that is one of the things we are getting paid for: taking the risk. Live dangerously and enjoy it. That's all we can do." This time, he said it without so much conviction.

"When everything settles down, we are going to have plenty of capital to run our wine business," said Monique with great glee, "and memories to savour."

The young couple returned to Paris that evening. M. Foch had handed Michael a package as they left Tours.

"This is for you," he had said. "You've helped my friends, and improved my standing amongst them. That's very good for business. Thank you."

"Well, that's a surprise," said Michael, as they settled down in their seats on the train and he opened the package to find a pair of gold cuff links.

"You see? I said that my father would like you. He obviously trusts you."

"He must do." *A lot of people trust me. I now must be capable of fulfilling their trust?* Michael thought to himself.

Michael waited on tenterhooks until the Sinister Port wanted him to go to England again, in spite of his worries over the money. He could do the two errands together. He was travelling backwards and forwards very frequently now, and the more frequently he went, the bigger the risk. The trip through Le Havre had shaken him up. Luckily, he did not have to wait long.

When he did get to London, he went to George's straight away. They discussed the previous operation. It was while he was there that word came through signifying that the consignment had got to Paris with no hitches. They celebrated the success with a bottle of good whisky. Relief lightened their mood.

However, George had other news. "Colonel Bouget has pledged the 12th Regiment to the generals. We got our stuff there not a moment too soon."

Michael quickly drove back to Wilton Street via Dolphin Square, where he was pleased to divest himself of the cash. Monique had been out shopping while he had been doing his errands and had bought some things that made the flat more like their home than a rented apartment. She, of course, still did not know the true nature of George. She was touched by Michael's attention to a problematic uncle.

They spent several days in England this time, mostly in London, where they went to the cinema in Leicester Square and to the theatre in Shaftesbury Avenue. Monique had come to love the theatre, so Michael took her to *Hamlet* at The Old Vic, but she found the language, although beautiful, a bit difficult, and Michael had to go over the plot with her afterwards. He would have liked to take her to *Romeo and Juliet*, but that did not seem to be on in the near future. Another visit was paid to Luba's Bistro, and they went to a Chinese restaurant, The South China, in the bottom end of Wardour Street, just off Shaftesbury Avenue. There were only a few such restaurants in London at that time, and Monique had never been to one in Paris. She was surprised by the variety and the quality of Chinese food. *It is almost as good as French cuisine,* she thought. She did know of a Parisian Vietnamese restaurant, but she had never been there. They decided they would visit it when they got back.

Michael thought it strange how many revolutionaries—Chou En Lai, Ho Chi Minh, amongst others—had served as waiters in Vietnamese restaurants in Paris, whereas in England, Marx, Garibaldi, and Lenin, expatriate revolutionaries, had sat reading in the British Museum. *Perhaps it says something about the relative cultures in France and England. In France, being a waiter is a skilled and honourable profession. Is a reader in a museum an honourable occupation in England?*

Eventually, Monique and Michael set off again for the coast, very happy, full of their metropolitan experiences. The ceasing of their city pleasures was always compensated for by the drive through the southern countryside on a warm, sunny day. Again, the sea was calm. Monique did not know if she suffered from sea sickness. She had never been tested. Michael was never sick. He must have been given the antidote in his genes.

When they were back in Paris, he took the first opportunity to visit Sinister Port. They were busy unpacking and cleaning the guns. Half had already been done and distributed to newfound supporters. Michael settled down to help with the rest. They were wrapped in oiled paper and preserved with very heavy, sticky grease, almost like plastic. Most of the weapons were Kalashnikovs AK-47s, but there was a German MG-42 machine gun, probably left over from the war. A heavier weapon like that, with its tremendous rate of fire, could be very useful.

When he got home, Monique wondered where he had got all the nasty sticky stuff from on his clothes. Some were beyond repair.

The next morning, after breakfast, Michael sat looking at Monique. His mind went over ideas that kept recurring. This time, he developed them further. His thoughts were becoming clearer. *My union with her is not just based on physical attraction. What Pierre has to say about women is a lot of nonsense. Monique could not have any dark secrets from me and I should not have a dark secret from her—albeit my secret is of different in nature. My duplicity worries me greatly. Without that barrier, which I have created, our two minds would be completely drawn together. I must get rid of it.*

He thought for a minute. Then, with determination, *I must come clean and share my secret right now. I will then have no doubts about our unity.*

"Monique, I have something to tell you."

"Oh, tell me later. Just enjoy the moment."

Chapter Eight

Pierre phoned. "Hallo, Michael. How are things going? How about meeting up and having some lunch? We have a lot to talk about, and it would be nice to have a chat about something other than politics. Perhaps paintings and subjects more casual than our usual conversations."

"It's a nice idea. Where do you suggest and when?"

"Do you know Double Blue? It's on the junction of Rue Adler and Rue Condorçet?"

"No, but I can find it."

"Perhaps tomorrow, about 1 o'clock?"

"I'll be there."

They were both punctual people, so they met as they went into the restaurant. The waiter came to see if they wanted a drink while they chose from the menu.

"I don't want to drink too much, otherwise I won't work this afternoon," said Pierre, picking up the menu, "but I want wine with my lunch to help it down, so let's see what we are going to eat first."

"A sentiment with which I wholly concur," said Michael, with mock sophistication.

Michael chose moules marinières as an hors d'oeuvre, followed by roast quail. Pierre had pâté followed by a venison pie. They had both let affluence turn them into moderate epicureans. It was a very good, honest restaurant, and the food was delicious. No wine would be ideal with everything they were ordering, which was diverse. They compromised on a light red house wine.

"I have just bought myself a Paul Klee."

"Wow!" Michael was amazed and slightly nervous.

"He is so witty. It is difficult to be humorous, and produce great art. However, he is the master. Very few can do it."

"I agree. You can count such artists on one hand. The only other person I can think of is Max Ernst."

"Sometimes Picasso comes up with a gem, *Fishing at Antibes,* for example, but only rarely does it supersede cartoonism when he's joking, and those are not his great works. He admits himself that he's a joker, and as I said before, it is only when he is emotionally moved that he becomes a great artist."

"It's the same in music," Michael exclaimed. He was delighted. It was reassuring to find that someone else had arrived at similar ideas as he had. "Satie can be witty and amusing," he paused, "and so can Berlioz sometimes. His writing is also sometimes witty. You should read his correspondence with Wagner." This diverted Michael's mind to another idea. "In literature it's easier. Many writers, novelists, and even poets can be amusing, and yet their work can still retain a profound quality."

"That's not surprising. Comedy is at the centre of literature. Words thrive on idiosyncrasy, and idiosyncrasy is close to wit," replied Pierre. "Also, literature is concerned with motive and causality, and a lot of motives are ridiculous and comical. Good stories can often delight in bizarre happenings."

"And what of wit? Is that a form of humour?" Michael highlighted a problem he had often considered.

"Wit is colour for the author. It is not really humour. I am sure you amuse yourself when painting, by indulging in some delightful colour combinations, purely for the sensual pleasure of it. It is not always dictated by the subject matter. It is self-indulgence."

"True." Michael was reluctant to admit this. He still took his art very seriously. "But one has to be careful it does not divert from the subject."

"If that is avoided, it is then that it can become great art. Take Shakespeare, for example." Pierre paused and continued, slowly, with a thoughtful air, "An author is essentially a wordsmith, and he sometimes amuses himself with the embroidery of words for his own pleasure, even when it is not dictated by the subject matter or the plot. Ideas form the substance of his work, and he expresses these with a plot of dramatic and sometimes bizarre happenings, but he allows himself some amusement on the way. Writing, like any solitary profession, can be lonely and sometimes boringly routine. We must allow the author some leeway for self-amusement."

Michael had a moment of uncharacteristic self-pity. "If literature is a succession of ridiculous and bizarre happenings, then my life is due for literary treatment. It has become full of bizarre happenings."

"Would you like it any other way?"

"Perhaps not." He paused. "When I think about what I have left behind, I am amazed." He gave a little laugh. "I have always told myself that one should live dangerously, but I wonder if things have gone too far." He paused again. "The life I would be living now, had I not left the BBC, would be boring in the extreme, but it would be safer."

Pierre grinned. "We have certainly given you the opportunity to live dangerously."

Michael matched his grin. He contemplated his past, nodding his head with each phrase. "I would be going to work every day, collecting my salary each month," his voice rose slightly, "and by now, I might be settling down with the girl next door, and looking forward to a new car every three years, and three children in the course of the next six."

"Do you have regrets?"

"Not really. Life now is much richer."

"And are you looking forward to three children in the course of the next six years?"

"No. I don't think Monique is interested in children. At least not at the moment."

"Be careful. Women are never what they seem. Their deep mysteries are one of their attractions, but that is where they are dangerous."

Michael gave another smile. "Well, I am living dangerously then, aren't I?"

Their food arrived.

Pierre continued, "However fresh and unconventional women appear, eventually they revert to type. They revert to the way they have been brought up. Monique has been brought up in a wealthy bourgeois family. I can see that. Be careful."

"Monique has left her bourgeois past behind her. We agree completely on how we want to live our lives."

"We think we know the woman we live with, and we expect that they will behave rationally, as we behave rationally, but they are much more in touch with their bodies than we are. They have to be. Not only does their position in society depend upon it," he changed his tone to one more sympathetic, "socially it is their biggest asset," then, reverting to his original rather pompous tone, "but it is they who produce the next generation, and they are enslaved by the function nature has put upon them. Their bodies continually make them aware of the fact. If their behaviour is not controlled by their emotions, as we men erroneously like to think, it is certainly immensely affected by their hormones, which control their emotions."

"What's the difference?"

"Their intellect intervenes between the two."

"Anyway, Monique is not carried away by her emotions and is not a bit like her background. She has made a point of breaking away, becoming a painter, and getting involved with someone like me."

"She does that to rebel against her parents, as all children have to at some point. One day, she will start to look for what she knows and has left behind. She will start to look for what makes her feel secure in a tumultuous world."

"And what is that?"

"A comfortable family atmosphere; a luxurious living style, a sophisticated social circle, where people make money and gossip about their children and new cars, and a safe place to bring up her offspring in the same way that she was brought up."

"She doesn't seem to want that. If she did, I would give it to her."

"Are you capable of giving it to her? Don't misunderstand me. I am not criticising you, but she will just subconsciously seek the aura which she knows, and has left behind. You come from a very different background. This, of course, is one of your advantages at the moment. As I said, sooner or later all children have to break free of their parents, and the earlier they do this, the better. Monique is fairly old for such a thing to happen, and so the break, when it came, had to be greater than wearing unsuitable clothes or stomping out in a temper over the time she came in at night." He pauses to take a mouthful of food. "She is a nice and sympathetic girl, and therefore instinctively she avoids a really violent break, which would deeply hurt her parents."

Michael leant across the table. "Let me top your glass up."

"Thank you."

Pierre took a sip and continued unabated, "Painting, and involving herself with you, shows her parents her independence, without hurting them too much. One day, when she has made her point, she might very well revert to the society she knows, takes for granted, and in which she feels at home."

"I hope not, but if she does, I am willing to adapt to her whim."

"I also hope, for your sake, that she does not."

"I think you have a very poor view of women."

"On the contrary, I love women," Pierre's demeanour was suddenly elated, then it subsided, "but I can see their faults. Perhaps I should not say faults, because they are not faults, but necessary characteristics for their role in life."

"What do you mean, 'their role in life'?"

"Society is women. We men are peripheral. Their friendships and social networks are the centre of mankind. If a couple meets another couple and the women do not get on, they never meet again. They choose the relationships. They control our circle of friends." He sips his wine. "They make the home. They feed us. They are responsible for the future. They give us birth, and they more often than not, bury us. We are here to supply the extra genes to procreate, and to defend them. We think we are in charge, but it is they who make the decisions and govern our lives."

"You have a very cynical view of women. What causes this? Do you not have a woman in your life?"

"Oh yes. I have several: sleeping partners, social company, companions."

"But not a lover?"

"I have had."

"Have had? What went wrong?"

"A lover has to be someone you can completely trust, someone who is there for you, and of whom you never have any doubts; someone who is on your side."

"Like Monique!"

Pierre ignored the remark, so Michael continued, "And you have never found a woman you can trust?"

"Oh yes! When I was a young lad, about your age, I was desperately in love with a young girl, and she was in love with me, or so I thought." Pierre leant back in his chair and a nostalgic look washed over his face. "She was ten years younger than me; beautiful, intelligent, and sexy," Again his tone changed, to a matter-of-fact level for a moment, "although we could not indulge ourselves so much in those days." His voice croaked a little. He recovered himself and went on. "Aware of the age difference, I treated her with kid gloves. She won a scholarship to the Sorbonne."

"She was intelligent?"

"She was very intelligent. I thought she ought to go. It was a shame to waste such a good brain. She was not so sure. She wanted to marry me and have children. Her self-image was based on that of her mother, a voluptuous earth-mother figure, whereas she was, in truth, an intellectual like her father."

"Shall I top up your glass?" Michael was keen for Pierre to go on. Here was a side of Pierre that he never showed.

Michael contributed diffidently to the conversation "Very few of us have the right self-image, especially when we're young." He was beginning to wonder if he had a false image of himself.

Pierre continued, "Anyway, eventually I persuaded her that she should take up the opportunity, and even drove her there on her first day. We were living in Rheims at the time. The parting was very tearful. She wanted to come back to Rheims with me, but I promised that when she had finished her degree, we could marry and indulge ourselves in domestic bliss."

"What went wrong?"

Pierre sat silent, with his head down. Michael was surprised that Pierre was so subdued. He was obviously reliving a very emotional period in his life. This was not the image Michael had of Pierre.

"She came home that Christmas and we had a rather awkward period. She still wanted to come home for good, and I still thought she should study. To give her confidence we got formally engaged. Her parents were pleased, and I thought everything was set up for plain sailing."

Pierre's expression deepened into sadness. "The next Easter, she did not return to Rheims. At least, she did not come to see me. I was worried and phoned her parents, only to find that she was there. She came round to see me, and told me that she had met somebody else, a young lad at the university, and was now in love with two people. I was devastated. We went through a very stormy period, and she consequently failed her next lot of exams. My feelings then were that we were both liable to lose everything. I would lose my loved one for nothing, and she would not have the benefit of a good education, for which I had made my sacrifice, if she was thrown out of the university. I decided to leave her alone to finish her studies, and then, when she returned to her parents; when she had got her degree, I would woo her again."

There was a long pause. Michael felt he could not interrupt. There was a strange atmosphere in the air.

Pierre recovered himself. "She never returned to her parents. A few days after I thought she must have come back to Rheims, I phoned her parents, to see what was happening, to be told that she had got married the week before, the day after she graduated."

There was another long pause. Michael had never seen Pierre like this. There were things about him he kept well hidden. He always appeared so self-confident and sophisticated. Could it be that the wine had brought to the surface things that were otherwise well sublimated?

"I was devastated." Pierre perked up and continued, "I have hoped ever since that her marriage would break up, and I could win her again, but there has never been an opportunity. I have met her once or twice, and I always felt like jelly in her presence. The irony is that she says that she thought I was trying to get rid of her. She completely misinterpreted my taking her to the university, and my sacrifice in leaving her alone to study. Years later, she said that she thought I did not love her, and if she had realised that I did, it would have been different."

There followed a long silence. Then he continued, "I dreamt about her every night for the next eight years. I could not get her out of my mind."

Pierre pulled himself out of his depression. His countenance visibly improved.

"Shall we get another bottle?"

"Perhaps a half."

"Waiter, do you have a half bottle of this?"

"Certainly, sir."

Michael felt he had to say something, and struggled for something appropriate.

"Do you still dream about her?"

"No. I can't say I am completely cured, but I've got her out of my soul enough to carry on with life."

"And you think this might happen to me?"

"Not necessarily, but make sure Monique knows you love her. Tell her!"

The half bottle arrived, and Pierre continued, "I thought that my actions would have expressed my love. I had a ring made for her exactly as she dreamt of it. I got a friend of mine, a jeweller, to discuss rings with her, without her realising why, and I had a beautiful coat tailored for her in the same way. Both gifts were prepared in secret. I thought my actions would speak louder than any words, but that is not enough for women, they have to be told in so many words."

By the time the lunch was over, and they had leisurely finished the wine, Michael had a completely different view of Pierre. He was a bit shocked. He had thought Pierre was so sophisticated, so much in control, so cool, and here he was an emotional creature after all. It made Michael very thoughtful. He realised that he had started to see Pierre as a life model, but now he would have to be reliant on himself.

After dinner that night, Michael observed Monique with new eyes.

"What is it like being a woman?"

She laughed. "Just the same as being a man, I should think."

"But it can't be. Your life chances are so different. I know you drive and are very independent, but most girls can't dictate the course of their life. They are very restricted both by society and nature."

She laughed again.

"We have more things in common than different. I like food and wine like you. I like driving fast cars, and sunshine, and the wind in my hair. I like making love."

She came round the table and sat on his lap.

"Ah! But is it the same for you? Do you experience the same sensations?"

"I should imagine so, but of course I can never know what you are feeling."

"Women can have multiple orgasms."

"So what? That is nature's requirement to widen the selection of the genes."

"What do you mean by that?"

She continued with a big smile. "Once a woman gets into a sexy mood, she wants it to go on. In *homo sapiens'* primitive state, soon after they had descended from the trees, she was happy to continue intercourse with anyone in the clan of reasonable presentation who was willing. A man making love is soon worn out."

"That does not strike me as a good enough reason."

She continued with her point, "This gives a chance for others in the tribe to take part, so there is a wider selection of genes in the sperm to compete and fertilise the egg. The strongest sperm wins. Perhaps the multiple orgasms could have evolved to facilitate this process, and so strengthen the species."

"You don't have to have an orgasm to conceive. That notion went out in the 18th Century."

"No. I know, but why else would a woman allow herself to be humped around, if it wasn't for the promise of extra orgasms, and nature to improve the species?"

"I have to admit I would not like to be humped around by anyone for an orgasm or anything else."

"You're not a woman."

"That's what I mean. Does a woman—do you—experience different sexual pleasures to a man?"

"Oh, you're far too serious about these things."

"But they are important. I want to know all about you. I want to know you completely. How can I know how to treat you if I do not know how you feel?"

"Well, you should treat me naturally, as you feel, not on some intellectual theory you have concocted."

"I can see that you have different emotions to me. Like most women, you are turned to jelly and "goo goo" at babies, whereas I see them as noisy shitting machines."

"You horror. Don't be so superior."

"I'm not being superior. I'm expressing what I've observed, and what I don't understand. Why do you spend three times as long as I do in the bathroom? Why do you spend so much time on your makeup?"

"I hardly use any makeup, and I spend far less time on it than most women."

"Exactly! That's what I need to understand. Why do they?"

"Well, women are dependent on their bodies. We love them, and we take pleasure and pride in them. They remind us of their existence all the time. Our standing amongst other women is dictated by how we look and carry ourselves. We compete with our bodies, whereas men compete with ideas and success, or so I am told." She got up and went to the window. "Whether we like it or not, our standing in society is dictated by the man we've attracted, and who has committed himself to us. You can't appreciate what pressure that puts on a girl."

"Men's standing is also affected by his partner. A man likes to be seen with an attractive woman on his arm. Socially, people notice if he has desirable company. It improves his standing," Michael felt her point had been easily negated.

Monique disagreed. "It's not the same. Amongst men, the kudos is fleeting, and if the man is a goon, it acts against him. He is written off as only a ladies' man. This is not given as a compliment amongst men."

"So you admit that being a woman is not the same as being a man?"

Monique took on an altogether more serious demeanour. "Yes, of course we are different. However, there are large parts of us that are the same. That is the human part, and the most important. Only the female part is different. I admit I do get a sexual thrill when others are attracted to me. They might be men or women, and even old men, and men I do not find attractive. The fact that someone desires my body gives me a kick. That might be a difference."

Michael had never realised that. His face registered a surprised confusion. "If a woman I don't fancy desires me, I find it just embarrassing."

She tousled his hair. "You are a funny old thing."

In Algeria, the military conspirators were meeting. The group was larger than before. The plotters were assembled in a small, smoky room. Smoking was usually frowned upon at military staff meetings, but they had already overstepped convention with their plotting, and this was not official.

"M. Soustelle here has just arrived. He has something to say about our support in France," General Massu said with an authoritative air, pulling the company together.

"Yes, I'm afraid the support is not as good as I had hoped. I tried unsuccessfully to get the Gaullist Party behind us, but they were very divided, and De Gaulle himself was not to be contacted. He would not see me."

General Salan, having been De Gaulle's assistant during the war, felt he could speak for him. "We don't need to speak to him. I am sure he thinks as we do."

Soustelle indignantly carried on. "I had to make a quick exit to Spain. Those traitors who are in power in Paris wanted to put me on trial for treason."

"Do you think we will have support anyway?" A slightly worried Colonel Peyat wanted to reassure himself.

"I am sure so. There are enough patriotic Frenchmen who see the iniquity of giving away half of France, who will rally to our cause."

Colonel Peyat spoke up again. "We have to be careful. As a student of history, and particularly the plan to invade England in 1745, I can tell you that the project failed because our Scottish Jacobean allies overestimated the support they were going to get in England. They assumed the English Catholics would rise up to support them against the Hanoverian usurpers, but they were wrong. You cannot rely on the supposed sympathies of a subordinate population."

"But you should not be affected one way or the other by the possibility of doubtful support," General Massu said, expressing himself in a firm tone. "We should have faith in our own decisions. We should do what is right, not what would be popular, and right is on our side."

Colonel Peyat was hesitant. Things were not working out as expected, but he came back to the idea that he had sworn an oath to obey orders without question… *But I am human. Should I disobey? No! I have to obey.* It was his duty, but he was very unhappy.

In Tours, another meeting was about to take place. It was a gathering of M. Foch's friends.

"We have been brought up to lead," said General Duchamp, who was waiting with Madame Muson and Albert Renier for the others to come to the meeting with the rest of the money that they wanted Michael to deposit abroad. "Look what a mess the proletariat make of things when they get control. Socialism? Pff! Evolutionary theory tells us that the strong are here to make decisions, and the mob are lucky that we pull them along with us to reap the benefit. They should appreciate, and thank us for it. We create the wealth, after all."

"You had better not let your neighbours hear you say that. Some of their ancestors led the mob in 1789."

"Exactly. Look what chaos that lot made of it."

"You can't say you would have supported the Ancient Régime."

"No. They were a degenerate lot. It needed a soldier with a bit of discipline, like Napoleon, to sort things out, and get France back on her feet. That's what we need now."

"The strong man? The superman?"

"Yes. Someone like De Gaulle."

"He's retired, and probably would not want to come back to this mess."

"Has anyone asked him?"

"Probably not. Nobody has the initiative."

"I could not get to see him," Soustelle interjected.

"We live in an age of mice, not heroes."

"When he sees what we have done to protect ourselves and France, he will understand. He will be with us. The occasion will draw forth the man."

"He would be a great asset, if he could be persuaded to take over."

At this point, the rest of the rebellious officers turned up, and discussion of details took over.

Michael went to Tours to collect the money from General Duchamp's group this time. He and Monique made a quick visit to the Manoir and then set off again for England. They went by Airbridge from Le Touquet to Lydd. Monique thought this was the most enjoyable route, as it was more personal, and it gave the chance of a pleasant drive through the Sussex countryside. She loved the smell of the hedges, the flickering of sunlight cutting through as they drove down sunken country lanes with trees meeting above, forming a roof. She loved the fresh air tugging at her hair as they crested a hill. That reminded her of her nurse, brushing it vigorously when she was a child. And she loved the excitement of speed. Michael was worried that at a small airport they might be more easily recognised, but there was nobody there they had seen last time.

It was nice to be back again in their flat in Wilton Street. Monique regarded it as the first home they were making together. Queens Club was not very far away, and neither Michael nor Monique had ever seen any top-class tennis, so they got some tickets. They went primarily because they thought it was the fashionable thing to do, now they were in funds, but Monique found she loved the tennis. The sun was always shining and the games were particularly exciting.

They diverted on their way back to the tube station, so that Michael could show her the back of Hammersmith School where Gustav Holst had taught mathematics and music. It failed to make a point to Monique. She did not know Holst's music. The French only played French orchestral music, plus Beethoven, whom God had mistakenly made a German. Michael resolved to introduce her to Holst and perhaps Benjamin Britten.

They now had a small fortune in the bank, so Michael got some tickets for the centre court at Wimbledon. They saw Lew Hoad defeat Ashley Cooper. Again, the sun shone and they indulged themselves with strawberries and cream, washed down with some champagne.

"You say that all these tennis players are amateur?" Monique was puzzled.

"Yes."

"But if they have to practice all the time, and travel round the world to different tournaments, how can they afford it?"

"Normal people can't. You have to be rich."

"That isn't fair."

"The world isn't fair."

"Then why do they not organise it differently?"

"The privileged class always want to keep things to themselves. They don't want competition from the common proles."

"We French want everybody to have an equal chance in life. That's what our revolution was about. Why don't the French players, and the other nationalities, object?"

"The English, or rather the English upper class, either invented most of the current sports or wrote the rule books. They are still dominating the governing bodies of most of them, and don't want any changes. Things will eventually change, of course, but as yet most people have not realised that England is not the world's great power anymore. The Suez crisis has come as a big shock to most Englishmen, upper and lower class, and they don't realise that the hegemony of the British Empire is over."

"You are always talking about class. Surely everyone is equal now?"

"I wish they were, but you cannot understand British society unless you take class into consideration. There are tremendous differences in wealth, income and social status. Monique looked puzzled.

Michael continued. "More than that, if you are not from the right family and background, you are never going to be accepted and get to the top in England. We chose the wrong side in 1789. Power in this country is still in the hands of six hundred families, and it doesn't really matter how much money you have got."

"We have a nice flat, in a posh part of London, and a lot of money now. Surely we are going to get on?"

"Only up to a certain point. Of course not every aristocrat is a snob, but enough are to exclude us from the top echelons of society. Do you realise that although the English cricket team contains both amateurs and professionals, the captain always has to be an amateur, and the professionals have to go out onto the pitch at Lords, cricket's headquarters, through a different door, and are not allowed through the Long Room."

"The English are a strange lot."

When they got back to France, Michael wanted to settle down to do some painting, but Monique thought they should go to their vineyards and start to sort out the wine production. Her parents were also asking when they were going to get married. Relatives had to be informed and plans made. The practicalities of life were taking over. They went to the Manoir.

Monique realised that under her father the estate and the wine production business had got into a mess. *Does my father realise that by treating this place as a hobby things have deteriorated? Is giving it to us his easy way out? If that is the case, I'll show him.*

Monique arranged for a couple of women from the village to come up to the Manoir and help with the grape harvest, and sort out the mess in the house. She showed Michael the outlines of the process of the making of wine. Michael was relieved that they had a modern vat to crush the grapes and make the juice. He had this old-fashioned romantic idea of crushing the grapes with your feet. That thought put him off. It was unhygienic, and he was pleased that he did not have to get himself mucky. He could not avoid the exhaustion of the harvest, however; endlessly cleaning bottles, and carting boxes of corks into the bottling room. There was no other help once the first lot of grapes had been picked. He and Monique worked from dawn to dusk. All thought of their newfound wealth and their comfortable way of life went out of the window. *This is almost as tiring as fishing.*

Michael had not expected such constant physical work when M. Foch had given them the wine business to run. All he wanted was to get back to Paris and his studio. But there was much more work to be done than he had bargained for. Monique was wholly immersed in the organising. He observed how much she enjoyed it.

"You don't seem to be interested in your painting anymore," he said to Monique.

"I am, but at this moment we have to get our business underway."

"To the exclusion of everything else?"

"If we want to make a success of it, we have to start now."

"I came to Paris to paint. It looks as though I am going to end up as a businessman."

"We will end up as business partners together, and then we can paint."

"Inspiration is an ephemeral child. You have to grab it, and give it its head at the first appearance. It is not something you can put in a cupboard and bring out when you feel like it. It is the master, not you. You have to be its slave, or at least its servant; otherwise it will depart and settle elsewhere. It will settle with somebody where it feels more appreciated." Michael felt his inspiration was being swamped by work.

Eventually, they did get back to Paris, but within a week of getting into his studio, just as he was getting into the rhythm of painting, Monique received a phone call from one of their village helpers and announced that they had to go to Le Manoir d'Espérance again.

"We have only just come back from there."

"These things can't wait. There is a time for each process."

"Painting can't wait. There has to be a time for that."

"You've been painting all this week. Surely we can go to Courtay now?"

"You don't understand, although you should, as a painter yourself. When you're painting, it takes over your whole life, not just when you're standing in front of the easel. Every minute of the day, your mind is filled with unusual perspectives, and combinations of colours, to say nothing of the subject matter you want to express."

"Well, you can think about that as we harvest the next crop of grapes. We have to test if the next variety is ripe yet."

"I would prefer to harvest the next set of ideas I have. They are just as important to process and get on to the canvas, as your grapes are to get into bottles."

"They are our grapes."

"I can't think about perspective if I am thinking about how to work the bottling machine."

"Do you want us to have a nice life together?"

"Yes! Of course."

"Then you have to sacrifice some of your time now."

Michael eventually gave in, and they went to their future home, but he was very unhappy about it.

Chapter Nine

Another week was spent preparing for the wine-making. Although Michael liked the fresh air, he could not whip up any enthusiasm for it on this occasion, or for the necessary business-planning. Luckily, they could return to the big city before embarking on the next process. Michael could look forward to some time at his easel. This enabled him to retain his cool demeanour.

They had only been back in Paris for a day when Michael got a message from Bertrand. He went to the Raymonds' flat to see him. *Everything conspires these days to stop me painting,* Michael thought.

Bertrand was looking very stern when he arrived. "Where have you been? We have some things to be collected from England."

"I have been at my girlfriend's parents' house in the Loire Valley."

"They're quite well off, aren't they?" Bernard asked. "What are their politics?"

"Oh, they are apolitical."

"Nobody is apolitical. That is just an excuse for hiding what you really believe but can't justify."

"Well, they are more interested in their family than in national politics."

Pierre jovially butts in, "A man without politics is like snails without garlic." He did not like things to get too serious, "without taste, in other words; without bite, without flavour."

Bertrand disagreed with Pierre as he usually did. "It is a man who doubts the strength of his own opinions, or a man who is unwilling to divulge his selfish interests."

Michael could not accept Bertrand's perspective. "He can't be called selfish if he is concerned to look after the comfort of those that depend on him. Surely that should be his first concern?"

Bertrand did not like making light of the situation like Pierre. His concern embraced the whole of society. His concern was with the whole state. He had always been a bit suspicious of Pierre, with his bourgeois background.

Michael addressed Bertrand. "But if we say that, why stop there? What about the whole of humanity? Or the whole of creation?"

"Creation can look after itself, and Lenin reasoned that if we waited for the whole of humanity to get itself sorted out, we would wait forever, and we would never make progress."

"You sound like a Stalinist," commented Pierre.

"I'd rather be a Stalinist than a Trotskyite."

Michael felt he had to interrupt. "Whatever my future in-laws' politics are, they would be neither for nor against us."

Bertrand knew exactly what that meant and needed to say it. "Those that are not with us clog up the process and are therefore against us. Anyway, let's not waste time discussing your girlfriend's parents' politics. We have something for you to collect urgently from England, and this time there is something we want you to take there. Go to this address." He handed Michael a slip of paper. "And collect a package from a man called Yves."

Michael was depressed but not able to show it. *Will I ever have time for painting? I resent this ever-increasing attention all my contacts are demanding. It does give me money; a lot of money I know, but I have come to Paris to paint. If I had wanted to make money, I would have become an accountant or a solicitor.* Nevertheless, he went to the Boulevard Voltaire by bus and found the address that Bertrand had given him, in a backstreet.

He rang the bell. Nothing. He rang again. The door was open, swinging ajar, so he went in. "Hallo!" He was standing in a very dusty workshop. It had a high ceiling, but there were so many things hanging from it that you had to duck your head to cross the room. There was just a narrow passageway between the junk on the floor, to lead you to another door in the far corner. "Hallo! Is there anybody there?"

A faint croaky voice came from the next room. "Hallo. Yes. I'm here. Come in."

Michael crossed the workshop and pushed open a creaky door, which knocked over a pile of sheet metal. "Oh, I'm sorry."

"Don't bother about that. What can I do for you?"

"Are you Yves?"

"Yes."

"Bertrand sent me."

"Ah, yes."

There stood before him a tall, thin man of indeterminate age. He looked old, but on close inspection, his face was smooth, or at least the upper half was smooth, for he obviously had not shaved for a week, and the lower half was covered in stubble. His hair was the opposite—long and soft, with a slight reddish tinge. Shabby clothes were hidden by a long blue apron, which stretched almost to the floor. He held in his long-fingered hand a cog, probably part of some sort of gearbox. Behind him stood a large frame full of cogs, some knitting into each other, but others quite free. This confirmed the gearbox theory. He was an apparition from the age of mythology. The man noticed Michael surveying the mechanism behind him.

"Oh yes. I'm inventing a translation machine."

"A translation machine? Haven't we already got that?"

"Got what?"

"A translation machine."

"A translation machine?"

"Yes. We call it a human being."

"Very unreliable. Subject to emotions. You can't depend upon them. However, the cogs do not always fit where I want them to. They are proving unreliable also." This was said with a sad expression.

"In that case wouldn't it be better to develop the concept electronically?"

"Also unreliable. There's nothing like hard steel. Can't be bent. Can't be influenced. Shows no emotion."

"How far have you got?"

"Well, there is a long way to go yet."

At this point a tin of nuts and bolts slipped off a sloping shelf in the corner, spreading its contents over the floor.

"Oh gosh, let me help you pick them up," said Michael, who was down on his knees very quickly.

"Oh, don't worry about that. Look at this lovely bit of engineering. I got it out of a dust cart yesterday." Yves picked up what looked like the inside of a car's gearbox and handed it to Michael. It was surprisingly heavy, and Michael nearly dropped it. "I intend to incorporate it into my machine."

Michael's hands were suddenly covered in oil.

"Oh dear. Here, take this." Yves handed Michael a rag. The rag was dirty enough to add to the muck already on Michael's hands. Michael looked for a place to put the gearbox innards down, but the whole place was cluttered with tools or pieces of engineering.

Michael handed back the rag as he questioned timidly, thinking of nothing else to say. "Does it fit into your plan?"

"What?"

"The gearbox, I mean. Does it conform to a part of your original drawings?"

"Oh, I don't worry about that. There are no drawings. It's too good to waste. It will fit in somewhere."

Michael could see that the translation machine was going to have a long gestation period, and he thought he would take a lot of convincing of its possible success.

"Bertrand says you have a package for me to take to England."

"Ah, yes. Another of my little inventions. Now where did I put it?"

At this point, Yves started rummaging around in a drawer beside his infernal machine. A pot fell out through a hole in the bottom, and this time small springs scattered all over the floor.

There was a remarkably neat package on the top of the chest of drawers. Michael played a hunch. "Could this be it?"

"Ah, yes. I had it ready for you." He handed Michael the package. "What did you say your name was?"

"I didn't, but it's Michael."

"Nice to meet you, Michael." Then in a louder voice, and raising up a clenched fist, "Long live the revolution!" He held out his hand to shake and say either 'Hallo' or 'Goodbye'.

Michael felt it better be 'Goodbye'.

"My name's Yves."

"Yes. I know."

"Of course, Bertrand told you."

"I am sorry to break up our conversation about translation, but I have to go."

As Michael left, picking his way through the outer workshop and putting the package in his pocket, he heard another crash and a tinkling of nuts on a steel sheet.

"Damn!" he heard from the inner sanctum.

I hope my friends don't have too many supporters like that, Michael thought to himself. He had taken an instant irrational liking to Yves, but he felt plotting with him could get very dangerous.

He went to England this time without Monique. She claimed that she had to do things for the wine business. One of the things was to see some wine dealers in Paris. It was a shame, for Michael had become used to Monique's company on his trips. It was her company on his travels that now made them enjoyable rather than tedious. Travel, when you start, is exciting and stimulating, but like all things, familiarity breeds contempt. He had reached that point. Travel was now a distraction from other, more worthy occupations, like painting, like indulging in the intimate company of Monique and life at home.

This time, he flew by Air France, so that he could partake of the better food. He did not intend to stay in London very long, just one night, so he could see George, return to Paris, and get down to some painting. Consequently, he had bought a return ticket. On the way back, the aircraft made a couple of extra circuits over Paris so that the passengers could finish their dinner. *Very French,* Michael thought. *They have got their priorities right. I wonder if there will always be such cultural differences between airlines.*

Monique's sister, who was waiting for him at the airport, stepped forward and kissed him. "I have the car outside." Beside her was a black-haired girl. Michael was worried. *Why no Monique? Has there been an accident?* He stepped forward to shake the girl's hand and be introduced. "Don't you recognise me?" she exclaimed. She then burst into laughter and took off a black wig, revealing Monique and her golden hair.

Michael was embarrassed and relieved at the same time. "I took you for a cousin."

On their way to the Champs-Élysées, Monique and Angelique chided Michael, who felt very guilty about not recognising her. However, she was soon bubbling with enthusiasm over the fact that she had secured a very large order from the wine dealers. Nevertheless, she admitted she was a bit apprehensive. Could a small concern like theirs supply such an amount? Nevertheless, she was determined to succeed. Michael reassured her.

A practical mood soon overtook her. Joking was over. "We will have to go to the Manoir and check how many empty bottles we have. Most probably we will have to order more. I have already had a word with a cork supplier, and he will be sending us 10,000 next week. There is a printer here that will print a label I designed while you were away last night. He will have 10,000 for us also by next week, and he will send them on to the Manoir. We will have to be there to receive them."

"Can't we stay in Paris for a bit?"

"We have to get the business started. We must be serious if we are going to do something with it."

"But we are destroying everything for money. When did we last go and see our friends at Mes Amis? When did we go and have breakfast at Les Deux Magots? When did we both spend a day in our studios painting?"

Monique was brought up short by Michael's protestations. She looked serious for a moment. The fact that Michael was not overjoyed by her success came as a surprise. She was a bit angry, but then she realised that perhaps she was getting carried away with the idea of being a successful businesswoman. Michael was serious. Perhaps he had a point. She did not want to lose him. "All right then, we could stay in Paris tonight, and go to Courtay later." Michael leant across and kissed her.

They made very passionate love that night. They were both suddenly aware that they were drifting apart. Neither wanted that, so the next morning they went down to Boulevard Saint Germain and had breakfast in Les Deux Magots. The same noisy group was still there, as though they had never been away, laying down the law to each other. Michael was amused. He wondered who they could be. They all seemed very articulate.

After breakfast, Michael and Monique rushed off to their studios and worked very hard, hardly stopping for lunch. Both felt the day's work was very successful, so they finished early enough to go down to the Seine and sit watching the boats go by as of old, before walking up to the old haunt where they had first met. It really was like it used to be, and they both enjoyed it. Their friends were very pleased to see them. The quality of the food had in no way deteriorated. They chose the dishes they had enjoyed in the past, and they washed them down with a larger than usual amount of wine. It was altogether a lovely day. They went to bed happy that night.

Monique thought the exercise had been worth doing and volunteered a further suggestion that she thought Michael would appreciate. "Perhaps we could stay another day here. The corks will not arrive until Wednesday, and we can sort out the bottles before the weekend."

"Whatever you think," said Michael. He appreciated her consideration for him and wanted to reciprocate. "I understand that you are keen to show your parents that you are capable, and I promise that we will show them their faith has not been misplaced."

"It's not just that. I want us to have a comfortable and successful life."

"We will have, and we'll impress your parents as well."

"Perhaps we could enjoy painting for a couple of days," she said with a drawn-out, thoughtful tone.

"Right. That's decided. As you say. We'll stay here, and paint, and live the life we used to live, and go to the Manoir on Tuesday evening."

"A good idea." *Yes! Things can be sorted out if you are honest and talk to each other.*

A night drive after the restaurant on Tuesday got them to Manoir d'Espérance late. It was not an unpleasant journey, as it was a warm night. They had the hood down, and the heater on to keep their legs and bodies warm. They both felt very snug. With absolutely no traffic on the road, there were not any hold-ups. The villages they passed through had long since gone to sleep.

At Le Manoir d'Espérance the following Wednesday, they were up early. Monique took charge. "Get all the bottles you can find, like those in the boxes in the stable, and put them in the sterilizing plant. If they won't all go in, stack them up outside, and then I will come and show you how the whole thing works. First of all, I must clean up the bottling room, and prepare it for the boxes of new bottles and the corks when they arrive. At the moment, there is no room to swing a cat."

Michael was very apprehensive. He had begun to realise that the work to be done was much more complicated than was at first apparent. *Monique appears to know what she is doing, but does she? She has helped her father, but always alongside the casual, more knowledgeable labour he had employed from the village when they made wine before. Does her confidence shield her real lack of experience? The wine has turned out to be excellent, but how much of that is chance? If not chance, it is probably the expertise of the local people M. Foch has employed. Does Monique really know what to do?*

Michael volunteered a suggestion with a certain trepidation. "There's so much work to be done, shouldn't we employ an expert?"

"If we are going to turn this into a prosperous business, we can't start off by spending all our money on outside labour."

"But there's so much to do."

"All the more reason for getting on with things."

Michael felt there was no use in pressing the point. He knew nothing about wine production, and Monique seemed to have confidence in herself. So, he succumbed to her will, as she had humoured him by staying in Paris a few days extra.

"There are a load of old sacks and boxes in front of the steriliser. What shall I do with them?" asked Michael.

"The sacks are probably rotten. I don't fancy using them for anything anyway, so throw them on the pile of rubbish behind the bar to be burnt. As to the boxes, see if any of them are useable, and throw the rest on the rubbish heap as well."

Just before lunchtime, Monique rushed down to the village to get some bread. They were both already tired and stiff, and pleased to have a break. They sat down for about half an hour and ate the bread with some farmer's sausage that had been hanging from the ceiling of the kitchen. They made coffee. Wine would have slowed the afternoon's work, as Monique pointed out. They had only just finished the coffee, when the man turned up from the station in Tours with the shipment of corks.

The bonfire was burning comfortably. Monique had found lots of other rubbish that she wanted out of the way. Michael was happier. He felt he had contributed. Directly the cork man had gone, she showed him how to work the steriliser. Things were going quite well, but there was so much still to do.

"It's very important that everything is done properly; otherwise, it will ruin the wine," said Monique with a schoolmarmish air.

This made Michael feel a bit like a little boy, although he maintained his cool, serious air.

"Once the bottles are being sterilised, you can come and help me prepare for the bottling," said Monique as she picked up another box of corks.

He did as he was told and then went and helped clear all the tables in the bottling room and gave them a good scrubbing down. He collected some barrels of last year's wine and rolled them round to the bottling unit. They were heavy, and his back by this time had become incredibly stiff. Painting in oils is a very physical pursuit and can be tiring, but the action is a continuous movement, a bit like dancing, not dealing with heavy weights and constantly bending up and down. Michael discovered muscles he did not know he had, and they were shouting at him.

Monique was worried. *Michael does not seem to be interested in our future. Does he not see how a successful wine company would secure the future for us and our family for the rest of our lives? Painting is so precarious. Can he not see that that could never guarantee to keep a family? We might never meet another Pierre. He should be prepared to put it to one side for a while and work as an amateur painter, and then perhaps take it up more seriously later on.*

Michael knew that inspiration was a selfish creature. If one did not give it the attention it demanded, it would go, and probably never return, however hard one tried to coax it back. He was surprised that Monique could not see this. *She is a painter herself. She must feel the urge to paint.* Nevertheless, he continued with his work as directed by Monique, but the resentment was building up.

When they returned to Paris, they again tried to placate their differences by going to their old restaurant several times. They sat by the Seine on many occasions, and they walked together through the town. Although they appeared to have patched things up, beneath the surface, their relations were far from calm.

One day, as they walked down the Champs-Élysées, Monique remarked on a strange little car she saw; a Mini.

Michael repeated what he had heard from his friend, a car enthusiast he knew, "I believe that's the prototype of a new English car. They say it's going to become fashionable and sweep the market. Although it's not flamboyant, it's going to be so easy to make it around town and park."

"Perhaps we should get one for short trips around Paris. We can get a blue card, and it will make shopping easy," Monique remarked.

If it's a prototype, it's not been kept very secret, Michael mused. He had little respect for the car industries' bosses, "Well, what's wrong with going by Metro?" He was worried by her growing occupation with material things, but he then had second thoughts. *Perhaps I should make a gesture. We can't afford to quarrel about everything.* He took a hard look at the car. *It is a strange-looking little thing, and looks too small to get into, but if she wants it...* "Alright then. If you'd like one. We'll have to see when it comes out."

"It's so cute. The manufacturers will make a fortune."

He decided he should take the opportunity to keep the conversation on a prosaic level. Emotions were raw and needed to be avoided. "They should, but there is such an incompetent management fraternity in England, they are sure to lose money on it. They never do their homework."

"That's stupid."

"I agree, but they are only interested in takeover bids to make them personally rich, with no regard for the products or their workers. Then they spend the money on buying a country estate. They desert manufacturing because they want to play at being 'the land-owning aristocrat'. It's all part of the class system. Their products do not interest them. It is not like that in Germany, say, where managers take pride in what they are making. There, the people in charge are usually engineers, chemists, or knowledgeable in something useful. It was like that in Victorian England. Then entrepreneurs and inventors that formed the companies took pride in what they were making. The country became prosperous as a result. The company boards in England nowadays neglect their duties. Most of them are people with titles, or people who want to get titles, who know nothing about engineering, accountancy, or anything useful for that matter."

Michael was getting going on his high horse, "Look at the motorcycle industry. It presents a perfect example. England had a flourishing business supplying most of the world's motorbikes after the war. But what happened? The couple who controlled BSA, Lord and Lady Docker, one of the largest motorbike manufacturers in the world, drove around in a gold-plated Daimler and spent their time giving sumptuous parties. They bought out all the other motorcycle firms, meanwhile neglecting BSA, and it went to pot. They never improved the designs, and so the Italians took over the motorcycle industry, introducing electric starting and multi-cylinder engines. The Dockers then complained about the unions. A management gets the unions it deserves. The same will happen to the car industry one day. You mark my words."

Pierre contacted Michael, as there was another task he wanted him to carry out. They met in a café. Pierre seemed very happy, back to his normal self, not at all like the last time they had met.

"You don't look so happy," Pierre commented.

"No. Monique and I are not getting along very well at the moment."

"How long have you been together?"

"I don't know. A couple of years."

"Well, there you are. Love does not last forever."

"Of course it does. Monique and I love each other very much."

"That heady intoxication you have experienced can only last one or two years. Then we all have to find another form of relationship."

"Nonsense. We are just going through a bad period. There are just a few problems."

"No. They are symptoms of something deeper. You now have to work on what you have in common, and construct a new supportive companionship. Things have changed. You will both have to make a big effort now, and it won't come easily."

"What do you mean? I like the relationship we have. There's no need to build something different?"

"Mankind has dealt with this same question for ages. How can we relate to one another, to someone of the opposite sex, when we are not regarding them in a prurient way or carried away in a romantic haze? That instantaneous intoxication you have already experienced never lasts." Pierre got into one of his pontificatory moods. "What holds us together? What is it that drives us to compromise our more selfish interests? I sometimes wonder if we are two different species. You have to ask the question of why men and women want to get together at all, we are so different, do we really enjoy each other's company?"

"Of course! Isn't that obvious?"

"No. Sensuality comes into it. True! Physically we desire the other, but thinking lust is enough, is a mistake. There must be other compulsions of a more abstract nature we enjoy in the opposite sex. However, they have to be cultivated, and often at the expense of ourselves."

Michael was struck by the fact that Pierre had re-sublimated all the unhappiness he had admitted in their last meeting. He was at a loss for something to say. He felt he had to respond. "You get nothing for nothing," was the best he could do. *Pierre does over complicate things,* he said to himself.

Pierre, however, was in an expansive, lecturing mood, and not to be stopped. "Is it the same for men and women? That is another question. Is it the same when we fool ourselves that this concern with another being is intensified to the level we call love?" Pierre paused while he thought, then continued. "Could it be the subconscious desire for immortality? There is a common interest at the basic primeval level; at the level of fundamental nature, where one's genes compel a person to reproduce themselves, and achieve an eternal life that our feeble bodies can never attain. We are deemed to die, while our genes strive to continue. It is all very simple. Then we excuse this by calling it love."

Michael's tone was a bit indignant. "What has the subconscious to do with it? I love Monique because she's a nice person and physically attractive."

"Don't discount your animal evolution. It dictates a lot of your behaviour. It makes us all hope to combine our genes with another for future survival. Maybe it is with someone we admire, or with whom we sympathise, but usually our behaviour is very primeval, however subconscious. Love is an excuse."

"I only want to be with someone I love."

The evangelising spirit in Pierre wanted him to show Michael the strength of hidden imperatives. "We are slaves to primeval forces we don't understand. In this, both men and women are the same, but the road to achievement is different. Men go for a nubile, fertile young body that can reproduce his genes in a healthy young child, whereas a woman wants a strong man who can protect and provide for her and their offspring. They both need each other, but the means of achieving their aims differs greatly. Women have relatively few chances of reproducing themselves. They are fertile from their teens to their forties, give or take a few years, but a man can, in theory, go on to have offspring until he is eighty. That makes a big difference."

"But he doesn't. How many men do you know that have had children when eighty?"

Pierre carried on regardless. "Even in her restricted period of fecundity, a woman can usually produce only one child at a time. Her body's strength in forming and bringing to birth an offspring takes most of her effort for nine months, and that effort requires her to rest for a while afterwards, whereas a man can impregnate several women in one day, and do the same again the next. His effort is minimal. He can therefore be irresponsible. A woman's ability to produce children is limited, and her commitment great. It's not surprising they favour monogamy."

"I thought you were cynical before, but you really reduce human behaviour to mechanics."

"It is important that we understand the subconscious compulsions that drive us. If we see those, we can then behave more rationally."

"I disagree with you. How can the number of children we can have affect our behaviour in our choice of partner?"

"We think we are in charge of our destiny, but we should know what is driving us. To understand this, we have to search for what a man and a woman look for, and what makes them interested in someone of the opposite sex. That will affect their strategy. I'll give you that, to a certain extent, that has changed with civilisation." He emphasised this. "In our primeval animal phase of evolution, perhaps it was enough for her to find a strong male, able to fight off any dangers, but as *homo sapiens* developed a brain and cunning, intelligence became more useful and important. Brute force was no longer the solution to all problems, and power in other forms took precedence, but women still look for a powerful partner in some form or another."

"In that case, why don't all women go for the same man?"

"Power comes in many forms; wealth, good looks, leadership, social position, cunning, talent, a successful career, and the form of power that attracts a given woman varies from one to another, often dictated by her background. We are not all the same. Her character, her upbringing, her social circumstances affect her choice, but power is the dominant factor in her interest in a prospective partner. Mark my words!" He turned to Michael. "Whereas men are not interested in powerful women."

"You're right about one thing. Unlike women, most men don't like powerful women." Michael said this with a huff and raised eyebrows. "But I am an exception."

"Quite right. I'm glad to hear it. Monique is a powerful woman." But Pierre was now unstoppable. "A man on the other hand, does not need a partner to protect and sustain him. He can be irresponsible and take no interest in his children, and have as many as opportunity dictates. He could scatter his seed to the proverbial wind. Like many animals, he could rely on numbers surviving to sustain his line, and some men are like that."

"But not all men. Very few in fact. I am not like that."

"I'm sure you're not."

Pierre stopped and wondered if he had gone too far. He had no pleasure in disillusioning his young friend. "Maybe—not all men. Nowadays a man has the possibility to adopt another strategy; quality not quantity, and concentrate his interest and affection in a small group; his chosen lover and her children, the modern nuclear family. This takes his interests and behaviour closer to that of the woman. In which case, the nature of the chosen lover he would wish to conceive with would be as important to him as he would be to the woman. Friendship and respect for the other person enters the fray. He becomes more discriminating, more civilised. That is what I am advocating when I say love has driven its course."

He took a deep breath and continued, "The woman he chooses would still have to be physically strong and able to bear children, and therefore he would still look for a young woman. That would not change. She would have to have childbearing hips and voluptuous breasts to feed the offspring. She would have to be soft and rounded. Men seem to find it impossible to resist the double curve of the breasts or the buttocks. But I give you, she would also have to be sympathetic and motherly to gain his deeper affection. Subconsciously, he would realise that if she was towards him, she would probably be towards their children. Intelligence in her would still not be as important, as he would be responsible for planning their way out of any problems in life. It's not irrational for men to go for attractive dumb women."

"Well, I don't know where to start. If you think like that about all these things, I am not surprised you don't have a regular loved one." Michael gave a friendly smile, but he was becoming harder. Life was beginning to turn him from a youth into a man.

Pierre now realised he had gone too far. *Am I sounding too bitter*? He softened his explanation. "We are conscious of none of these things, and all of them cannot explain this feeling that we recognise as love." *Can I really explain the unexplainable?* "Love as we define it is total illogical obsession with another. Medieval witches thought they could evoke love with magic potions. Perhaps they could. Did they understand love better than we do?"

After this long diatribe, Pierre relaxed. There was silence for a minute while Michael digested it.

Monique's physical attributes cannot completely explain the affection, or indeed the love she generates in me. I am sure of that. It might be magic.

The rest of the meeting was taken up with more prosaic things, but on his way home on the bus, he mused over what Pierre had said.

Pierre is not right. Monique's physical presence does cause a tangible tingle in my blood to the extent that I want to cry, but that is not all. Pierre has a truncated view of the relationship between men and women. He sees nothing but the physical side. Every movement that Monique makes excites me. That's true, but I am interested, indeed excited by her ideas. Her views are so much in tune with my own, I find it uncanny. Our love is the love between two human beings. Equals! I am enraptured by her. What is certain is that I can't explain how she can have such an effect on me to the exclusion of everything else, but she does.

He got off the bus. *In one respect, perhaps Pierre is right. Perhaps there is such a thing as magic? Nothing else could explain my imprisonment by her existence.*

On returning home, he found himself explaining to Monique the need to make another trip.

"Who do you have to go to England for this time? I know it's not for my father's friends. Their business is all done." Monique was getting irritated by these frequent interruptions to her plans. "It must be the other lot. Who are these people? What is their business that demands your immediate attention? What are they up to?"

"I have taken on this job. I have to do it."

"Why?"

"Because I gave my word. I am committed."

"We don't need the money now. My father's friends have seen to that. Why do you put their business above your painting, and our future?" She was angry. "You complain about working to secure our future?"

"It's a matter of keeping faith. I can't break my word."

"But you can break my heart. Who is this strange Uncle George of yours? Does he really exist?"

"George is as much alive as you or me."

"But he is a very strange uncle."

"Come with me to England." Michael hoped that a few days in London, enjoying the theatre and the galleries, would calm Monique down.

She thought for a moment, then agreed to go.

They went.

He was wrong.

They arrived in London in a thick fog. You could hardly see your hand in front of your face. They were lucky to get a taxi to take them back into London from the airport, and that was only because the driver wanted to get home that night. It was three hours before they were dropped off at a tube station, near to where the taxi driver lived, and it cost a small fortune.

"I can't drive safely at walking pace," protested the cab driver.

Monique was in a very grumpy mood. "I don't know why anybody wants to live in this god-forsaken place," she stared wistfully out of the window. "Or why I came here with you."

Michael was not happy with life as it had become either. He had been surprised and worried by the fact that Pierre was not the man he thought he was. He was much more complex. And now Monique had changed.

But am I the man I thought myself to be? I am certainly not the man who left the BBC. They say you grow up once you have children, but living dangerously can also age you quickly. Life now has to be taken very seriously.

The generals were meeting again in Algiers. It was a larger group than ever before. General Salan addressed the assembly.

"Well, I think you know what we are all here for. De Gaulle has let us down. He won't see us. Let me therefore introduce you to our organising committee. General Challe, C-in-C of the Army of Algeria, you already know. General Jouhaud is I-G of the air force, and will provide us with essential air cover if necessary, and we have now been joined by General Zeller, CoS of Armée de Terre, along with myself. You all know who I am. We are taking over the rule of Algeria, and all orders must come from us from now on. Plans are now completed, and Colonel Argoud here will be setting off to organise things in Paris. Await our orders. Soon we will all be on our way to Paris, to inject some sanity into France's destiny."

Chapter Ten

Life had been so great, but now it was all slipping away. Where had it all gone wrong? Michael could not really blame Monique. He could see she was doing what she thought was right for them, but could she not see the cost? *Why does she not realise that she is destroying our relationship? There are more things in life than money and luxury. Yes, I have come to enjoy our new-found wealth. I like the nice flats, the expensive restaurants, and the posh car, but I like more the satisfaction that comes with self-expression. Material comfort is ephemeral. Surely she can see that from her father's experiences.* Michael would be happy with her as a wife, and a couple of children, without all the trappings of bourgeois comfort, as long as he could paint. He did not want to go through life, and the brief episode he would spend in this world, without leaving some sort of mark. He needed to paint.

Monique was very worried. *Things are not going well, and it had all been so promising. I know that Michael is not a selfish creature, one of those men that expect the world to revolve around them, but he does not seem to understand. The world is a pitiless place. You have to fight to survive. Father has offered us a marvellous opportunity. Any normal young man would have jumped at it and rejoiced. With a little effort even now, we could be comfortable for the rest of our lives, but he does not appreciate it. Can he not see that a painting career is so ephemeral? The fashion of today can be gone by tomorrow.*

Michael was becoming more irritable by the day. He woke up at three in the morning, when confidence is at its lowest ebb, and lay awake for hours. His relationship with Monique was under great stress, and he could see no way of dealing with it. The weight of secrecy was heavy on him, and he had nobody to discuss things with.

What have I got myself into? If only I had someone I could talk to. I have given my word to tell no one of my various commitments, and yet I long to share things with Monique. She would understand and sympathise, I am sure. Or would she? I am now breaking the law in more ways than one, and in more countries than one. Worse than that, I am betraying my own morality. Carrying money out of the country breaks French law. That has been exciting. But carrying guns into this country is a different kettle of fish? Guns are made to kill. I do not want to kill anyone. Even people with whom I disagree have a right to life. But what if they wanted to kill me? What if they wanted to kill or enslave someone I loved? Then I have a right to fight back, to prepare myself to protect them. I do not love people like General Duchamp or Bertrand. I distrust and dislike both of them. What I do is not for them. No! Moving General Duchamp's group's money was for Monique and my future, and those guns would be used to protect us, and our future, and what I believed in, democracy and freedom. They are principles worth defending, even at the risk of denying my own scruples.

He tossed and turned. He dozed. He awoke again. *General Duchamp definitely stands for everything I despise. Am I doing his bidding for greed? I am certainly not doing things for him and his friends out of principle. Even if not out of greed, am I not just indulging my lust for adventure? Do I break the law and my principles for selfish reasons? Monique already knows about that part of my behaviour. We already share that secret. Can I tell her I am gun-running for the left? She will certainly disapprove of that.*

With the lack of sleep, Michael's character changed. The great warmth that Monique had felt, and that had attracted her to him, diminished. She was therefore becoming as upset and as quarrelsome as he was. *He is not the man I first met. What has changed him?*

Michael needed to escape into his painting. In that other world, he might relax. With resolve, he confronted Monique. The tone of his voice was firm. "I'm going down to my studio today, and I hope not to be disturbed. Perhaps I might get at least one day to do what I came to Paris for." Then with a more reflective tone, as he realised he sounded angry, "Are you coming?"

She looked sadly at him. *This is definitely not the man I had fallen for.*

Michael was affected by her sad look. "You could do some painting too," He said with sympathy, but he realised that if he did not put in a tremendous effort, he was gradually going to be weaned away from his painting altogether. He was determined not to let that happen.

"No. I want to tidy up here a bit first. I might come later." Monique realised that if she did not put in a great effort, they were going to be driven away from each other, but she could not face the prospect of making up to him yet, not as she felt at the moment.

Michael caught a bus to his studio. He wanted to think, and the fresh air at the back would clear his head. He needed a strategy. He had too many secrets: from General Duchamp's group, from the Sinister Port, from Monique's father, from Monique, from everybody. Two diametrically opposed groups had him working for them, and the woman he loved was going off at a tangent chasing an unworthy goal, which was never going to make them happy. *I have to keep secrets from everyone on the pain of what could possibly be death.* He had commitments to them all. He was piggy in the middle. If only he could share his burdens, it might be easier.

The painting did not go well. He was working on a semi-abstract based on a group of people he had seen by the Seine. They were not exactly clochards, but they did not look prosperous, and as he had watched them, a wealthy-looking man with an attractive woman on his arm had passed by. The idea was to portray the juxtaposition of wealth and poverty in our modern, supposedly prosperous, world. The subdued red from the background that he wanted to smoulder through the blues and browns, to give the picture a threatening atmosphere, was consistently too dominant. Perhaps it was the wrong red? Normally, he could choose his pigments without thinking. It usually came subconsciously, but his sense of colour had gone wrong. To add to his troubles, he was running out of cobalt blue. Why!? It could not be because he had been painting too much recently. Normally he would have gone and helped himself to some of Monique's, but in the present circumstances, he felt unable to. Until he could get to the artist's suppliers, he would have to substitute something else, and there was not really an alternative. *I do not want to stop painting now I have started, just to go and get supplies, but whatever I do without the proper pigment is going to be false.* His patience was finally exhausted when he knocked over a jar of turpentine. *I don't deserve all this trouble.*

Monique arrived after lunch. She did not come straight into his studio as she usually did. He could hear her knocking around in hers. Eventually, she did come in. She stood in front of the canvas he was working on.

She gave comment, "The red is too bright."

"I know."

"You should use an Indian red, not cadmium red."

"Who is painting this picture, you or me?"

"I was only helping."

"I don't need help at the moment."

"I thought we had agreed that we would criticise each other's work?"

"Yes, but not at the moment."

"Well, if you don't want my help, I can spend my time better elsewhere." She made to go.

"Don't be so childish."

"Who's being childish? I try to help, and you bite my head off."

"You are not helping. You are just getting at me. You don't want me to paint. It might upset your plans."

"Don't be so silly. You're just like some child. If you can't do what you want, when you want, you get upset."

"I can see that my painting is not going well. I don't need you to tell me. If I had not been made to spend so much time chasing your business plans, I would not have got out of practice."

"What do you mean, 'Chasing my business plans?' They are plans for our future, both our futures. I am not just thinking of myself. I am doing it for you."

"Well, I don't need it. I am happy with my future in painting. I did not leave the BBC to end up as a second-rate businessman in a provincial town in France. I know nothing about making wine, or selling it to make a fortune, so I am not going to spend my time doing it badly, while what I can do well, I leave to wither away."

"Nobody has made you do anything. My father made us a very good offer. We both agreed to accept it. Most men would have been grateful, but you don't appreciate it. You are not prepared to do anything to make the wine business a success. You just want things to fall into your lap. You're just lazy."

"Lazy?! I am not lazy!" Michael was exasperated. "But there is only a certain amount of time in what we call a life, and it is too precious to waste. I don't want to waste it making money."

"You enjoy money as much as I do. You have enjoyed the good food, the fast car, the comfortable homes. Don't now get precious and pretend you are superior to worldly luxury."

"You're right. I have been seduced by comfort, but material wealth is soon gone. It can be taken away. Look at your father's history. How many times has he had to start again, only to lose it once more? Are we…"

At this point, Monique stormed out of his studio, slamming the door and shattering the glass panel. Michael was furious that she should walk out as he was saying something, and break the door in the process. *That will have to be paid for.* He put down his brush, wiped his hands on a turps rag, and followed her into her studio.

"Have you got no manners? There's nothing more rude than walking out on someone who's speaking to you."

"It's not necessary to stand and listen to childish nonsense."

At this moment there was a call from the door.

"Hallo. Can I come in?" Pierre emerged in the doorway.

"No you can't. Bugger off!" Monique snapped back.

"I'm sorry," Michael answered.

"I can see I have chosen a bad moment," said Pierre, with a shocked look on his face.

"Yes. We have a problem."

"I'll come back another time."

"Is it important or just social?" Michael enquired.

"It is a bit urgent. We wanted you to take something extra with you to England in a hurry. But I can come back, perhaps tomorrow."

"No, let me have it now. As things are, I might not be here tomorrow."

Monique scowled.

"Well, here it is. I'm sorry to come at such an awkward time." Pierre placed an envelope on the table.

Monique turned to him, her face was red with anger. "Yes, you should be sorry. Perhaps you should marry him. He is more interested in you than me."

"I did not mean to interrupt. Forgive me!" With that, Pierre left; his face red, his head confused, his heart sad.

"What is it that that lot have on you? It's too much to go to the Manoir with me, and yet you go off and do their bidding at their first summons."

Michael's mood subsided quickly. "There are things you don't know about. I have tried to tell you, but you have changed the subject before I could explain myself."

"You can't explain yourself. There is no excuse for what you've done. Every time I want you to do something for our good, it is too much trouble. You have got to do your painting, but when they want you to do something, you can drop everything."

"That's unfair. I have worked myself to exhaustion for the wine business."

"With a very bad grace."

"I have tried very hard. The whole business is completely alien to me, but I have tried."

"Not very hard."

"Very hard."

"You're lazy!"

"I'm anything but lazy."

"What is it that they have on you? Are they blackmailing you or something?"

"Of course not, but I share some of their beliefs."

"What? Are they religious fanatics or cult protagonists? I have never heard you come over all spiritual."

"No, political beliefs."

"What political beliefs do you have, apart from complaining about the freedom of a Frenchman to sleep on the street?"

"You know as well as I do that France is teetering on the edge of civil war."

"There's not civil war. There's just a load of troublemakers encouraged by an incompetent government."

"That's not true. France is threatened by a coup. Fascist elements are mobilising to rob the people of their democracy. The generals in Algeria are threatening to invade France. Right-wing fanatics have not learnt the lessons of Hitler and Franco."

"What nonsense."

"Fascism is on the march and its adherents are fools who have no regard for humanity."

"How can you come out with such folly?"

"Fascism destroys everybody in the end." Michael's face wrinkled up with concern, "People think they can control it. They see it as a way of getting rid of those who disagree with them."

"The troublemakers."

"They're not troublemakers. They are the people who cherish freedom. Selfish 'Gentlemen of the Right' are the troublemakers." Michael spluttered. "Fascism will destroys its own in the end as well as the people it seeks to destroy." He cleared his throat. "It starts by destroying its opponents, then the neutrals, then its own supporters. Nobody is safe once the forces of evil are free. These generals want to mould France to their selfish ends, not realising that those ends control them, not they the ends. They are ignorant and blind. I want to defend the people and the things I love. Everything will be destroyed, including our lives, if they are not stopped."

"You do talk nonsense!"

Michael's tone changed to one that had an element of pleading. "If the generals in Algeria invade France, as they intend to, and try to take over, there are some people who won't let this happen, and I intend to help them."

"You? What is it to you? What have you got to do with it?"

"I intend to help defend democracy and society."

"You've never taken an interest in society before. You're not even a Frenchman. You should be thinking of people close to you. You should be thinking of your family; of those that love you."

"People who love me would understand my position."

Michael took a deep breath. He wanted to get Monique to see things as he did, but how? He continued in a soft voice.

"I have chosen this country for my home, and I cherish it. It is a highly civilised society." His voice gained vigour. "But as a human being I have a duty. I do what I am doing not just for France but the whole of humanity. I am a free man and I intend to stay that way. Moreover, I intend to help others preserve their freedom. I intend to defend your freedom."

"Oh, you do sound high and mighty."

"No, I'm not high or mighty. It is to stop others who do see themselves as high and mighty that I act. I have joined like-minded people who treasure freedom."

"So you have been plotting behind my back, organising some counter-coup with other discontents, while I have been striving to secure our future. I do all the work and plan our life, while you just plot a revolution."

"Nothing of the sort! I have been helping to secure a free future for us both; for you and me. If the generals have their way, you won't be able to say, or think, or do what you like."

"I've lived through the German occupation. You just have to look after those around you."

"That's selfish. We are all part of the human race."

"I thought you did this courier job to earn money so that you could stay here, but apparently you were trying to solve the world's problems. Do you see yourself as a sort of angel?"

"Don't be silly."

"I thought you were working to stay here for me, but all the time you were satisfying your political ambitions."

"I have no political ambitions."

Tears were appearing in Monique's eyes. "I thought our relationship was what was important to you." *I must not cry! I am a strong person.* She then shouted, "Whereas, in fact, it was just a cover for you to interfere in French politics. Perfidious Albion. Never trust an Englishman."

"Now you're becoming hysterical."

"How dare you call me hysterical!?" Her sorrow turned to one of anger. *Thank you for making me angry. Tears are now banished.* "When women express something they believe in strongly, why do men always accuse them of being hysterical?" She felt very betrayed. She had striven to make their future marriage a success, while all the time he had been deceiving her, plotting while she worked, betraying her, her family, her family's friends, her class. Yes, as an Englishman he ought to know about class. Whether he likes it or not, he is in a privileged group of society, and he should realise he has to defend it, or the 'great unwashed' will sweep it away in their envy.

"I have hated deceiving you. There are many times I have tried to tell you what I was doing, but you always changed the subject, and the moment passed. I am not against you and your friends. I have worked for them transferring money to secure their future."

"For cash. For your benefit, not for theirs."

"For our benefit. For us."

"You have used me. I have been just a cover."

"Not at all. I came here to paint. I found you, and life was a paradise. The generals threaten that paradise, and I have to defend it."

She was not listening to him. "I feel used and cheap and I hate you." She crossed the room, picked up a vase, and threw it through the window. There was a loud crash. Glass sprayed everywhere. The silly thought crossed Michael's mind. *That is two panes of glass we will have to pay for*. Before he had time to resolve this thought, the concierge appeared.

"What is going on here?"

Michael was placatory. "I'm sorry."

Monique was not. She screamed. "Get out!"

The concierge withdrew.

"If you are going to behave like an animal, I am going."

"Go! I never want to see you again. I hate you! You bastard!"

Michael returned to his studio. *So much for my day's painting*. There was no hope of carrying on now. He stood and stared at the wall with unseeing eyes. He would go back to the flat. He quickly cleaned his brushes with automatic movements. His thoughts were elsewhere. They were running over what had been said, and what had been meant. *How have things got so out of hand?* He washed his hands and left.

Monique was sobbing. It was unlike her. She was stronger than that. *I am not the crying type*. She hated weepy women, but she had been so deceived. *How could he? How could he pretend to be helping my family, when all the time plotting with the opposition, those that would do us harm?* She was sad and she was angry, and she was going to make him pay.

It was evening when Monique returned to the flat. Darkness had fallen, but Michael had not switched on the lights. After drinking some coffee, he had just sat in an armchair thinking for most of the day. Twilight had passed him by without him noticing. Monique switched on the light.

"Are you still here?"

Michael was shaken out of his thoughts. "Shall I get you some coffee?"

"I want nothing from you." Her eyes were screwed up in an expression of hatred.

"I am sorry. I never wanted to deceive you."

"But you did, and for a long time. How can I ever trust you again?"

"You can trust me in everything else. I love you. That has always been true. There is no deception there."

"If a man is deceitful, he is deceitful. There are no half ways. A couple has to be open about everything. They should share their life. They should share their thoughts. They should share their actions. Will I ever be able to believe what you tell me is true? Regardless of any political differences, it is the difference in our willingness to trust one another that rankles."

"I was wrong. I admit it. Can't we start again as though nothing had happened?"

"No! Your word is your most precious possession. Once the purity of that has gone, it can never be retrieved. Even if I wanted to, subconsciously I could never believe in you again."

"We are young." Michael was racking his brains to find a way to ease the situation. "Everything seems straightforward when you are young. One day you will realise that nothing is as simple as it appears. Other people's lives depended on me keeping a secret, and I had given my word that I would protect their preparations to defend themselves from what might be a bloody mess. I promised not to tell even my closest friends."

"We are not friends. We are lovers."

Michael ignored her and continued. "I kept my word to them. That proves I can be trusted. In guarding their secret, I have proved my trustworthiness. Eventually, I would have told you. I tried several times. It was just a matter of time. I always wanted to. Keeping things from you has weighed heavily on me."

"Not heavily enough."

"Can't you see I was caught between two states of good faith, my promise to them, and my commitment to you?"

"And you chose them in preference to me."

"No! I kept your parents and their friends' behaviour secret. What I was doing for them was also illegal."

Michael felt he was being unfairly treated, but he also had feelings of guilt, which weakened his position. He hoped some penitence on his part would ease the situation.

"Now everything is out in the open, surely we can start again with a clean slate."

"Is everything out in the open? How can I know that? What else haven't you told me?"

"You know there are other good qualities as well as sincerity, and one of them is compassion. I am asking you to forgive and forget what has gone before Let us start again."

"No. There are angels around that might be able to forgive you, and even weak women who are willing to be deceived and sat upon, but I am not one of them. I'd like you to get out of my chair, out of my flat, and out of my life. I never want to see you again."

Michael got up from the chair, went into the bedroom where he put most of his clothes into a bag, leaving his curly-brimmed bowler, adding some books and a photo, and left.

Monique sat in a chair for some time. She went and made some coffee and thought about the events of the day. *What is the truth of what Michael had been doing? Has he just used me as a cover? How deep has been his involvement in this plot to cause a civil war? For how long had it been going on? Is he really involved with people who would rob my father of his hard work yet again?* It had been a crazy afternoon, and she had not been able to sort it all out in her mind yet. *I have been very rude to Pierre. That was not necessary. And what does he know? He gives the appearance of a sophisticated man of the world, who was wise and someone you could trust, but is he one of that group, and a key to a lot of things? Perhaps I could find out from him. If there is trouble brewing, and there is danger to my father, perhaps he would know, and I could warn Papa.* She lifted the phone and rang. "Hallo, Pierre? I am sorry I was so rude to you today. I want to apologise. Could we meet?"

Chapter Eleven

Tears filled Michael's eyes. He jumped into his car, threw his bag on the passenger's seat, and slammed the door, not because he was angry, but because he was in a hurry. He was in a hurry to get away. He could not believe what was happening. Paradise was slipping through his fingers. He had found the perfect woman. He had found what he wanted to do in life. He had money enough to live comfortably in a beautiful city, and now it was all disintegrating in his hands. What had brought it about? If there was a god, it was a cruel god. The Greeks knew about that. Half their literature was concerned with hubris, and the way the gods reaped their revenge.

He sped through the northern suburbs of Paris at a pace that would get him arrested, but he did not care. Luckily it was a bit late, and most of the police had gone home, or were occupied in catching burglars. His mood oscillated between sorrow and anger.

What should I do now? Probably the best thing to do will be to proceed as normal; carry out my obligations. I have the package that Pierre brought. If I carry out that errand, I will not have to think about my course of action until later. Pierre, Claude, and the rest depended upon me. I cannot let them down.

Political problems did not matter so much to him anymore. Personal problems can shut out the great problems of the world at large. *I will carry on automatically until a way forward presents itself. And it will.*

As he cleared Paris, it started to rain. It was not just a shower. It came down in torrents. The angels were sympathetic to his mood. They were crying profusely. It was going to be a long, tedious night drive to Boulogne. It would give him a lot of time to think. But that was the last thing he wanted to do. All his thoughts were black, and his mind was going so fast that attention to the road did not occupy his consciousness enough. He could not stop himself thinking. The speed of the drive could not leave the speed of his thoughts behind.

Where had it all gone wrong? Monique is a painter. She knows how much painting demands. And yet she has been tempted, diverted, by the idea of being a businesswoman. She is greater than that. She should see the folly of succumbing to the material world. She should see that money is an illusion. There are greater things in life than money and success. Those are ephemeral and can disappear in an instant. Art educates the soul. It enriches life and makes it worth living. An enriched person carries their treasure with them. That cannot be taken away. There is no substitute for self-improvement, so why is Monique straying from her vocation? She is intelligent. She is sincere. How has she become diverted by the promise of material things? Is Pierre's forecast coming true? Is she reverting to the values of her childhood? No! She has already left those illusions behind. Nevertheless, the material world has seduced a potentially great person?'

He suddenly had to slam on his brakes. A car came out of a side road. He skidded sideways on to the pavement. He threw his steering wheel to the right, turning his wheels into the skid. He stopped just short of a bollard. *Damn!* The other car just sped off down the road, its occupants oblivious to the disruption they had caused. *What are they doing out at this time of night? Frenchmen, at least Frenchmen in the countryside, should have gone to bed. They are obviously fools, not looking where they were going.* His anger, for the moment, was diverted on to the other car drivers.

Perhaps it was not altogether an unfortunate incident because it had distracted him from his dark thoughts for a moment, but only a moment, for those thoughts now came rushing back with renewed vigour.

He drove off the pavement. Although he could offer some reasons, none completely explained the extreme situation that his relationship with Monique was in.

He passed Montdidier. All were asleep. A bit later, he came to Amiens. He went through the town, which was deserted. He slowed down anyway, as he knew the annoyance of being woken up by speeding traffic. Fast traffic echoed through empty streets. He still felt he was on the side of the good. This proved it, so that made the quarrel with Monique not his fault. It was lucky he slowed down, for he noticed a police car resting in a side street. Automatically, he felt guilty, and his pulse increased. However, its occupants took no notice of him; they were probably asleep, like the rest of the town. It was now a sleepy town, whatever it had been in the past, and it had been very important. He was glad he did not live in a town like this, where history had passed it by. *This is the sort of place where most people live,* he said to himself, *looking after their families, attending to their crops or pursuing their craft, and letting great things happen elsewhere. It was the privileged few that live in great cities like Paris or London, where the big issues of human history now take place. In fact, most of the world's population still live in villages, not even towns, and have no effect on world events*. He realised that he was privileged in that he lived at the centre of things, and he did appreciate that, although dealing with reasonably big events appeared to have ruined his life. The thought crossed his mind that perhaps the unprivileged were better off after all. He wanted a family and domestic bliss with Monique. *But would I be satisfied just with family life... No!*

He was also aware that he was privileged in more ways than one. *Most people go through life never knowing what they want to do with it, whereas I have found my vocation, and I have found the woman I want to share it with. Not many people succeed in that. Not only that, but the woman I have found knows, or should know, how it is to live the life I seek. That is exceptional luck, but now it is all being thrown away, mainly because Monique cannot see my point of view.* He negotiated a sharp turn. *Or perhaps she might be just a little bit right.* The same thoughts kept repeating, but there was no way of banishing them from his consciousness.

He suddenly saw a light. It came from a wayside café. He had just passed Flixecourt and still had a long way to go. From the vehicles parked in the forecourt, he deduced it must be a lorry drivers' halt. He stopped and parked his car. The rain was still pouring down, so he made a quick dash for the café door. As he entered, he noticed a Routiers sign. He had been forced into a lucky choice for his stop.

Inside, he came into a different world. It was full of bright light. A juke box competed with a high level of dialogue and laughter. Some drivers were playing a game of pool or snooker at the other end of the room. He went to the counter and ordered some coffee. There was cooking going on behind a hatch, and it smelt very good, but he had no appetite. His stomach was all screwed up. However, he thought he had better eat something, as he had eaten nothing since lunch, and that was a long time ago. He had been too upset with the events of the day to think about food. Adrenalin had kept him going, but that would run out soon, so he ordered a baguette. He took his coffee to a table in the corner, sat down, and regarded the company. Most of the drivers were dressed in blue overalls with a floppy beret, or a cap that looked like a beret. If they had been English, they would probably be wearing brown, but blue was the French colour. He speculated why. Most had worn blue at the battle of Waterloo, and although they had lost that battle, they were still proud of the fact that they had won most of the previous battles against the aristocratic dictators of Europe. They brought freedom to the masses. Things had never been the same after the end of the French hegemony of Europe. After the revolution and Napoleon, nobody again could ignore democracy. The whole of Europe was indebted to them for that.

A waitress brought his baguette. It was tasty. He enjoyed it in spite of his emotionally induced sick feeling. He felt altogether better as he left the café and got into his car again. The rain had eased off a little, and the road was much clearer as he drove away.

Nevertheless, the events of the previous day forced themselves back into his consciousness. The food and coffee had perhaps given him a respite and a slightly different perspective. *Have I in fact been too hard on Monique? She was doing what she thought was right for our future. Perhaps I should be pleased. Even if she was wrong, it was her thought that counted. Her motive was that of someone who wants the best for those she loves. Perhaps I should go back and try and make things up.* He slowed the car a bit. *No. That would not be sensible. Best let it settle. Let things calm down. Anyway, I have a job to do. I have embarked on going to England, and only a weak man changes direction halfway through a process. Perhaps, later on, if I explained more carefully my position and apologise, she will see the error of her ways as well. We have both made mistakes.*

On the other hand, how could she say I am useless and selfish? She has been really spiteful. I have tried my best. Surely she could see that. Perhaps she did not want to see it. She wanted all the glory for herself. She was intent on showing her father what a great businesswoman she was. Perhaps she was trying to impress herself. It is not usual for a girl to be economically so astute. She is exceptional, and this is a way she can show it to the world. With a successful wine business, the world would have to recognise her talents. They would beat a pathway to her door. He noticed a large lorry going in the other direction rather fast. *We men do not have this problem. If we have talent and succeed, it is recognised. We do not have to emphasise the fact, and if we fail, nobody notices. For women, it is the opposite. If they fail, people notice it, and delight in their failure. Maybe I am being too hard on her. On the other hand, she was trying to dominate me. Most women try that at some phase in a relationship, especially intelligent women. A man should stand up to that. I am not going to be subjugated to her will all the time.* Then another lorry with the same name on the side rushed past. *It is a pity, for I had thought we had a perfectly balanced partnership. Maybe that is impossible. Perhaps there always has to be one boss in a relationship, otherwise it will not work. Locke thought that. And he thought it should be the man.*

Michael drove on through the night and eventually, the sun started to peak its way above the horizon as he cleared a ridge. It announced its arrival, with a golden haze in the sky at first, and then, having warned all watchers and put them on alert, it jumped from its hiding place in all its glory. Streaks of gold shot across the sky, dividing the rain clouds that were brushed aside in its powerful awakening.

Things always look more beautiful when you are sad. And I am sad. Perhaps the senses are more acute. Perhaps it is in contrast to dark inner thoughts. Whatever the cause, the emotion induced by beauty is more intense. These moments often remain in one's memory long after the cause for sadness has departed.

He drove on past Nouvion through dawn's early light. The populace was stirring. Tractors were started up, and hay carts were dragged on to village roads. Michael had to be more careful, but he did not slow that much. Anger and despair drove him on.

He was approaching Neufchatel-Hardelot when he noticed several police cars either side of the road. He slowed. It was a roadblock. There was a car in front of him. They waved it through. The policeman to the side was consulting a clipboard, and then, glancing down at his number plate, said something to his companion. Michael's pulse started racing. The other policeman stepped out and raised his arm. He stopped.

"Good morning. Michael Daubeney, I believe?"

"How do you know that?"

"That's not difficult with a car like yours."

"But how do you know that I have a car like this?"

"That's our job. Would you step out of the car?"

Michael complied.

"Can I see your passport?"

Michael leant back into the car and retrieved his passport from his bag. Another policeman of obviously higher rank came up, and the first one handed him the passport.

"It has a lot of stamps in it."

"I travel a lot."

"I can see that. You must be very rich. So this is your car. Can I see the papers?"

Michael again stretched back into the car and got the log book and his international driving licence.

"How much money are you carrying?"

"I don't know." He drew his wallet from his pocket and looked inside. "About 10,000 francs."

"And the rest?"

"What rest?"

"The rest you have probably hidden in your car."

Thank goodness I have finished taking things out of the country for M. Foch's friends, Michael thought.

"There's no money hidden in my car! What makes you think that?"

"We have reason to believe that you have been smuggling. I'm afraid we are going to have to take your car away to inspect it. Perhaps you would like to step across to our other vehicle, and we can take you back to the police station. There are some questions we would like you to answer."

"You're making a big mistake. You'll find nothing in my car or on me. You're going to look very silly... And I have a boat to catch." However, his confidence was undermined by his conscience. His words came out without much conviction.

Michael walked across with the police sergeant and got into the police vehicle.

"Could we have the keys to your car? A colleague will drive it back to the station."

They set off in a procession, the car Michael was in leading the way. It was a fairly long drive. They did not go into the local village. Eventually, they stopped in a courtyard, where Michael was led into the back of the building that formed the front of the police yard. He had no idea where he was. He noticed his car being driven into a garage at the other side of the yard. He was shown into a small office. It was bare, save for a table and two chairs, one either side of the table. *This is an interrogation room,* he thought.

Now left alone, he was suddenly feeling tired, in spite of his heart pumping faster than usual. He wished he felt fresher and had his wits about him. There was nothing he could do but wait. He dozed in and out of consciousness.

Eventually, after several hours, the police officer came in. "Well now, what have you been up to?"

"What do you mean, 'What have I been up to'?"

"We know you have been smuggling. What have you been smuggling?"

"What do you think I have been smuggling?"

"That's up to you to tell us."

"On the contrary. If you think I have been smuggling, you must know what it is, and it's up to you to tell me."

"It will be much better if you come clean and tell us everything. We probably know it all anyway, so co-operation might help your cause."

"If you probably know it, you don't need to ask me."

"We'd like to hear it coming from you."

"Have you found anything in my car?"

"Not yet, but we have plenty of time."

"You'll be wasting plenty of time."

Michael wished he did not feel so tired. He did not know what they knew. They obviously knew something, but what? One of the two groups that he had worked for had given him away, but which one? Whichever one, he did not want to let them know about the other. Then he would be in even worse trouble. He would have to stall until the police gave themselves away.

"You're a painter, I believe?"

"True."

"A painter with a lot of money."

Michael was thinking how to answer that when his interrogator continued.

"Painters do not usually have a lot of money unless they are up to something else."

"That's because you have a bourgeois perspective on the arts. You think an artist has to starve and suffer to produce great works, but that idea is a product of the 19th Century, when the nouveau riche took over, who were very ignorant. In the past, a lot of painters have been very rich indeed. Rubens, for example."

"I am not here to discuss art history with you. I don't think you realise how much trouble you are in."

"No. Tell me."

"No, you tell me. What have you been up to?"

"Well, I have been living in Paris and painting pictures."

"And travelling a lot."

"I have been travelling."

"That takes money."

"I have sold some pictures."

"How many, and to whom?"

Michael's mind raced. Did they know about Pierre? Were they aware of the Sinister Port group?

"I can't remember. Various people. As a good bourgeois, you must know that artists are disorganised and never keep any records."

"Artists don't usually keep a posh sports car either."

Again Michael's mind sought some explanation. Did they know the source of his money? Did they know about the right-wing group and their deal with him? *I need a lead to try and divert them.*

"I have a rich girlfriend."

"Yes. We know about her."

A horrible thought flashed across his mind. *Monique is the only one who knows where I might be going. No! She would never do that.*

"She has a father with no morals. He collaborated with the Nazis." The policeman said this with a sneer.

So that was it. Had his interrogator said too much? *It looks as though my left-wing conspiring friends fed the police information in revenge? But what for? To what purpose? Bertrand had been very interested in M. Foch's politics, but the others were not vindictive.*

The policeman developed a nonchalant air. "But he's a respectable citizen now. We all have to forget the past. None of us came out of the war smelling sweetly. Let bygones be bygones."

"So what are your bygones?"

"We are talking about you, not me."

"If we are talking about me, I have nothing to say."

"I am sure by the time we have finished, you will say a lot."

"I might have a lot to say to someone about wrongful arrest."

The interrogator laughed. "You are not in England now, you know. I can't be threatened."

"What is your name?" said Michael with a stern voice.

"That won't do you any good, but my name is Sergeant Bucolin."

"I'll remember that."

"Ah. So you do have a memory. Perhaps you could remember the names of those behind your activities."

"We have not yet established that I have any activities," he paused. "Apart from painting."

"I can see that you consider yourself smart. You know we learnt a lot from the Germans. It was probably the only benefit we got from the occupation. They taught us how to get information out of people."

"You know, I had the impression that you had probably co-operated with the fascists. You would make a good Nazi."

"I think I'll leave you for a bit. You can think about what you are going to tell me. I really don't like hurting people."

The policeman left. Michael was pleased. He felt so tired. The light was still on, and it was a bit bright, but he was so exhausted it did not matter anyway. He dozed.

There was a bang. He jumped. The metal door of the room clanked as a couple of policemen came in. "You're not supposed to sleep. You're supposed to be thinking about things."

They pulled him to his feet and started walking him round the room. For a few moments, he became really awake, but then his exhaustion overcame him. He dozed, even though he was being walked around. His interrogator came in, and the supporting policemen plonked him on a chair and left.

"Well now you've had a couple of hours to think about things, have you got anything to tell me?"

"A couple of hours? You left only a couple of minutes ago."

"Oh dear! Other faculties as well as your memory seem to be amiss."

"You can't try that old trick on me. You left and came back immediately you saw me dozing."

"I'm afraid you are deluding yourself. Perhaps it is because you need sleep. I'll leave you again to get some more rest. I'll leave you to fully recover, and then perhaps your memory will return."

He left. Michael looked around the room.

If only there was a window in the room, I would be able to judge the time. They are trying to confuse me. I know I have not slept for more than a few seconds. I can hear activity in the yard. It must still be early in the morning, but then there would probably be activity in the yard all the day, so that is not much use.

He collapsed on the bed and immediately fell asleep.

Chapter Twelve

He had no idea how long he had been asleep before two men entered, woke him up, and took him to another room. He noticed during his transfer that it was light outside, but as it was overcast, he could not tell what part of the day it was.

His new room was about three metres by four metres. It was very much like the former room. This one had a window high up, but it had been blocked up on the outside. The only light was given by a bare bulb, very bright, that hung in the centre of the room. There was a bed with a thin mattress, a pillow, and two blankets. In one corner was a chair, and in the other a bucket, which was presumably for bodily functions. No sooner had he looked round the room than two policemen brought in a wooden table and stuck it against the wall. A third came with a second chair.

Michael sat on the bed and contemplated his situation. *If this is what living dangerously brings you to, perhaps I ought to get another motto.* As he was thinking what that should be, he fell fast asleep.

There was a bang. He jumped. The door of the room clanked as a couple of policemen barged in. "You're not supposed to sleep. You've been given a chance to revive your memory."

Michael had an inconsequential thought. *They have very gruff voices. Most predatory animals have gruff voices. Lions roar and dogs bark.*

They pulled him to his feet and started walking him round the room again. This time his tiredness overcame him immediately. He fell asleep even though he was being dragged around. It was the same routine. The interrogator came back in, Michael was slammed down on the chair, and his walkers left. The interrogator sat on the chair at the other end of the table.

"Well, now you've had plenty of time to think about things, have you got something to tell me?"

"I have to tell you that you left me only a couple of minutes ago. Don't think you can confuse me by keep on coming in before I have had time to sleep."

"Why should I want to confuse you? I want to hear the truth from you."

"You wouldn't recognise the truth."

"How about these friends of yours? What are their names?"

"I have lots of friends. Which ones are you talking about?"

"Those that you're plotting with."

So it is the left-wing group the police know about, Michael thought to himself. *The use of the word 'plotting' suggests politics, and I never actually plotted with the wealthy lot, the friends of M. Foch. I only carried their money for them. On the one hand, if the police know about Claude and his group, it would probably not have been that group that told the police about me. They wouldn't risk incriminating themselves. Then on the other hand, it might have been just one of them, or a plant, perhaps Bertrand. I've never liked him.* Michael then considered the alternatives more coolly. *It is just as unlikely that General Duchamp and his friends would put me in the hands of the police. I might talk and incriminate them. Unless of course they want me out of the way, now that I have done everything I could for them. They probably have sympathisers in the police.*

"Why should I be plotting?" Michael brought himself back to the present.

"A lot of people are plotting these days. We live in difficult times."

"But I am English. Why should I plot in France?"

"Exactly. Why are you plotting in France?"

"I am just a painter, as I have told you. I have no need to plot."

"Let's talk about your girlfriend. What is she up to?"

Michael's thoughts immediately jumped. *So it was her who informed on me. No, if they are asking about her, she can't be on their side. On the other hand, the fact that they do know about her means she may have been in contact. Or are they just fishing?*

"I don't think she is up to anything apart from painting, looking after a family business, and planning to marry me."

"Marry you, eh? I'm afraid you are deluding yourself. Perhaps it's because you still need sleep. I'll leave you again to get some more rest."

He suddenly left. Michael looked around the room. He collapsed on the bed and fell into a deep stupor.

Two men rushed into the room and woke him. "Come on, it's time for breakfast."

Michael felt terrible. Again, he was sure he had only just dozed off.

"Nonsense. I don't want food; I want to go to sleep," he protested.

"You've been asleep for hours. It's time for breakfast."

The men put his food on the table and left. He dozed off.

The two men clattered in again. "Wake up! It's dinner time." They deposited more food on the table, more in keeping with lunch or an evening meal.

Michael felt even worse than before. He was sure no time had passed. They had embarked on a course to drive him crazy, but he was going to hold onto his sanity. *We have a natural clock in our bodies. That is going to keep me in contact with reality. My stomach tells me that the two meals left on the table are a lot of nonsense. I have no appetite. I have no thirst. My body is more reliable than my captors' suggestions, but they obviously do not realise that.* However, his body also told him to sleep, and he could not resist its command. Again, he dozed, and again the two men and his integrator came in.

"You have not eaten any of your food. I know what you are up to. If police inspectors come to see you, you are going to claim that we starved you, when we are trying to look after your welfare. We had better not leave this here to go mouldy. It could cause all sorts of infection, so we'll clear it away." With that, they took the food and left.

I have to hold on to reality. If reality fails me, I might say anything. My stomach tells me that time has not passed, but that might be confused. I have driven for a night, and eaten at that café, something I'm not used to. Also, I did not eat much yesterday. I have been so upset. Can I rely on my stomach? He had an inkling of doubt.

He looked around the room, and the bucket caught his eye. That was it. He had a strong bladder and only went to pee three or four times a day. That would be his clock. He did not need to pee yet, so time had not passed as they said. He only ever went to empty his bowels once a day, after his morning cup of tea. That would be his way of counting off the days. *That is if they keep me here for long. They think they are smart, but they will not be able to confuse my timekeeping. That is one weapon of theirs I have neutralised.*

The next time the interrogating sergeant came in with the policemen and woke him up, he gave them a big smile and taunted them. "It's not working, is it?" The sergeant could detect a new confidence in his eyes. He was not sure why, but the present course was not a success. He could see that.

The sergeant vacantly scratched his chin. His body language betrayed his confusion. "I can see we have a smart one in you," he said. "However, it is not always good to be smart. We will have to try other methods of getting to the truth."

"I thought you had the truth. That's why I am surprised you keep on asking me questions. Either you have some information, albeit false, that you want me to verify, or you know nothing and are fishing in the dark."

"Well, O.K., I can see we have to try another approach. The Gestapo taught us a thing or two. I think we will leave you to rest now, and start afresh later on. In the meantime, you can think about what you are going to tell me, and speculate on how good you are at resisting pain."

Directly the policemen left, Michael fell asleep, and awoke to a dark room. The light had been put out, and he felt refreshed. This time he had slept for some time. He could feel that. He needed a pee but had some difficulty in finding the bucket in the dark. Relieved, he then sat on his bed and thought.

He was in a mess. What was certain was that someone had given him away. The police had been waiting for him. They knew who he was, and what car he drove. M. Foch's friends would probably not know that, so it was unlikely to be them. On the other hand, it could be, because they were the ones that were least involved and friendly towards him. For them, he did not matter. Once he was no longer of any use, they would have no compunction in giving him away. The Sinister Port, on the other hand, needed his activity still, and they were people with whom he had a common sympathy. They were all birds of a feather, in it together. He had served them well. They must know that. But they had given him a package to take to England and knew he would be travelling. Was the package a plant? What was in the package? He felt it next to his ribcage. If it was they who had told the authorities, he would feel particularly betrayed and bitter. But then being betrayed was being betrayed, whoever did it. One group was no worse than the other.

The only other person who could have done it was too horrible to contemplate. Monique probably knew where he was going, when, and which route he would most likely take. But she would never betray him. Would she? No, it was unthinkable. He lay back on the bed and stared at the blackness in the direction of the ceiling. She had been very angry that he had held a secret from her. It appeared that that was more important to her than the fact that his politics did not coincide with hers or that he was not interested in the wine business, although these things certainly added to her displeasure.

I can understand why she is angry. I should have told her earlier. But that could not be enough to betray me to the authorities. We have shared a bed together. We love each other, or have loved each other. Could love die that quickly? Could it be defeated by a simple thing like not sharing a secret? They say love and hate are neighbours. No, Monique would never give me away, even if she was angry with me. The feelings between us are too deep, too warm. What about her father? Perhaps he does not want her to marry me after all. No, that theory does not hold up. He wants someone to run his vineyards. It hurt him to see his investment unused, as Monique has pointed out.

That brought Michael back again to Monique herself. *No! I refuse to believe that it could be her.*

Was there someone else who was more likely to have done it? Probably Bertrand. Michael had never really taken to Bertrand. He was the cool, planning type. He had questioned the Fochs' politics. Perhaps he had seen them as potential enemies, as people who would naturally support the generals when they came. He was the sort of person who would see anyone who was not with him as against him. Those types were never to be trusted. But Michael had no evidence to support that view. What about Pierre? No, he was not someone who was vindictive. He was cynical, of course, but that was only about the behaviour of women. The other members of Sinister Port were good, straightforward, working-class souls who would not be so devious. That brought him back to Monique again. "Hell hath no fury as a woman scorned." Shakespeare knew a thing or two, but he had not scorned Monique. He wanted their relationship to continue. It was she who was breaking it up. "Get out of my life!" she had said. But would she put him into such danger? Would she be so spiteful as to drop him in such trouble? Maybe she did not realise the trouble she was dropping him in. Maybe she unwittingly gave him away. It was all too much. He had to stop thinking.

The darkness stimulated the same thoughts to go round and round in his head. With no other senses stimulated, he could only think and sleep.

Eventually, after some considerable time, the light bulb went on, and the sergeant entered.

"Have you come up with anything to tell me?"

"Yes, I have got something to tell you. I want to see the British Consul."

"Oh, the British Consul will be too busy at the moment. Things are hotting up. We are on the verge of chaos. French society has taken leave of its senses."

"I still have the right to see my Consul."

"You have no rights. We suspect you might be a spy. In which case, we have the right to take you out and shoot you."

"Who do you think I could possibly be spying for?"

"That's for you to tell us."

"This is ridiculous. You know nothing about me. Somebody has given you a rumour, and you are fishing to see if there is anything going on that I might know about."

"We know that you associate with some very unsavoury people."

"Who?"

"You know who we are talking about."

If only I did know. However, it appears that they don't know and are only fishing. Their bluff has gone on for too long. It has no substance.

The sergeant continued. "I can see we are going to get nowhere with these word games. I give you credit. You are too clever, so we are going to try something else." With this he drew some contraptions out of his bag. "Do you know what these are?"

"No."

"Thumb screws. Very old-fashioned, but very effective. They administer minor damage, but significant pain. One of the things the Nazis taught us was that the most effective way to administer torture was gradually, step by step, with plenty of time for the subject to think about things in between."

"Don't you think I have had enough time to think about things already? I cannot recall anything that might be of interest to you?"

"Well, if at the end of our little sessions, you still don't tell me what I want to know, I can only assume you have been trained in interrogation avoidance techniques, and are therefore a spy. In which case, we would certainly have to shoot you."

"You'd never get away with it."

"If there is rioting in the streets, and the shooting starts, no one is going to take any notice of an extra body."

Michael had a slight worry that he might be right. *Civil wars always allow for the settling of old scores, and very few people are ever brought to book afterwards And who is going to miss me?*

The sergeant continued. "We are wasting time. Give me your left hand."

Michael presented his hand, and the sergeant clamped the contraption on his thumb.

"Is it comfortable?"

"I thought the idea was that it should be uncomfortable."

"Only when I decide. I am solely in charge. I will administer pain or not, according to how you co-operate."

At that moment, the sergeant turned the screw, and Michael felt an excruciating pain shoot from his thumb, through his wrist, and up his arm. Michael felt anger bubbling up inside him, but he must not let it get the better of him. He had to remain calm.

"You see. I am in charge." He turned the screw again, and Michael felt his thumb joint crunch, and blood trickled down his hand.

At this point, one of the other policemen came in. "I think you should come. Things are happening very fast. The radio is giving out a series of special announcements."

The sergeant rose. "You see, things can hurt," he said as he turned to go, "and we have some even more destructive little gadgets. Think about it. Tell me who you are co-operating with, and all this pain could stop. If not, who knows? We might have to put you up against a wall." With that, he left.

Michael was left alone again to think. He managed to get the thumb screw off. It had made a mess of his left thumb, and it was incredibly painful. Would he be able to stand much worse pain? He did not know. Nobody knows until it happens. Whoever was responsible for putting him in this situation had a lot to answer for. The evidence pointed to Monique, but he could not bring himself to believe that she could do such a thing. The incident at Le Havre suddenly came into his head, when she was interrogated by the customs. Had they got something on her, and had she done a deal? No! Now he was becoming paranoid. He was getting involved in crazy theories. He went and lay on the bed, nursing his hand in a handkerchief. There was nothing he could do but wait. He was a pawn in the hands of the master chess player: Fate, who would decide all.

It was several hours before the sergeant returned. Michael had heard much activity outside. Physical and emotional pain vied with each other for his attention. In his mind, he had gone over all the previous thoughts again, with no greater success. Would he ever know who had given him away?

Sergeant Bucolin entered. He wore a surprisingly worried expression this time. "Things are happening. Apparently, they have offered De Gaulle the presidency again. He has accepted on certain conditions. The generals in Algeria who are on the verge of invading France are only holding back until the negotiations with De Gaulle are completed. They are led by Salan, Zeller, Massu, and Challe. This puts me in a difficult situation. I have enemies." He turned slowly and took things out of his bag. "Here is your passport, and here is mine." He held the two passports up, one in either hand. "Now I believe you have illegal ways of leaving France and entering England. You can have yours back if we go together, and you take me with you to England."

So it must be Sinister Port that has given me away! Michael laughed. "What! Do you expect me to believe you? This is just another one of your little tricks. Is this not just a trap? You obviously like playing games. Look at my thumb. After the way you have behaved, why should I trust you?"

"Because you have to!" The sergeant had the air of someone who knew he was in a commanding position. "I am your only chance of getting out of here."

Michael was really angry now. *How dare he think I would co-operate at all with him, after what he has done? The arrogance of the man! But then he is a policeman. What can you expect?* However, he kept control and answered calmly.

"This would be, a nice way of finding out my contacts."

"It would be, but you have to take me on trust. There are those higher up than me who are determined to deal with you and your friends in a much harsher manner than me. They have known about you for some time."

"Which friends?"

"Your friends."

Michael's mind was racing. *He really does not know which group. He is still trying unreasonably hard to disguise his ignorance.*

"Tell me who you think I am associated with, and I might consider your proposition." *At last, here is a chance of finding who has betrayed me,* Michael reasoned to himself. *If he is clever, he will give me just enough evidence to make me think he knows more than he does, but that will let me know who has given me away.*

"I really don't know. I have only been carrying out orders. What I do know is that we are both in trouble, but if we co-operate we can get out of it."

"You really expect me to fall for that? I view you and your type with contempt."

"Your contempt does not worry me. You have to take this opportunity. It's your only chance."

"So what are you going to do if you get to England?"

"I have a sister who lives in London. She is married to an Englishman. Look, you don't have to like me. You just have to trust me."

"Trust you!?"

"If I told you I grew up in England during the war, would that let you chauvinistically trust me more?"

Michael quickly weighed up the options. Unfortunately, the sergeant was right. *He will have to trust me as well if only half of what he is saying is true. It might be my only chance.*

Then calmly, "Well, I will need to make a phone call to England. It has to be a secure phone. Not one that can be listened into."

"That can be arranged."

The sergeant left and returned with a phone, which he plugged into a small socket in the skirting board. He went out again and returned almost immediately.

"Right. It's fixed. Make your call."

"Won't the others outside be listening in?"

"They have all gone home. They are almost as worried as I am."

"So I could attack you and walk out of here without any deal?"

"How far would you get?"

"It might be a better bet than trusting you."

"It might not be. We can leave here together in a police car, and nobody will stop and question us. We can go to wherever you need to go."

Michael eyed the sergeant with suspicion. *He might be my best chance of getting out of a hole – or the only chance.* He weighed things up. *My prospects here look pretty black. If I contact Charley to arrange a rendezvous, it will be in code, albeit a primitive code. I will navigate, and I do not have to tell him, presumably doing the driving, the where and when of the rendezvous. The initiative is then with me. Once in the car, he will presumably be out of touch with any superiors. We will be on equal terms. I can take my chances when the car stops, if need be.* "Alright then. Pass me my jacket." He winced as he took the jacket and tried to look inside the nametag. "I can't do this. Read me out the number on the back of that tag."

The sergeant did as requested, while Michael dialled it on the phone. It rang. A strong Sussex accent answered, "Hallo, Charley Adams here."

"Charley? It's Michael. Am I pleased to hear you? I am in a bit of trouble." He then remembered he had to sound normal.

"Trouble?"

"Yes, we have an emergency with the menu. I don't suppose you could deliver three kettles of your best fish, mostly turbot, or brill and Dover sole, to the bread shop tomorrow morning could you?"

"Well, that will be a bit bloody tight. You are in a hurry, are you?"

"Yes! Very! Various unforeseen things have come up, and I have been let down badly."

"Three kettles are going to be difficult to get my hands on straight away, but I could let you have say… seven large cod to be going on with. I could get those there by tomorrow morning."

"Seven will do nicely. You'll be well paid for them. We'll pick them up from the bread shop. Usual place. Seven."

"OK. Now I'll have to get my bloody skates on. Oh sorry, we said cod, didn't we?" He giggled.

Michael turned to Sergeant Bucolin, grinning all over, "You know, English puns are worse than the French." Then, more seriously, "Right. For better or worse, the stage is set. You are going to need to look like a fisherman. Have you got some suitable old clothes?"

"You are worried about trusting me, but I will now have to trust you. I presume we are going to meet a boat. How do I know you won't leave me behind on the shore?"

"I am a man of honour." Michael grinned.

The sergeant raised his eyebrows.

Michael continued, "I don't know where we are, or the route we will have to take, but drive north. Give me the map, and I will direct you once I see a land mark. How long will it take to get to the coast?"

"It depends which coast you're talking about, but the north coast, I presume; about two hours."

"We will have to be there at seven o'clock tomorrow morning."

"It might be tight. It is already gone 2am. We will need about two hours to get anywhere on the north coast from here, and another twenty minutes to sort things out. I will have to dump the police car inconspicuously somewhere, and walk to your rendezvous point, and I will need to change out of my uniform into the old clothes. There are a few things to be done here to allay suspicion. That is going to take another half hour."

"Good." Michael was now committed, whatever happened. *Fate must take its turn.*

"I will come for you at about four. It will be necessary to handcuff you, in case we are stopped. If that happens, I am transporting you as a prisoner."

Chapter Thirteen

Michael was bleary-eyed when Sergeant Bucolin woke him up. He was still very wary about the trip. Maybe it was a trap of some sort? But he had nothing to lose. He could see no other way out.

"Here. We won't be able to stop," the sergeant handed him a package. "So I have brought you some bread and cheese. Get into your jacket before I put these handcuffs on you."

"Is this the sympathetic fascist I have not seen before? Bread and cheese, eh?"

"I'm not a fascist. You have no idea where my sympathies lie."

Michael did not have to waste time dressing. He had worn the same clothes for a couple of days now. He was beginning to feel uncomfortable in them. *I might not need to change into my old clothes on the boat.* He amused himself with the thought. *I look pretty shabby in these, and I probably smell bad enough to compete with the fish.*

They went out and got in a police car, which was parked directly outside. Michael looked wistfully at the garage he had seen his Austin-Healey driven into. "It's a pity I have to leave my car behind."

"Yes, but how far do you think you would have got in that? Every policeman in the north of France will be looking for it."

"There was not specific information then that I was coming your way? You set up a road block as a matter of routine?"

"That's right. It was general information passed to everyone from central command."

"You did not get a phone call from a woman telling you about me?"

"No. What woman? As I say, it was a general warning to look for you and your car going north. Whichever route you had taken, you would have been stopped."

Michael quickly reasoned that that was evidence that it was not necessarily Monique that had given him away. That pleased him, but he could not stop himself churning the possibilities over in his head. *She could have phoned police headquarters, of course, but it opens up the possibility again of any number of people informing the authorities. The fact that she knew the routes I might have taken is no longer relevant.* He was really relieved. He hated thinking that the person he loved had betrayed him. Of all the individual people it could have been, she would have hurt him the most, and delivered psychological pain far deeper than any physical pain he had suffered.

"It is a nice car. I have always fancied having one like that," remarked the sergeant, with an envious look in the direction of the garage. "Where did you get the money to pay for it?"

"You won't mind if I don't answer such a question, just in case this is all a big ruse to get me to talk. I am taking a risk in trusting you at all, but I only trust you so far."

"Don't forget I am trusting you as well. We are now in this together." He used English for the first time. "As I believe you say, 'We swim together, or we sink alone'."

Michael was a bit surprised. *He answered in English.* "That's only a nautical version, and I suspect one that has suffered in translation. The real version is, 'We hang together or we hang alone'. Your version has lost its linguistic beauty."

"Ah, yes. More witty and more pungent." The sergeant grinned. He obviously liked it. "But we've got more important things to deal with than cars or philosophy." He plonked a map onto Michael's lap and pointed to their position.

Michael quickly got his bearings, then reverting to French, "Right. Turn left and take the D940 going north."

Sergeant Bucolin accelerated.

They were quickly out into the countryside, speeding along at quite a nice pace. Michael took a long sideways look at his chauffeur.

"What are you going to do in England?"

"I'll get a job."

"How is your English?"

"Good enough. I spent the war in England as a teenager."

"So what was all that about the Gestapo then?"

"I had to frighten you."

"You didn't succeed."

"I could see that. I was just pretending, but you were impressed by my acting? Other policemen who instructed us in interrogation techniques had associated with the Gestapo, and they unofficially passed various tips on. I did my National Service in French Indochina. I saw the techniques being used there, and I was told to use them on you. I'm sorry."

"Saying sorry is hardly enough. You have made a mess of my thumb."

"That'll heal."

Michael thought for a moment, staring at his neighbour. *What made you suddenly change your mind? Why did you suddenly want to get away?* Michael had been very surprised, but, of course, pleased. *It's lucky that he changed his mind after only one day, or I might have ended up a real mess. There's no knowing what else he might have learnt from the Gestapo.*

The sergeant sought to explain himself. "It is the sudden change of regime that worries me. It is not De Gaulle himself I am worried about. It is some of his minions. And more importantly, it is some of the generals in Algeria—Zeller, Challe—and some of their henchmen that concerns me. I have some very nasty enemies."

Three cheers for De Gaulle anyway, Michael thought.

"What did you do that made you enemies?"

"You won't mind if I don't answer that."

They passed a police car that was pulled up off the road. Michael could feel his muscles tense up. Sergeant Bucolin waved. The driver of the other car stirred himself, and waved back.

After about an hour, traffic started appearing on the road. They had to watch their speed. Half-asleep tractor drivers started emerging from the gateways of farmyards, without looking too hard for fast traffic, which they never expected to appear at this time of the morning. Birds were pecking at the road to get grit into their crop. The odd cat returning from a night's sport, hunting mice and voles in the haystacks and dung heaps, was taking a leisurely stroll on the way home, and had to be avoided. The car lurched round several of them, using up one of their nine feline lives. Michael was relieved that Sergeant Bucolin was a better-than-average driver. *It would have been ironic for me to end in a road crash.*

Now forced to travel at a slower speed, a police motorcyclist passed them. The rider seemed to take a good look inside their car. Michael tensed. Sergeant Bucolin waved and the cyclist moved on. Michael's pulse returned to normal. "Do you think he was suspicious? He seemed very interested in us?"

"No, he was just doing his job. It was just routine."

The sun started to rise again. It was reminiscent of Michael's drive the day before; before the police had picked him up. He was less emotionally disturbed now. He had other things to worry about. His physical safety now took precedence over his emotional welfare, but the beauty of the rising sun brought some of the pangs back into his heart again. *Who has betrayed me? Why had not Monique understood? Could she possibly be the culprit?*

"I am eating my bread and cheese now. We might not get a chance later on." With that, the sergeant rummaged around in his bag, which was down by the side of his seat, brought out his food, and started eating.

I hope he is a very good driver. Driving one-handed is a special skill.

"I'll join you," responded Michael, but with handcuffs, he had difficulty in retrieving his food, so Sergeant Bucolin leant across and got it out for him.

"So, Sergeant Bucolin, if we are in this together, what is your Christian name?"

"Jérôme."

"Well, Jérôme, let's hope our mutual trust pays dividends."

They drove on in silence for a while, then Jérôme started shuffling around in his seat, as someone who was tiring and had to wake himself out of an approaching stupor. After all, he also had not had a night's sleep. Flashes of unconsciousness were overtaking him and had to be fought away. He had to say something, and all he could think of was, "Well, we must be more than halfway there, wherever it is we are going. So far, so good."

Michael saw the problem and felt it would be wise to engage him in a conversation. "Don't be such an optimist. We have to find the boat and get on without looking suspicious."

"I would not have had you down for a pessimist, taking as many risks as you have."

"What risks do you think I have taken?" Michael was not yet 100% sure that this was not a wheeze to get information out of him, and he was still intent on getting a hint of who had betrayed him. If he could find out what risks the sergeant knew about, he might be able to work out who had given him away.

"Going in and out of France illegally is a risk in itself."

"What makes you think I have entered and exited illegally?"

"I have been informed, and our present journey confirms that the information was correct."

"Informed? By whom?"

"By my superiors."

"And who told them?"

"I have no idea."

"None whatsoever?"

"None whatsoever."

They drove on. Michael's thumb hurt. He regarded his driver with a certain amount of hatred. *I must not fall victim to hatred. He is not an ogre. But why does he now betray his better nature? Is it a ruse? If he has principles, why did he not betray them before? That's what the whole German nation tried to use as an excuse. Like him, they claimed they were only obeying orders. But then, did I not betray my principles when I carried money for that right-wing group?*

They continued in silence for a while. Michael felt the need to keep Jérôme talking. He was struck by the reasoning that he had to be an optimist. It diverted his darker thoughts for the moment. *Is it necessary to be an optimist to take risks?* "I have never thought about whether I am optimistic or pessimistic," he offered. "There's no point in worrying about such things." He searched Jérôme's face for a reaction.

"Oh, there is. If we know how we are inclined, we can modify our behaviour. I would say you were definitely optimistic, taking all the chances you have, and thinking you could get away with it." He grinned, "And look where it has got you."

"It got me to France. It got me doing the thing I like most: painting. It made me rich."

"Ah! It made you rich. How, I wonder? What have you been up to?"

"No, I wonder what you think I have been up to."

"You have been smuggling."

"Smuggling what?"

"That is what I did not have time to find out. Pity! I was looking forward to some promotion, had I succeeded."

Michael ignored that. "It got me a beautiful fiancée, whom I love."

"But does she love you?" the sergeant interrupted with a slight smirk on his face.

Michael was shaken by this remark. *What does he know about Monique?* he thought. *Why does he keep bringing her up, and question her love*? He turned and scanned Jérôme's face. It gave nothing away. *Perhaps I am making too much of it.* He decided to pursue a less painful course. "Well, if nothing else, it got me an Austin-Healey, which you would have liked and will probably never get." Michael could say this with a smile which was almost a laugh.

"And you have had to leave that and your beautiful fiancée behind."

"Well, what are you leaving behind? Who are you leaving behind?"

"You don't mind if I don't answer that."

"So you have secrets too."

"I have nothing to regret."

"In that case, I'm sorry for you. At least I have had love and pleasure."

"And where are you now?"

"In the same mess as someone who has never had these things."

"Yes, luckily you are an optimist. I am impressed. You can put the rosiest picture on events. It gives you energy for action. We are not out of trouble yet. We might need that energy. Let's hope your optimism is not ill-placed."

It was not long after this exchange that they came up to a roadblock. Michael felt his pulse quicken. Police cars were parked diagonally either side of the road. Several motorcyclists were astride their bikes. And there was a bevy of pedestrian police with torches, stopping cars.

Sergeant Bucolin went to drive on through, but a policeman stepped out and vigorously waved him to stop. Michael felt his throat go dry.

"I am taking this prisoner to Boulogne for questioning," exclaimed Sergeant Bucolin in a very authoritative voice. Michael's heart was suddenly pumping hard. He made sure his handcuffs were visible.

"Can I see your warrant?"

Sergeant Jérôme Bucolin produced his police warrant from his pocket. "What is the problem? Has something happened?" he enquired. He received no answer. The policeman perused the document in silence. His expression was stern, and he took an age. He looked at Sergeant Bucolin and at his photo.

Michael was apprehensive. *Have they discovered the police station we left is deserted?*

"Thank you, Sergeant Bucolin," said the policeman, as his voice changed from official, to one of confidentiality and explanation. "Everything is happening at the moment. We are on the verge of civil war. We have to be on our guard against saboteurs and you were not posing as police."

"Yes, I understand," Sergeant Bucolin's voice changed to conspiratorial and matched that of the examining policeman.

Another car drew up behind them, and the policeman quickly waved Jérôme and Michael on in order to attend to it. Michael relaxed. He realised he had been sweating. Jérôme let out a sigh of relief. "That was a close one."

"You looked very calm."

"Only on the outside. You were not sitting where I was sitting. I can assure you I was anything but calm."

"Well, you handled it very well. You are a good actor. I might start to trust you."

"Remember, we have to trust each other."

Another few miles were covered, Michael was feeling more cheerful. "We just have to get on the boat now. I see that you worked out that we were probably going to Boulogne. We will be there soon."

"We have to hide the police car, and disguise ourselves. And walk into town. And avoid police patrols. We are going into the town, the port, aren't we? Remember, the story of a policeman taking a prisoner to headquarters will no longer hold water when I am in civilian clothes."

"Oh, that should be alright," said Michael.

"You really are an optimist."

"You're not sitting where I am sitting." They both laughed.

Michael thought for a few minutes. He could see Jérôme was beginning to tire again, and he had to keep him talking, even if it was vacuous. "Tell me, what did you mean by my girlfriend might not love me?"

"Nothing really, but a beautiful young woman always has suitors, who admire her and want to make love to her. That is always flattering, and flattery is the most difficult thing to resist."

"Have you seen her?"

"No."

"Then how do you know she is beautiful?"

"That's easy. It doesn't take much reasoning. We have a tendency to choose our equals as a partner, so that we can relax. I assume that someone with good looks and great sex appeal like you, would choose a similar partner, and I have learnt from your interrogation that you also have a big ego. You have self-confidence. That's something else women go for. That, and with your looks, you must be desirable and have a very desirable partner."

"How can you judge my ego?"

"You have the strength enough to allow you to resist my questioning. You are not intimidated easily. Also, I can see that you are one of those people that have command of yourself. That also has an appeal for the opposite sex. That will last. You will carry that into old age. There are those that are attractive just when young. Their youth and their prettiness make them desirable, but there are those that have a deeper inbuilt attraction they carry with them throughout life. It is inexplicable."

"Monique's attraction is certainly inexplicable."

"Monique, eh?" Jérôme grinned and continued, "They may be men or women. The aura follows them into old age. They are always attractive, even as they lose their looks. It's an advantage and a disadvantage, as are most things."

"How can attraction be a disadvantage?"

"Well, possessors suffer more temptations than most of the rest of us. Many offers of relationships or affairs come their way. It's their choice whether they take up the offers, but they have to be strong to resist. Over-indulgence degenerates the soul. Only fools over-indulge, but then, most people are fools."

"Monique is no fool."

"I'm glad to hear it. As I say, such people tend to choose someone of like attraction as their stable partner. We feel at home with someone we feel is our equal. Then it is down to the depth of their love for that other, and the strength of their character, as to whether they cheat. Let's hope Monique's love is deep."

Michael mumbled to himself, "Monique would never cheat."

"As I see that you have this quality of deep attraction, I therefore can assume your girlfriend does. How strong is her character?"

"She is a very strong character," said Michael with great confidence.

Michael contemplated what Jérôme had said for a minute. "I'm glad you think I am attractive to women. I was never particularly aware of it." He gave a self-satisfied chuckle.

"Your sort never are. You take it for granted. You erroneously think everybody has the same opportunities."

"I never cheat."

"Probably not."

"And Monique would never cheat."

"Probably not."

There was a short silence while Michael gathered his thoughts. "But you're right about my fiancée. She is extremely attractive, but we love each other and would never cheat on one another."

"I hope you're right."

Michael was worried. *Could he really not have seen Monique and know so much about her? No. Logistically, they could never have met. It must be pure speculation on his part. Would his superiors have said anything about her attraction, even if they had seen her? She could not have physically gone to the police in the time available. That's for sure. But she could have phoned?* Fatigue was making his thoughts very confused.

The countryside looked beautiful in the early morning sunlight. Michael was touched. He shared his thoughts with Jérôme. "France is in real trouble. Such a beautiful country should not get itself into political trouble. It makes me cry."

"We only cry for ourselves."

"What do you mean? I sympathise with the French people, and the disasters that will befall them, if things come to the worst."

"No, you don't. You only cry for the thought that you might be mixed up in things, and lose your current privileged position. You imagine your problems and possible pain, and you cry in anticipation. We think we are sympathetic, but we always cry for ourselves."

"You really are cynical. You can't imagine that anyone could feel the hurt of others. Some of us are worried about our fellow human beings. No one is just an individual. We are part of humanity. When we cry, we cry for others. When we laugh, can you not see that we are enjoying a mutual feeling of pleasure with others?"

"On the contrary. We laugh because we think something is funny, and it is funny because a disaster is not happening to us. Most humour is based on cruelty or misfortune. If it is not slapstick comedy, which is patently sadistic, it is based on someone's stupid behaviour, misadventure, or misunderstanding; or peculiar idiosyncrasies. We are truly self-centred. We laugh because the tragedy is befalling someone else, and not us."

"I can't accept that all humour is based on cruelty. What about wordplay and puns?"

"I am not sure that wordplay comes into the category of humour. Few people laugh. Even there, we are self-centred. The perpetrator delights in the fact that they have seen verbal connections that the others have missed. No. We are always totally selfish and self-satisfied, I'm sorry to say."

"You don't sound very sorry to me."

"Oh, I am. I am." He nodded and lowered his head.

Michael turned over in his head what Jérôme had been saying. "Thank God I'm not as cynical as you."

"There's no point in thanking God. He doesn't exist."

"You surprise me again. I didn't suspect you of being an atheist."

"There's a lot you don't know about me. I see religion as one of the myths perpetuated to instil a belief in fatalism; to maintain the status quo, so that those in power will not have to employ so many people like me."

Michael is surprised. *What am I hearing?* It kept him quiet, while he digested it.

"If you disapprove of what you do, and what other people like yourself do, why do you do it?"

"Money! We all have to live. Sometimes we all have to do things we do not really approve of." Michael felt a pang. "And are we not all more than one person in the same body? It depends which one is dominant when opportunities present themselves. Are you without evil?"

"No, we all make mistakes, but I would like to think I would not torture someone."

"Until you are ordered to do it by a superior, you don't know."

"I have sworn an oath to obey my superiors."

"You have the luxury of never having to obey orders without question."

"You're wrong. I have done two years National Service. I was drilled to obey orders there without thinking, but I would like to think I would not have done anything evil or immoral."

"But were you ever tested?"

"No," Michael paused. "But you can't be blamed for what you haven't done or put the blame for what you have done on other people—on your officers. That's what the Nazis tried. We all have to take responsibility for our actions. Without the foot soldiers willing to do their bidding, the bosses would not prevail."

Jérôme felt he had to answer. "I am not proud of everything I've done, but we sometimes come to places we don't want to be by small steps."

This rang a bell in Michael's experience. *Small steps*. The difficult position he found himself in had not been planned.

Jérôme continued, "As Freud said, 'We are all murderers in our imagination.'"

Michael was curious about something Jérôme had said earlier and wanted to return it. "So you would like to do away with religion?"

"Certainly."

"But then 'the powers that be' would have to employ more people like you." *It's religion that makes most people behave well.*

Jérôme shrugged his shoulders. "More work." He grinned.

The esoteric conversation was interrupted by reality. Houses started to appear more frequently. They were approaching the outskirts of Boulogne.

"I thought it would be Boulogne." Jérôme's face glowed with self-satisfaction. "Now, where can I hide this car?"

"Perhaps in some wooded country lane before we get too far in."

"No. Anybody coming across a deserted police car miles from anywhere would immediately be suspicious. They have patrols covering the edges of towns. It will be better in a back street, not too far in."

He then jumped with a sudden realisation. "I know an illicit strip club. Nobody will be suspicious of an empty police car outside there. The occupants might be inside enforcing the law."

They grinned at each other.

"Enjoying themselves?"

"Enforcing the law."

"Or something."

"Or something."

They soon found the club. With difficulty, Sergeant Bucolin got into his old clothes in the back of the car, and changed to 'Jérôme.' He released Michael from the handcuffs. They got out, put the police uniform in the boot, and locked the car.

"I will have to call you Jérôme from now on." Then, looking at his accomplice, Michael added, "You don't look much like a French fisherman."

"You don't look like a Frenchman at all."

"Perhaps we had better split up. A Frenchman and an Englishman together in the early morning is going to need a bit of explaining."

"No fear!" exclaimed Jérôme. "We are travelling into town together. I am not letting you out of my sight."

"I suppose a torturer would be foolish to trust his victim."

"I am sorry about your hand."

They walked on quietly into town, making good headway. Suddenly, as they rounded a corner, they saw a police foot patrol. They turned quickly in order to go off in another direction, but the policemen had seen them.

"Hoy!" They heard a call behind them and both started to run. Loud footsteps of police-issued boots echoed down the cobbled street they had just left. They doubled back down a side alley.

"I am wearing police-issue shoes."

"There's nothing we can do about that now, I'm afraid. The shoe shops aren't open yet."

They ran for a bit, and then, turning a corner, they nearly ran straight into the patrol. They turned and ran off again down a back alley to a chorus of "Stop!" At a dead end, they vaulted a wall, finding themselves in a small garden. Then tried to adopt a nonchalant air as they let themselves out of the front gate. In surprisingly quick time, they found themselves at the harbour. The patrol seemed to have disappeared. Charley's boat was nowhere to be seen. Michael was dismayed. "What time is it?"

"Just gone half past seven."

"We're late."

"So are they."

"They could not have come in and left so quickly, could they?"

"No. Let's both be optimists."

Michael's heart was beating loudly, and he thought he could hear Jérôme's.

Suddenly, to his great delight, he saw a fishing boat entering the harbour. His heart rose and then sank again. It was not Charley.

They stepped back into the darkness between two sheds to wait.

"What time is it?"

"Two minutes after you asked last time."

Again, a boat appeared off the harbour arm. Michael left the refuge to get a better look. The sergeant pulled him back.

"We'll know soon enough."

The boat rounded the lighthouse and entered the harbour.

"It's Charley!"

"Good. Now we have to keep calm. A customs man might come out and see them."

Sure enough, someone came from the office at the end and walked along the quay to where the boat was tying up. A conversation took place between the customs officer and Charley, but they were too far away to hear what was being said. Eventually, with a lot of smiles, the customs man left and went back to his warm office.

Jérôme held Michael's arm. "Now we have to be very casual. Do you smoke?"

"No. Why?"

"If we just stroll along the jetty, we might seem to be up to no good, but if we saunter along smoking, it will look as though we are just having a break. This is where a policeman's eye and experience can be an asset."

He drew a packet from his pocket and handed Michael a cigarette. He lit it, then lit one for himself.

Michael coughed. "Don't do too much of that, or you will give us away."

They strolled out and walked down the quay to where the first boat had docked. Here, Jérôme engaged the young lad adjusting the warps in casual conversation.

"So, what's the weather like outside today?"

"It's alright at the moment, but it is supposed to be getting worse later."

Michael stood back a bit. He did not want his French accent to be tested. Jérôme and the boy shared a joke and laughed together.

The skipper came out of his cabin and joined in. They all seemed very happy.

"You must have had a good catch?"

"Not at all. It was poor. Not worth staying out for with the barometer falling."

"Nevertheless, you seem happy."

"There's no point in being anything else."

Michael was far from happy. He was very nervous. After an eternity, the sergeant broke off the conversation, and they carried on down to Charley's boat.

Charley hauled himself up on to the quay. "I thought that was you I saw there, but I was expecting to see you alone," he said as he approached Michael.

"This is Jérôme. I want you to take him with us. He is in as much trouble as I am."

Charley scrutinised Jérôme. Michael jumped in. "You will be well paid."

"It's not a matter of money. It's just if he's a bloody policeman or customs man or something."

"I can vouch for him."

"O.K. then."

Charley looked up towards the customs office. "One of you slip down now, preferably Jérôme, and you, Michael, as you're so obviously English, can go with Jim to take the fish to the market and get on when you come back together. We have only two kettles. It's not much, but we could not fish on the way here, or we would have been late. We had to have some excuse for docking, so I brought fish all the way from Hastings."

Jérôme sat down on the bollard, and then casually slipped down to the deck to help Jim up with the fish.

"What have you done to your hand?"

"Oh, just a little accident."

Michael took the kettles, and then, when Jim jumped up, went off with him to the market, carrying a kettle each. Charley got Jérôme to hide behind the gear in the cabin.

"We don't want the harbour master seeing too many people on board as we leave. It's a bloody good job I only brought Jim."

He cleaned up his cabin.

"So, you're a Frenchman?"

"Yes."

"France is in a bloody mess at the moment. I have been hearing all about it on the wireless," Charley said this very cheerfully.

"You could say that." Jérôme's mood was markedly different.

It seemed an age before Jim and Michael returned. Michael jumped down to the deck, and Jim doubled up the warps before he followed him. Michael thought he saw their police pursuers coming into the port.

They cast off and headed out round the breakwater. Charley waved as they passed the harbourmaster's office. Someone gave a feeble wave back, but nobody seemed very concerned.

Chapter Fourteen

They cleared the harbour. There was a sou'westerly blowing, not too hard, but enough to make it choppy.

"It's supposed to be blowing up. Let's hope we can make good way to Hastings before it gets too bloody bad." Charley quickly brought the helm round to steer nor'west.

Jérôme was looking a bit green. He was not from seafaring stock. Charley didn't think any Frenchman was from seafaring stock, except perhaps for those from St Malo, like Loik Cuek. He laughed. Very soon crewman Jim joined Jérôme at the back of the boat. They were sick together.

"The bloody entente cordiale," exclaimed Charley.

"I don't think it's very cordial at the moment," remarked Michael.

Charley laughed. "I don't know why Jim persists in fishing. Directly it's above a force bloody 4, he spews up. The name of Adams doesn't seem to do him any bloody good."

Michael was more sympathetic "Nevertheless, he has to keep up family traditions."

Charley took on a sad expression. "One day there might not be any bloody family traditions to keep up. At the moment, there's plenty of fish about, but there's these bloody new great factory ships that just scoop up everything, dredging the seabed and ripping it up, killing every bloody thing, and most of what they catch goes to make bloody fertiliser." He nodded his head. "No! One day there might be no fish to catch, and no bloody family tradition."

As they went further northwest, they lost the protection of the Normandy coast and the Cherbourg Peninsula. The sea was whipping up. Charley was more serious now "We had better tie everything down. We must be hitting a force 7."

They battled on for an hour or so.

"Is it getting dangerous?" Michael was a bit worried.

"Oh no, It's not even an 8. We've been out in much worse than this. We've taken force bloody 10 and survived. And that was further down the Channel, where we were getting the big Atlantic rollers. Here, the waves are shorter. There's no danger. She's a bloody good boat."

The boat might survive, thought Michael, *but will I?* He was being thrown all over the place. Having one gammy hand did not help. Jim and Jérôme were still being sick over the stern. Jim had lashed himself to the stern fishing gear, and then helped Jérôme to do the same. Charley had put on a life jacket and tied himself on to the compass binnacle. He gave Michael a safety harness, and a life jacket.

"Don't inflate the bloody thing until you get washed overboard, otherwise it will get in your way and stop you getting out from under the boat, if we capsize."

"This is dangerous, isn't it?" Michael was looking a bit white, not with sickness, but with apprehension.

"Oh no. This is nothing. We'll be alright. The biggest danger will come when we have to cross the bloody shipping lanes. In this weather, the cargo ships will have difficulty in seeing us, and the lookouts are drunk most of the bloody time anyway."

At this moment, a large wave hit the port bow, throwing it violently to starboard and stopping the boat in its tracks.

"We can't make enough speed in this bloody sea to clear the bloody lanes, so we'll have to aim at the stern of one of them and hope to get round the back and away before the next bloody one comes along. There ain't much bloody room between them. They're travelling at 15 or 20 knots. They come up the Channel like a string of circus elephants, grabbing each other's tail in a bloody high-speed queue."

They were clear into the centre of the Channel by now, and the weather was doing its worst. The rain was not falling—it was travelling horizontally, and so dense you could hardly see the bowsprit. A lobster pot broke loose. Michael went to retrieve it. Charley grabbed him.

"No! Leave it." It was swept over the side. Charley grinned. "I can't afford to lose you. I might not get bloody well paid."

The rain was mixing with the spray coming up from the sea and forming stinging projectiles. Michael sat down in the back of the half-cabin for protection. He braced himself between the wall and the floor. He hoped the two at the back were alright. He could not see them, but they had tied themselves down, and Jim was very experienced, even if Jérôme was not.

Suddenly a little bird, a firecrest, zoomed on to the boat, into the cabin, and perched on the cable of Charley's radio. There it stayed, not worried about humans as much as the elements. It chirped incessantly and shat all over Charley's chart table. Charley just laughed. He was being thrown all over the place, but he did not seem to care, and took most of the violent movement in his legs, which he kept bent. Michael took note of that.

They suddenly saw a great ship emerge out of the haze. Charley swung the helm round and then back again, heading for its stern. Everything clattered.

"Are you alright out there?" shouted Charley.

A faint cry came from the back of the boat. "A bit fucking wet, but alright."

The only soul that was not thrown by the sudden manoeuvres was the bird. *I suppose they must be used to their perches being thrown around in high winds,* thought Michael.

They passed under the stern of the large vessel, and as they cleared away, they could see another ship looming up behind, just as Charley had predicted.

"Is that us clear of that danger now then?" asked Michael in a timorous voice.

"No, that's the westerly lane. We still have to cross the bloody lot going east."

The weather did not abate. It had probably got up to a force 9. They passed the other shipping lane without seeing anything, although Michael was convinced he could hear a large vessel. He was on tenterhooks all the time.

They pressed on for another hour or so. The planks creaked. The tackle rattled. An extra-large wave crashed over the port stern, washing the fishing tackle and ropes across the deck, and the boat shuddered. Ominous squealing noises came as the cabin tried to free itself from the deck, but as Charley had said, it was a damned good boat. There was a thump and a swish as the prow hit each wave. Hour after hour, the chaotic symphony continued.

Charley started singing a sea shanty. The weather did not seem to worry him. He used the full power of his voice, but you could hardly hear him over the din.

"What shall we do with a drunken sailor?

What shall we do with a drunken sailor?"

When will this all end? thought Michael. *It has been going on far too long. We must be near the Sussex coast by now.*

Suddenly, the little bird emerged from the cabin and set off north into the storm and the haze.

"We must be nearing land," remarked Charley. "That's a bloody relief."

So Charley was worried after all, thought Michael.

"See if you can see the light up on West Hill."

"I can't see anything but spray. It might as well be night."

"Is that the light on the end of the harbour arm?" Charley enquired, pointing across the port bow.

"No. I can't see anything. Oh yes! That's certainly a light."

"We have to get that in line with the one on West Hill, and that will guide us in."

"I can only see the one light."

"Are those the cliffs at Rock-a-Nore off our starboard bow?"

"There is certainly a presence looming there," Michael replied.

"Good. She knows her own way home now." Charley patted the top of the helm affectionately.

After another five minutes, they could see the harbour arm on their port. It did not afford much protection, as the wind had backed round to the south. Charley turned the boat to face at right angles to the shore and put the engine at full speed ahead. She lurched forward. The wind and the waves chased her in. Great waves, like mountains, piled up behind her. At the last moment, just before touching the beach, a giant wave picked up her stern and swung her round 90 degrees, parallel to the beach, and over on her gunwales to a 45-degree angle. As the next wave crashed over the top of them, sending spray and spume in all directions, Charley swung the wheel to face the culprit, and took her out again.

"That was bloody nasty. We could have been rolled over and capsized." Charley had dropped the show of bravado. A mixture of spray and sweat was dripping from his now brown-grey face. The ruddy hue of his Saxon ancestors had succumbed to anxiety. Michael was pleased. Charley was human after all. Only gods and idiots have no fear.

Michael was grabbing on hard to the side of the cabin and the base of the compass binnacle. *What an irony,* he thought, *after all I have been through, to come to an end so near to safety. That can't possibly be.*

"Let's try again." Charley was looking serious. He had regained his composure.

Jim had found a new energy from somewhere and had gone round to the prow, making slow progress, step by step, as the boat lurched up and down. He was hanging on to the foremast, and, clutching a steel cable, he clipped himself on.

"Here we go again," shouted Charley as he put her into full ahead.

They rushed at the beach. There was a clunk as the boat hit the shingle this time. Jim, with amazing agility, unclipped, jumped off, clutching the hawser that was threaded through a hole at the base of the stempost, and gave it to the Boy Ashore, who appeared from nowhere. He attached it to the cable he had hauled down from the winding shed. On a given signal, the slack was taken up. Michael and Charley came jumping off just as another gigantic wave rolled over the stern.

"I hope Jérôme is alright."

"I lashed him well on before I left, and he is semi-conscious anyway, so he won't know what is happening," Jim replied.

Jim, Michael, and Charley picked up logs and placed them under the front of the boat as it was wound up the beach. It slowly made its way up the shingle slope, sliding on the greased logs, and leaving them at the back, behind it. Before the sea could come and seize the logs, they grabbed the short rope handles that were attached and retrieved them, rushing them round to the front, where they were put down again. The process was wetter than usual, but that did not matter, as everybody was as wet as though they had swum across the Channel. The boat itself afforded them some protection. The only real danger came when they had to retrieve the logs from the rear, and some of those were sacrificed to the sea, rather than risk life.

Eventually, the boat was up over the crest of the beach. They took it up higher than usual, as they wanted it to be completely safe, and the storm was raging hard. If the giant waves crashed over the rim of the beach, they could do a lot of damage to anything within range.

A grey face looked over the gunwales. Jérôme! He was not feeling very well. "I think I'll go back to being a policeman."

"A policeman!?" Charley's voice was full of alarm.

Michael was quick to reassure him. "It's alright. He's one of us."

"I bloody well knew it. I could smell a policeman in Boulogne."

"This is an exceptional policeman. He has helped me out of a spot. He may have saved my life."

They sat down for a minute on the stade, utterly exhausted, and then got back on the boat, surveyed the damage, and tidied up.

"I have got to get some money. Is there a bank handy?"

"Yes. There's just one bank left in the Old Town, in George Street. Hurry and you'll just catch it," said Charley.

Michael's trip to George Street was agony. Every muscle ached and he had to stop every so often and sit down.

A man stopped, "Are you alright, mate?"

"Yes. Thanks." He hoisted himself up and staggered on.

At the bank, he drew as much out of his account as the clerk would allow him, and he gave it all to Charley, except for enough to get him and Jérôme, by train, to London. Charley was very pleased.

"You don't realise what a good deed you've done," said Michael. "You may have saved two lives."

"Well, that's good. I've always hoped to go to bloody heaven."

Once in the train, when they had recovered, Jérôme addressed Michael, "Thank you. I was not sure I could trust you, but the fact that you did not give your fellow plotters away, gave me hope."

"You did not know who betrayed me then? You didn't know where your information had come from; who the plotters were?"

"No. We were only told that you were mixed up in politics, and you had been smuggling."

"So you did not know which side of the political spectrum I was on, or what I had been smuggling?"

"No. If I had known that, my questioning would have been different. Now, if I knew, I would tell you. I don't know." He thought for a moment. "Although perhaps I think it may be better if you don't know. Sometimes it is better not to know the truth. The truth can hurt. I am not going to tell you which side of the political spectrum I am on either. It would be nice if we could part friends."

"Friends? Well, yes. Maybe."

At Charing Cross station, they shook hands, smiled at each other, and parted.

Michael thought it would be reasonably safe to go and spend the night in the Wilton Street flat. He had nowhere else. Nobody would have been organised enough yet in France to look for him there, although he would not be able to stay. *I will have to abandon it tomorrow.* Nevertheless, he went up the stairs with some trepidation. His worries were unfounded. Luckily, there was some food in the fridge that had not gone off, so with a couple of the tins from the cupboard, he managed to get himself a good meal. As he was deeply exhausted from the Channel trip, he fell asleep as he finished his food, and his head fell onto his empty plate. He did not know how long he had slept, but he woke after a bit, stripped off his clothes, got into bed, and slept soundly.

The next morning, he went first to his bank where he drew out a large amount of money, and then went and had a big breakfast. Next, he went and opened another account at a rival bank, retaining just enough to see him through the week.

What shall I do now? I must start a new life. Whoever has given me away might continue to pursue me. I know too much. I can't go and see George, in case it was the left-wing group that had wanted to get rid of me, and I can't look up any of my friends from the BBC, in case that gets back to George. I don't have to worry so much about right-wing people. They are going to be easier to detach from. I hardly knew any of them, and we certainly have no friends or acquaintances in common, except of course for Monique's family. Yes, there is Monique's family, and they know about the flat. I will have to get all my important and personal things out of there and settle up with the landlady. The rest will have to be abandoned like my lovely car. My first priority has to be flat-hunting.'

He bought a paper, searched the property pages, and at the third attempt, took a small flat on the edge of Hampstead Heath, near South End Green. He had enough money in his two accounts to last him for some time, so that was not a worry. His damaged hand was worrying him though. A doctor was needed. He caught a 24 bus down to Camden Town. His mind went over all the possible people once again who could have betrayed him, and in spite of himself, he kept coming back to Monique. She had the knowledge of his whereabouts, and she had a motive. He went past a surgery. This stopped his speculation; he got off the bus, and went in.

"How did you do that? It's nasty, but you'll live," said the rather jolly doctor as he bandaged his thumb.

"Oh, a wooden box fell on it."

"It must have been a big box to crush it like that."

Camden Town had always been a cheap place to shop, not like Belgravia, so he stocked up. He would probably not miss the high life. *Cheaper prices will make up for any frills,* he thought to himself.

He went to the Post Office and posted to George the package that Pierre had given him. He did not want to let his left-wing friends down, even if it had been one of them that had betrayed him. If it was, they would have to find out who was treacherous for themselves. He was finished with politics.

Back in his new flat, he lay on the bed. He wondered what life was going to have in store now. How was he going to cope without the love of Monique? He needed to start painting again quickly to take his mind off things. All those lovely pigments and materials he had to leave behind. *Never mind.* He had access to money. *I can soon get some more.* But he could not get another Monique.

He foresaw the future with sadness and apprehension.

So, this is what living dangerously brings you to.

Chapter Fifteen

The year is 2020. A middle-aged Michael is sitting in his armchair, looking out of the window at the gorgeous view. He is speculating on how beauty is wasted on the young.

The phone rings. He picks it up.

"Is that Michael Daubeney?"

"Yes."

"You don't know me, and I am sorry to bother you, but did you know Monique Foch?"

Michael hesitates. "Yes."

"I'm Pierre, Monique's son. I have bad news for you, I'm afraid. My mother died five weeks ago. We found instructions in her papers that you were to be informed if anything happened to her. I'm sorry I did not contact you before, but we did not know who you were, and we had difficulty in finding you. Were you a close friend of hers?"

"Yes." He pauses. "When we were young." He pauses again. "She's dead?"

"Yes."

Michael feels a shudder shoot through his body.

Pierre continues, "There is also a gold chain she always wore round her neck, with a single diamond on it. Along with her instructions, she said it was to be sent to you."

"She always wore?" Michael is puzzled for a moment.

"Yes. I think she had had it made out of a ring."

"Oh!" An expression of realisation comes over Michael's face. He gropes for something to say, and then an idea hits him. "How about your father?"

"I never knew him. He died soon after I was born."

"Well, thank you for letting me know. When is the funeral?"

"It was two weeks ago."

"Oh." Michael's head drops. "Please accept my condolences. I'll send you my address for the gold chain. I would like the chain to remember her by. Where can I reach you?"

"At Le Manoir d'Espérance, Courtay, Indre et Loire."

"Thank you for letting me know."

Michael stands for a few moments, gazing sightlessly out of the window. He puts the phone down gently. He cries.

Postscript

In 1958, De Gaulle accepted power, actively promoted by the right-wing, including the generals in Algeria, and passively accepted by the left. The Fourth Republic collapsed, and he organised a new constitution for the Fifth Republic. For the second time in his life, he was elected President in 1959.

The right, including the generals, expected him to use them to put down the Muslim revolt in Algeria. Instead, he held a referendum there, which gave a majority for self-government. In spite of several rebellions by the Pied-Noirs and the generals, in 1962 Algeria became an independent state. Generals Salan and Calle were tried, convicted of treason, and condemned to death, but later De Gaulle pardoned them.

The action of the novel takes place during the last phase of the old francs. Just after this period, new francs were introduced by De Gaulle at a rate of 100 to 1. This was later incorporated into the Euro.